PAGAN WARRIOR

BRITAIN: THE SEVENTH CENTURY

GODS AND KINGS

M J PORTER

M J PUBLISHING

Copyright notice
Porter, M J
Pagan Warrior
Copyright ©2015, 2022 Porter, M.J
All characters and events in this publication, other than those clearly in the public domain, are fictitious and any resemblance to actual persons, living or dead, is purely coincidental.

ALL RIGHTS RESERVED. No part of this publication may be reproduced, stored in a retrieval system or transmitted in any form or by any means without the prior written permission of the author, nor be otherwise circulated in any form of binding or cover other than that in which it is published and without a similar condition being imposed on the subsequent buyer.

ISBN:9781914332180 (ebook)
ISBN: 9781522060536 (paperback)
ISBN:9781914332166 (paperback)
ISBN: 9781914332173 (hardback)

Cover design by Flintlock Covers

❦ Created with Vellum

CONTENTS

Cast of Characters	vii
The Anglo-Saxon Chronicle AD617 (E version)	xi
Prologue	1
1. AD630 – Penda	5
2. AD630 - Cadwallon of Gwynedd	10
3. AD630 - Penda of Mercia	13
4. AD630 - Edwin of Northumbria	17
5. AD630 - Osfrith of Northumbria	21
6. AD630 - Eadfrith of Northumbria	25
7. AD630 - Eowa of Mercia	28
8. AD630 - Eanfrith of Bernicia	35
9. AD630 - Osric of Deira	39
10. AD631 - Penda of Mercia	44
11. AD631 - Cadwallon of Gwynedd	51
12. AD631 - Edwin of Northumbria	59
13. AD631 - Eadfrith of Northumbria	63
14. AD631 - Eowa of Mercia – The lands of the Hwicce	70
15. AD631 - Eanfrith of Bernicia, The Pictish Kingdom	75
16. AD631 - Penda of Mercia – Gwynedd	82
17. AD631 - Cadwallon of Gwynedd – Gwynedd	90
18. AD631 - Edwin of Northumbria	95
19. AD631 - Osfrith of Northumbria	105
20. AD631 - Eadfrith of Northumbria	110
21. AD631 Winter - Eowa of Mercia	114
22. AD631 Winter - Eanfrith of Bernicia	123
23. AD632 Early Summer - Penda of Mercia – Gwynedd	129
24. AD632 Summer - Cadwallon of Gwynedd	136
25. AD632 Early October - Edwin of Northumbria	140
26. AD632 October - Osfrith of Northumbria	147
27. AD632 October - Eadfrith of Northumbria	150
28. AD632 October - Eowa of Mercia	158
29. AD632 October - Osric of Deira	168
30. AD632 October – Eanfrith of Bernicia	172
31. AD632 - Penda of Mercia – The Battle of Hæðfeld	177

32. AD632 - Edwin of Northumbria	191
33. AD632 - Cadwallon of Gwynedd	200
34. AD632 - Eanfrith of Bernicia	214
35. AD632 - Osfrith of Northumbria	216
36. AD632 - Eadfrith of Northumbria	230
37. AD632 - Eowa of Mercia	234
38. AD632 - Penda of Mercia	239
Epilogue	245
Author notes	249
Meet the Author	253
Books by M J Porter (in series reading order)	255

For the history haters in my family, the 'roll your eyes' nearly teenagers, A and M, the 'please don't take us to another pile of rubble and expect us to get excited about it' fans.

*Thanks for putting up with me.
I love you.*

CAST OF CHARACTERS

This is a book of many characters and names. I apologize now. I've not yet penned a novel with a Game of Thrones style cast but this battle lends itself to it. To tell the story of such a great battle, I must introduce as many of the combatants as I can in order to do it justice. Hopefully, the below will help any who get lost. As a point of note, two characters share a confusingly similar name, Eadfrith of Northumbria, and Eanfrith of Bernicia – cousins, and historically accurate, and so their names have had to stay.

Cadwallon and Penda's allies
  Cadwallon, King of Gwynedd (British kingdom)
  Penda, of Mercian heritage (A Saxon kingdom)
  Cloten, King of Deheubarth or Dyfed (British kingdom)
  Clydog, King of Ceredigion (British kingdom)
  Eiludd, King of Powys (British kingdom)
  Clemen, King of Dumnonia (Modern day Cornwall)
  Domnall Brecc, King of Dal Riata (Part of western Scotland and Ireland)
  Beli, King of Alt Clut (Strathclyde – south-west Scotland)
  Eanfrith of Bernicia (North East England – bordering with

modern-day Scotland – the kingdom of Northumbria comprised the kingdoms of Deira and Bernicia, and extended into what we would today believe to be Scotland)

Edwin and his allies

<u>Edwin, King of Northumbria</u> – (the kingdoms of Deira and Bernicia combined)

His children – <u>Osfrith</u> (who has a son, Yffi) and <u>Eadfrith</u> with his first wife, <u>Cwenburh of Mercia</u> the daughter of the previous King of Mercia.

His children with his second wife, <u>Æthelburh</u>, aren't mentioned by name, but his second wife is the sister of the King of Kent

<u>Eowa, Lord/King of the Hwicce</u> – the Hwicce was a smaller Mercian kingdom to the south west, bordering with the early British kingdoms in what would become Wales.

<u>Osric of Deira</u>, Edwin's cousin (son of Æthelric of Deira – Edwin's uncle) (Deira is roughly modern-day Yorkshire)

<u>Eadbald, King of Kent –</u> his daughter is married to King Edwin of Northumbria

<u>Cynegils, King of Wessex</u>

<u>Sigeberht, King of the East Angles (modern-day East Anglia)</u>

<u>Oswald of Bernicia –</u> Edwin's nephew (roughly modern day Northumbria, but extending into modern-day Scotland and also to the west.)

Other Kings

<u>Rædwald of the East Anglians</u>, bretwalda (wide-ruler) over Britain before Edwin, and his ally until his death

<u>Æthelfrith of Northumbria</u> (Edwin of Northumbria's brother in law – married to his sister Acha and so the father of <u>Eanfrith of Bernicia</u> and <u>Oswald of Bernicia</u>) dies at the Battle of the River Idle in AD616, so making Edwin by conquest)

<u>Cinioch, son of Lutrun</u>, Pictish King (615-634) – not named in the book

Warriors

<u>Osfrith's warriors</u>; Actulf, Hahmund, Godfrid

<u>Edwin's warriors</u>: Eoif, Eomar (Eoif's son), Liefbrun, Ohtred, Alhred, Sigward

<u>Eowa's warriors</u>; Aldfrith (Eowa and Penda's fathers friend)

<u>Penda's warriors</u>; Wiglaf, Herebrod,

<u>Cadwallon's warriors</u>; Walaran

<u>Osfrith's warriors</u>; Godfrid, Hahmund, Actulf

<u>Gunghir</u> – Penda's horse

<u>Sleipnir</u> – Eowa's horse

THE ANGLO-SAXON CHRONICLE
AD617 (E VERSION)

Here, Æthelfrith, King of the Northumbrians, was killed by Rædwald, King of the East Anglians, and Edwin, Ælle's offspring, succeeded to the kingdom (of Northumbria) and conquered all Britain except for the inhabitants of Kent alone, and drove out the princes, the sons of Æthelfrith; that was first Eanfrith, then Oswald and Oswy, Oswudu, Oslaf and Offa.

PROLOGUE
AD629 - CADWALLON OF GWYNEDD

I wipe the blood from my face with my leather-gloved hand. It does more to smear than completely remove the sticky substance sheeting my eyes. I smell afresh the tang of recently shed blood.

I'm hidden away in a copse of trees, far from the battle line but close enough that I can make out the tiny figures, ant-like, crawling around the field of death.

My foster-brother and overlord, King Edwin, is victorious, and my rage is intense.

I should have won this battle. I should have belittled him and taken away his haughty title as overlord of these lands; the title he claims much to my disgust.

He pretends to his New God, his Christianity, as though it makes him worthier for such dominance. He forgets that I was a Christian long before him. Long, long before he even considered his marriage of convenience. A marriage that legitimised his claim to the throne of Northumbria in the eyes of Eadbald, the Christian King of the holiest kingdom of Kent. The brother of the woman Edwin took to be his second wife.

Men rush through the thick and gnarled trees around me, as

though they're being chased. Their faces are streaked with blood and mud, gore and snot. I shout to them to tell them no one follows them. That they should come to me, stand as my guard. But they're blind in their terror and don't heed my words.

I'd thought they were better warriors than this.

I'd thought they were as committed to killing Edwin as I am.

Yet, I'm the one cowering in the cover of the forest already. Perhaps, I should have led by example.

I can blame only myself for this abysmal failure. I underestimated Edwin, thought him no more than my foster-brother. I underestimated the number of his allies. Of how many men he could call upon to stand and fight in his name.

I had no idea the tactician he'd become, using my strategies against me.

So far, the only mistake being made is that he's not following the retreating men. He's not sent his men into my forest hideaway. That means I'll live to fight another day. That is an oversight.

I watch on with narrowed eyes, thirstily drinking in all that happens before me. I expect to be forced to run for my life at any moment. The last of my few remaining warriors stagger through the tightly-packed trees. Their footsteps are heavy and laboured. I'm sure that those on the blood-stained battlefield must hear them, but they don't even raise their eyes to look my way.

A horse rushes through, and then another, eyes crazed with terror, a shrill whinny of fear. I slap them on their rump in encouragement, pleased they know their way home. Horses are valuable, almost as prized as men. Certainly, more highly prized than some I could name. I'd rather take them home with me than leave them for Edwin.

As I think his name, I fancy that one of the warriors on top of his horse looks my way from the battlefield. I glare into the dimming daylight, wondering if it's him seeking me.

If I were closer, I'd see his steely eyes, thick full beard and moustache: his long brown hair, stubborn chin and bent nose. But I'm too far away. I imagine them easily enough.

I consider what he sees when he glances my way? Does he notice his far younger foster-brother or just an enemy? Does he laugh at my shame or soberly tuck it away and hope to understand my actions and motives?

Disgusted with my thoughts, I once more smear the muck from my face. My nose is bleeding. I have a split gum. My hair is coated in blood, but not mine. No wounds gush from the top of my head. My arms are sore from where I've been fighting all day. My body is starting to shiver with the shock of it all.

A tap on my back and I spin in fear, pleased when the eyes of my brother, Cadfan, meet mine. He's as riddled with exhaustion as I am, his chest heaving tightly beneath a split byrnie. He holds his seax and shield, grimacing around his pain.

"Come, we must leave," he commands. I know he's right. We need to make it back to our own lands, away from the watchful eyes of Edwin, even if, for now, he's choosing not to follow us.

We need to regroup, and I need to decide how I'll overwhelm him once and for all.

He's my much older foster brother, but he's no more qualified to be over-king of this island than I am, and I mean to prove it to him.

Once I've recuperated and found myself some allies as staunch as his own.

1

AD630 – PENDA

The (exiled) Court of Cadwallon of Gwynedd, Priestholm

My men follow me as I stride from my horse to meet this king who dares to demand my attendance upon him.

My anger guides my steps. I let it pool within me, build slowly. When I finally meet him, I'll tell him exactly what I think of him and his belligerent messenger.

I've heard of this Cadwallon, loser and subordinate to the alleged 'great' King Edwin of Northumbria. Huh, I could teach him a thing or two. Not that he listens to anyone other than the priests of this new religion, or rather the old faith that now sweeps this island as though it were a fresh one.

I keep to my old Gods. They're fickle and unreliable compared to the new but old God who did little but die for those who followed his teachings. He killed no one. He accomplished little in his short life. I wish for greater notoriety.

I hope Cadwallon doesn't speak to me of faith. I wish to talk about war, not matters of belief.

The hall towards which I stride is well built and has clearly been a permanent feature for some time. Yet to the rear of it, I see construction on another building. The post-holes are being dug deep into the stubborn ground by sweating men. Massive tree trunks are being worked upon, the scent of sawdust scenting the air. This royal site is filled with busy activity, even if rumours on the mainland tell me that Cadwallon is running for his life. I think King Edwin is overly boastful when he claims Cadwallon's lands as his to rule.

One day soon, I'll have a hall as magnificent as this. These craftspeople will beg me to let them build for me. And it won't be on an island either. Islands are simple to defend. Are an easy place of retreat. I plan on having far more land to call my own than a tiny little island. I plan on defending my palace without the aid of the natural barrier of the crashing sea waves that bring with them the smell of the ocean.

I feel the smile spread across my face at the shining future I foresee. As though to punish me for such thoughts, I trip over a discarded piece of wood in my distracted state. I feel my irritation coalesce and swell, but it leaves me swiftly. It's not the craftsman's fault I'm too busy with my thoughts to look where I'm going.

Cadwallon's warriors stalk my every step, and I watch them with some interest. These are the men who let King Edwin humiliate them. I'm surprised that Cadwallon keeps them with him.

And yet they look the part. Fierce and watchful, even though all they do is walk beside me. I consider what happened that day? I speculate as to why King Edwin overwhelmed them? I reconsider my derisive thoughts about Cadwallon and his men. If these finely dressed and well-equipped warriors with as many weapons as they need could not beat King Edwin, then why should I be able to?

I'm no more than the brother of a successful minor king, the son of the now-dead leader of my tribe. I don't have the vast resources with which Cadwallon can accumulate. Even now, in exile, his war band outnumbers mine by at least two to one, and that's merely all I can see.

Cadwallon's warriors creak as they walk, their leather byrnies tightly laced around their wide frames. Faces are fierce, and eyes are hard, unflinching. I swallow against a sudden rise of fear. But I've come as an equal. I need to stand my ground and not buckle under such a show of strong fierceness and steadfast devotion. I must live up to the reputation that's preceded me and made a king seek out my assistance.

Before I enter the hall, ducking my head as I enter through the low doorway, the cold, flat eyes of the warrior who walks closest to me takes my weapons. I don't like handing over my seax, my war axe or my shield, but I do so, noting the appraising eyes of the warrior as I hand him each item. He lays them reverentially on a rough wooden board and then moves to take the same from the rest of my warriors. I feel consoled that he handles my weapons with such respect.

There are murmurs of complaint from my men, but I'd told them this would be necessary. Men who come armed do not come to make peace. Ever. And often unarmed men don't, but that's only a passing thought as I stride into the great hall, one I might remember in the future if I don't get my way.

It's a chill day outside, but the smoky warmth from the well-stocked fire assaults my senses. I cough a little dryly as my eyes adjust to the dim lighting.

The hall is sparsely populated. I see Cadwallon standing close to the hearth, and his face lifts in greeting. This isn't the first time we've met, although I'm not sure he'll remember the last occasion. After all, I was just a warrior then, not a man who led warriors. My reputation has grown in recent years. Pity my brother, Eowa, eclipses me.

Striding towards me, Cadwallon's face creases in a tight grin of welcome that never quite reaches his eyes. Yet, his handclasp is warm enough, his dry skin against my cold hand, almost making him wince.

"Penda," he says in greeting. I nod to acknowledge that I am he.

"Lord Cadwallon," is all I respond. I'm keen to see what he wants to say to me.

"My thanks for coming when I extended overtures of friendship." I see there are to be pleasantries before we begin. I relax my tense posture a little as I glance over his shoulder and see the curious faces of small children and mighty warriors amongst those within his hall.

"It's my pleasure to speak with you in person. I've heard much about you."

"And I have about you. I see that most of what I've heard is probably true." I laugh at that. I wonder what he's heard of my exploits. Is it that I defeated the father and son kings, Cynegils and Cwichelm and gained the land of the Hwiccan kingdom for my brother? Is it that my brother and I do not always get along? Or is it perhaps just a man making small talk when faced with a warrior far more physically dominating than himself?

"Their speaking too often mangles rumours and fact," I say a little courteously. It would not do to mouth the truth, that Cadwallon is no great warrior or strategist, and that's why he's reached out to me across the contested border.

He's momentarily still as I speak the platitude. I believe him back at the battle with Edwin a year ago.

"Yes, they are," he muses, signalling for mead and food and indicating that I should sit with him on a bench before the vast roaring fire—super-heated blues dance at its centre. Cadwallon is a man who knows how to impress his audience and his warriors both.

My men are loosely alert close to the doorway. Their hands hover near where weapons would usually lie at their waists. I watch Cadwallon's eyes slide over them as though he measures them all and is grudgingly impressed.

Then his eyes clear, and he's looking intently at me, eyes bright.

"But we must speak of the future, not the past, of an alliance and the death of King Edwin."

I'm smiling now. The death of Edwin would be a great thing for me. It would create a vast power vacuum amongst the Saxon kingdoms. I'd be more than happy to step into that breach. Hopefully, with Edwin's death, my own damn brother will die as well, leaving the path clear for me. The nobler brother and the better man.

"Yes, the future," I say, lifting the elaborate drinking horn and swallowing deeply. I pass the horn to Cadwallon, eyebrows high. His smile almost reaches his eyes as he too drinks deeply, his gaze never straying from my face.

2

AD630 - CADWALLON OF GWYNEDD

The (exiled) Court of Cadwallon of Gwynedd, Priestholm

Penda is a giant of a man. I don't believe it's just a physical thing. No, instead, he exudes confidence. I'm a little envious as I sit and watch him drink and look around my hall with his quick looks.

His eyes tell the story of his envy, and it's only that naked need that makes me wary. Is he like this with everyone he meets? Does he crave everything that others have?

I know the story of his battles with the father and son kings. I know that he and his brother are often disunited in their goals. I consider what woman birthed such fiercely independent and proud men. Perhaps she was a Goddess and not a woman after all?

My flight of imagination amuses me, but I keep my smile in check. I'm trying to convey a composure I'm not sure I feel.

I want this alliance.

No, I need this alliance.

Of all the men and would-be-kings throughout this island, it's

Penda who wins the most battles. It's Penda who rides with the most confidence and grapples for what he wants. I require his raw energy and desire to beat King Edwin of Northumbria.

It seems as though every day, I hear new tales of Edwin's greatness and his prowess. It fills my mouth with bile. I've replayed those events from last year so often in my mind that I could relive it, moment by moment, if I wanted. Still, I can't see where I made a mistake, where I let him beat me?

Penda will give me the rawness I need. He fights like no other; his tactics are always surprising and devastating for his opponent.

"Do you have any thoughts on how we can defeat King Edwin?" I ask blandly, as though it's not the thing that keeps me awake each night, tossing and turning as I replay every scenario I can think of; that deprives me of the joy of my woman.

"Yes, I do. We need to bring him far from his land, cut off his retreat and then cut off his balls." Penda gurgles around the drinking horn. I know my eyes widen a little in horror at the evident joy he sees in battle. I want Edwin dead. I don't necessarily want him to suffer. Or do I? I reconsider. I don't much care as long as he's dead.

"And how do you suggest we tempt him far from home?"

Penda stills a little at that and glares at me, his ice-blue eyes intense.

"I thought I should leave some of the planning to you."

Damn. I really wanted him to come armed with an idea. If Edwin suspects I'm trying to force a confrontation with him, I know he'll not come, no matter how much I antagonize him.

We were brothers once. He knows me too well.

"That disappoints you, My Lord?" Penda asks with a slight taunt. I question what he sees on my face.

"No. Well, a little. I'd like someone else to prize Edwin away from his precious Northumbria. I fear he'll guess my involvement if I cause it."

Penda's satisfied smirk slides from his face as he assesses my words.

"You make a good point, Cadwallon. I'll need to think on it more."

That surprises me. I'd envisaged some rage from the warrior, not reasoned thinking. Perhaps, he's more than just brute strength after all.

"Edwin has no problem fighting away from Northumbria. I think he relishes it knowing that he can exact revenge on people who don't call him their Lord. It's luring him away that's the problem. He thinks himself a gracious king. One is keen to turn to diplomacy to get what he wants. One too happy to use religion as his justification."

"But he has no problem using his sword when he wants to."

"Yes, when he feels his honour has been impugned."

"Then we'll have to do just that."

"What?" I say, wondering what I've said that'd cleared Penda's face of its worrying thoughts.

"Do something that he's honour bound to retaliate against."

3

AD630 - PENDA OF MERCIA

The (exiled) Court of Cadwallon of Gwynedd, Priestholm

I still haven't decided what I think of Cadwallon. He seems to be both kingly and not kingly all at the same time. He comes with everything a king should have apart from confidence. Perhaps Edwin's defeat did more than send him running with his tail between his legs? Maybe it made him forget what it means to be kingly?

Either way, this potential alliance can be used to my advantage. I'd do well to have a sturdy ally. Someone who, whether he realises it or not, is considered a king worthy of emulation by many men. What Cadwallon has, others desire. The fact he still holds much of his lands, despite his failure is proof of the loyalty of his men. And that he inspires fears in others. They've not come to make good on his humiliation. That intrigues me.

I could have come as an enemy. Ridden roughshod over this weak king, but I didn't realise how enfeebled he was. Now that I've met him, I'd rather call him a friend than an enemy. My anger at his messenger has dissipated. I'm far more intrigued by what he plans than my initial fury let me think.

His reputation, combined with the success that I'll bring to our endeavour, will ensure we're both regarded as the highest of kings, the most distinguished of warriors. We'll be men to be feared. We'll be united in our purpose.

Food is brought and placed before us. I appraise it carefully. It seems to be good beef, dripping with its juices. I eat it eagerly, and Cadwallon watches my face with interest, grinning when I swallow the food quickly and reach for more.

"It's my favourite," he offers by way of an explanation. "My wife knows the recipe, the herbs, the exact way it must be cooked. She keeps it a secret from everyone. She says she'll always claim my stomach that way."

I nod in delight at the strange little tale. I've not yet taken a wife. I don't much know if I want one. I like variety in my bed.

"Do you not demand that she tells you?" I ask around a mouthful of the delicious meat.

"Where would the pleasure be in that?" he asks. I start to understand him a little more. He prefers to be taunted, have things held away from him. He likes to strive to accomplish the things he achieves. He doesn't want everything to be easy. I'm pleased. What we have planned won't be easy. Provided we both try for it, dream of it, desire it, we'll accomplish what we want. Edwin's death, and possibly my brother's as well. If that's not too much for which to hope. If my brother, as I imagine he will, becomes a problem instead of a stubborn thorn in my finger to be born, his death will become imperative.

"You'll join with me in forcing King Edwin back from my lands?" Cadwallon asks the question that must have been burning his mouth with the desire to ask it. That's why it's taken me two weeks to get here. I've avoided as many of Edwin's warriors as possible and then taken a ship to the island of Priestholm, where Cadwallon is regrouping. Edwin's men scour the land. I know they didn't chase Cadwallon from the battlefield, but they hunt for him now.

Edwin also likes to make things difficult for himself.

I believe he's realised his mistake in letting him go.

The bloody idiot.

"I will, My Lord. We scouted where we could on our way here. I assume you also know where Edwin's men are based."

Cadwallon chuckles at my formal response. My words mask my love of slaying my enemies and decapitating any who step in my way.

"First, we'll take back Mon, and then the land of the Britons. Once they're gone from there."

"And the land of the Middle Angles," I interject quickly. I don't want to send Edwin's warriors their way. There are many amongst the Middle Angles, as we Saxons call the new kingdom, I call family and friends.

"Yes, or, we can send them further north, to Chester and then they'll be almost within their kingdom."

"That would be best," I concur, and he grins at me.

"You have designs on the Middle Angles?" he queries. I shrug. It's not really any of his concern whether I do or not.

"I'm barely even a prince yet, let alone a king," I say. My words make him laugh, his hand hitting the table loudly. His delight shocks me.

"Penda, there's no need to hide your pretensions from me. I don't want the land of the Middle Angles. I just want bloody King Edwin dead and gone."

"You don't wish to be an over king like Edwin or Rædwald before him?" I demand, confused, and not enjoying it.

"No, I don't. I mean, don't misunderstand me, if I could be, then I would. If all the kings and war leaders dropped dead, then I'd be king there. But I don't look for it. Why would I?"

"I want scops to compose poems of my battle prowess, to tell tales of me, fill the heads of foolish young warriors with my name."

Cadwallon raises his drinking horn to my words, his merriment gone.

"I want the same, and I, you'll be pleased to know, already have scops who can do that for you."

I almost smirk at that, but I stop myself. I'm a bloody warrior, not a tittering child.

"One day, I'll have scops," I say instead, maintaining my façade of the mighty warrior.

"You will, my Lord Penda, you will."

I've never yet heard my name with 'Lord' preceding it. I like that, and Cadwallon, damn the man, knows it as well. I try to cover my brief flare of joy, but he's laughing again, not at me but with me, and I join him.

I like Cadwallon, I decide at that moment. I might not be his equal yet, but I will be.

4

AD630 - EDWIN OF NORTHUMBRIA

Ad Gefrin

I've rewarded my men handsomely for their overwhelming victory against the foolish Cadwallon last year. Not that it was any great hardship for them. The men of my war band live for war and plunder, jewels and women. I try to prevent their love of the women, but I don't think they live by my example. Not that I always blame them. But still, when you beat someone into submission, it's best to make sure they can pay their tribute when it's next demanded. Angry men make poor adherents. I know that. My men don't, though.

My hall is a wondrous thing. Yeavering, the farthest north of my royal residences and my favourite. The rawness of its surroundings and its contrariness calls to my nature. When the wind blows hard from the eastern sea or the western mountains, I can imagine the wood of the great hall bowing under the pressure. The shrieks and howls are ungodly. They remind me of my old Gods. The ones I worshipped before being made to turn to this new God.

I don't much know if I like my new God, but he seems to like me, so my second wife and my priest assure me. There's no need for me to love him, providing he watches out for me, and he has, for the last three years.

But back to Yeavering, Ad Gefrin, as the locals call it. When the sun shines, when the weather is fair, my palace in Yeavering is far more pleasant but just as contrary. It can go from bright sunshine to heaving rain in the blink of an eye, black clouds rolling in and turning day to night. I wonder if a woman decides upon the weather? It would make sense to me, although not one who follows the new God. No, a woman who follows the spiteful, self-centred ways of the old Gods must decide the weather. I admire her and almost wish I could be as irrational as her, only I'm a king and a Christian king at that. I must be magnanimous.

It pisses me off.

My men are feasting well from the tribute gained from the northern lands just this past month. The northern kingdom grows fine cattle that are easy to tempt away from their true masters. The beasts are a little slow and too stupid to realise that the men on horses are not their true masters. I grin at the thought. Cows and Gods. I'm in a strange mood today.

My elder sons have joined me for this feast. Osfrith and Eadfrith are not perhaps as I would want them, but I hope to bend them to my will. They'll need to be strong men if they're to hold my kingdom after my death. They'll need to learn guile and deceit and how to kill men with a stare, not just with a sword or a war axe.

As sons go, they've not disappointed me. Yet. I suppose there's always time. But whilst they have their war-bands to support them and my permission to raid where they want, provided it's in the north and not south of the mighty Humber River, they're content. They're men in need of much more shaping. They need the experience. But they've not filled me with enthusiasm for their futures.

My new wife sits with her women. She's refused to sit beside my other guest, Lord Eowa, a warrior from the south, a bloody-thirsty man and one who fought with me against Cadwallon last year.

He tries to mimic my gracious ways, but he's little more than a war-chief at heart. He has a small hideage to claim as his own, thanks to his brother and the loyalty of the men and women who live on the land of the Hwiccan kingdom. He's defended them well in the past. I think that he could be as great a threat as I am one day. That's why I keep him close and have him as my ally. It'll be best for my sons and me if Eowa looks on the hegemony of Northumbria favourably. He grows in power enough to leave his kingdom and visit mine. Enough that he eclipses his brother, Penda, the better warrior but not the man who'll be the king of the Mercian kingdom, with my help.

I have no problem playing this man for a fool if I must, but I'd rather not. I almost like him.

"Fine beef," he says at my side, and I chuckle at his thoughts that so closely resemble my earlier ones.

"It is, yes. It always tastes better when it doesn't come from your own herd."

He grins at that, his face crinkling around his eyes. He might be a younger man than I, but he's spent so much of his time outside, trying to find his enemy, that he carries lines around his eyes that mark him as far older.

"I agree, My Lord Edwin. Always better. You keep a great hall here, isolated as well, and easy to defend."

"I'd like to take credit for its placement, but my forebears first built here. The buildings aren't original because the weather takes its toll on wood and turf, but the site is the home of the royal family of Northumbria." I don't acknowledge that I killed the last king of Northumbria, the man who could truly claim that his forebears built this site. There's no need. Everyone knows about the battle on the banks of the River Idle.

"I wish I had somewhere so magnificent to call my own, but my family isn't as well established as yours. It's never likely to be if my brother has his bloody way," he offers, his tone turning sulky as he speaks.

Ah, Penda. The mighty warrior brother of Eowa. I've never met him or seen him, but I've heard of him. He stands over six feet tall, and he bristles with weapons. I wish I'd managed to ensnare that brother, but I'll have to make do with the one I have. Cadwallon, so I hear, has his hooks firmly into Penda. I've cursed my luck many times since Eowa told me the news on his arrival, but there's little I can do now.

There'll be another battle and soon at that. Provided Cadwallon only has Penda at his back; I'll be victorious.

Bloody Cadwallon.

He should have been brotherly towards me, but then, perhaps our relationship is the same as other siblings I know. We're foster brothers, but we hate each other, just as Eowa and Penda do. There's a certain irony there.

Mothers and fathers should have only one child, never more. It would do away with sibling rivalry and place the dynasty in jeopardy. As a brother, I resent it. As a father, I know the importance of securing a dynasty. Life can be a real bitch.

"I'm sure with time, you'll be able to settle in one place and build a palace as great as this one." I soothe the fractious voice of Eowa but store the information away. I like to know how the minds of the men I hope to trust work if only so I can undermine them when the time is right.

His rivalry with his brother could be his undoing.

It might be mine as well.

5

AD630 - OSFRITH OF NORTHUMBRIA

My father is making an arse of himself again. I'm watching him carefully, trying to decipher what he's saying to the bastard beside him, but I'm failing miserably. I wish I were sat beside him, but he's ensured I sit with my men instead. It's supposed to be an honour for them to feast with me, but I know it's just an excuse so he can speak to Eowa without me.

I don't know what he's planning, not yet, although I have an idea. I wish he could see me as an ally and not his son. But he sees me only as his son and his potential replacement. He gained his throne through stealth and deception. He watches everyone around him as though they mean to do the same to him.

King Edwin exudes confidence and power, but I've seen him when he's weak and his defences are down. I've seen him rock with fear and grief, especially when I was a small boy. I've never spoken to him about it. The knowledge is a more significant weapon when I keep it to myself. He wasn't always such a successful king, and that motivates me. I might not be anything yet, but it doesn't mean I won't be in the future.

I can rise as high as he has. I won't need older men with coarse clothes and the smell of the dead around me to do it.

My father is a vigorous man. He rides at the front of his war band and thinks nothing of it. He doesn't hide behind any other but takes responsibility for all his actions, even the ones I think are terrible. Today he's clean-shaven. In the past, he wouldn't have been. This new God asks strange things of men. His lack of a beard shows he has a stubborn chin, a bent nose and a full mouth. Easy for him to lie with lips such as those.

My brother, Eadfrith, is sitting with his war band as well. He looks as angry as I am, not that everyone else would know that. You have to know my brother to determine what he's really thinking. His face is like a mask, like the faces of Gods etched onto the stone markers, only ever able to look one way, see one thing. Only he sees everything and keeps it deep inside him.

He's a devious bastard, Eadfrith. It's better if we're friends rather than enemies.

"Who's that?" Actulf says to me, pointing with his cow-horn drinking horn at Eowa. Actulf is my childhood friend. I speak my mind to him. Every man needs someone they can trust and on whom they can entirely rely. I think my father used to turn to Eoif. But now, he's made to speak to Paulinus, the man who converted him to the new God on the instructions of King Eadbald. Paulinus, the bishop of our land, not that I know what that actually means, other than he can sit beside my father, unlike myself.

"Eowa, from the land of the Hwicce."

"Is he the one with the brother?" Actulf asks, his mouth filled with food as he does so.

"Yes, Penda. They're enemies at the moment. I think my father hopes to make him an ally."

"Why does he need an ally from the Hwicce? I thought he was king there already?"

"Well, yes, he is, so I don't know. I believe he's so used to intrigue now that he can't turn away from it."

"Is it Cadwallon he hopes to attack again, with Eowa's help?"

I consider my friend's words. He's a man of action and battle. He wears his weapons with great pride, and they mark him as a man, in his opinion. I'm always surprised that he even understands the undercurrents at play within my father's court.

"It must be. But you know. He keeps his secrets from me."

"Yes, I know. There's no need to go on about it again." His tone implies that he's undoubtedly heard enough about my opinion on how my father keeps me ignorant. I smirk at him, and he grins.

As I say, Actulf's my friend and my confidant. He can speak to me as he wants.

"Oh, watch out," he says, his head nodding towards my brother, who's making his way towards me. "What does he want with you?" Actulf asks sourly. He doesn't much like my brother. He never has.

"Well, we'll find out soon enough," I rebuke, and his face turns downwards. But like the issues with my father and me, he knows that the discussion of my brother and he does not need voicing again.

I appreciate that we can respect each other in this regard.

"Brother," Eadfrith says, sliding onto the bench next to me without being asked. Actulf is forced to make room for him.

Eadfrith's younger than I am, but we look alike. Sometimes people confuse us. He's taller than me, if only slightly. His hair is a shade or two darker, but really, that's all I can say to differentiate us. It's in our temperaments that we're opposite.

He's almost smiling as he clasps my arm in welcome, but as he leans closer to me, his words show how angry he is.

"Why the fuck's that jumped up Hwiccan war chief here? What the hell's the king plotting now?"

My brother always refers to our father as 'the king'. It makes me smirk, but it masks his simmering anger at the man. My brother finds Edwin's Christianity to be contrived. He despises our father's new Christian wife.

"War with King Cadwallon?" I ask, and his eyes narrow as he settles himself beside me.

"But we beat him and exiled him to Mon. Why do we need to fight him again?"

"Why don't you ask 'the king'?" I taunt. I'm rewarded for my irony by a heated glare on his otherwise passive face.

"Why don't you fuck yourself?" he hisses. "Oh, that's right, because you bloody can't, and likewise, I can't ask 'the king' anything. If I spend any time with him, I just want to kill him. It's his voice. It grates whenever he opens his mouth."

"Why do you stay?" I ask. The feud between my brother and my father is no secret. Everyone knows they tolerate each other only because they have to.

"Because here I'm the bloody king's son, and I have honours that I'd have to fight for anywhere else. You know that now stop goading me."

"Are you saying, little brother, that you're not good enough to carve out your own land to call your own?"

Actulf chokes on his mead at my words, and he turns away from my brother's scrutiny. As I say, Actulf dislikes my brother, and the feeling is mutual.

I hold my hands up to defray the situation. I really shouldn't needle him, but, well, he's my brother, and it's my right.

"I'm sure we'll find out soon enough."

"I don't like it," he groans, and I shake my head at him. He's no stranger to battle and war, and yet, well, I think he'd rather not have to forge his career in the spilt blood of other men. I don't share his squeamishness.

6

AD630 - EADFRITH OF NORTHUMBRIA

My brother Osfrith. I still don't know what I think of him, although I love him, as I should. Whether I like him or respect him is another matter entirely. I'd not follow him into battle. I know that for a certain fact.

The king. Now him, I hate. It's that simple. I used to try and hide it when I was younger, but as soon as he became a king, and I became a warrior of some renown, I forced the issue and the king? Well, he won on that occasion. I should have left, Osfrith's right, but I stayed. Now, the king and I warily circle each other like two wolves worrying the same piece of carcass. Neither of us wants to take a bite in case the other attacks us whilst we're distracted.

Eowa. I know of him, but I know more about his brother Penda. Now he'd be a better ally for the king to covet. Eowa has skilled warriors, but Penda is a skilled warrior. It's a vital distinction. But I know the king has lost Penda already. He and Cadwallon are already forging an agreement. It's the worst kept secret amongst our people. The king thinks no one knows and that he still appears strong with Eowa at his side.

I'd love nothing more than to point out his error, but then he'd have won something from me, and I intend to give the king nothing. Not one thing.

The news of Cadwallon's open rebellion has filled me with hope. He's the man that could help me belittle the king if I could only find the courage to stand against the king and openly defy him.

The realization that I find it so hard to do more than harbour my resentments against the king has made me doubt myself. Why can't I just rise against him? Why can't I just kill him in his bed? The fear is that at some deep level, I actually love him. I resent that and work twice as hard to hate him.

I know what he'd say if I ever approached him about it. He'd tell me that his new God speaks of the affairs of men's hearts. That love and hate are the same things, only turned on its head.

Fuck the bastard.

I wish I could hate him and not appreciate the truth of his words.

Now my brother, him, I can love no matter our differences. I think he's weaker than I am. Yet we both work to undermine our father, and that takes strength.

The king watches everyone around him, expecting betrayal at every turn. Not that I blame him. Twice, men have tried to kill him, assassinate him in cold blood. It's only his rage that stays my hand from attempting the same. He's ensured that everyone in Northumbria knows that only weak men kill strong kings in their sleep, while they pray or whilst they bed their women.

If he'd been less vocal about assassination, I'd have killed him long ago and made my brother king in his place. Or perhaps I wouldn't.

I'm not convinced that Osfrith and I would be able to rule together.

Northumbria is a new kingdom. It would be easy enough to divide it back into its constituent parts. Perhaps he could have Bernicia, and I could have Deira or vice versa.

Maybe we could make war against each other after our father's death and settle it all once and for all.

My brother is watching me with his intelligent eyes.

He knows me, and he knows how I think.

I'll have to be more careful around him.

"We should speak to Eowa. Let him know we would make better allies than the king."

Eadfrith's eyes open wide at the talk of treason in my father's hall. He chokes in shock.

I grin at him in delight.

That'll teach him to think he knows my thoughts.

I turn back to glare at the king and Eowa, unsurprised when I feel the heat of the king's gaze on me.

He thinks he knows me as well.

He's very, very mistaken.

7

AD630 - EOWA OF MERCIA
THE NORTHUMBRIAN COURT – AD GEFRIN

I'm not yet sure what I think of King Edwin. He's everything everyone says he is. A man other men admire. Yet I don't believe we share much in common. I think he desires things that I don't.

I want my land confirmed as my own and my people to be safe from overlords, war and famine. I get the impression that King Edwin wishes to be more of a God amongst his people, for all that he pretends to this new religion, this one God, whom he should be humble and obedient before. I've made sure I know what this God preaches and expects from his followers. I'm not convinced by Edwin's act, and neither, I think, are many people within this hall.

There's a wise man sat close to us as we feast and drink and regale each other with tales of our military prowess, each one mightier than the one before. It's a competition, I know it is, and Edwin will win because I've fought in a handful of significant engagements in my short time. He's a much older man than me, and he's fought for every piece of land he now claims to rule. No doubt, as I gain in notoriety, that will change. I think many of my clashes will be against my brother, just as Edwin's were against his brother by marriage. But that's something to mull over another day.

Men who want to be kings need to know how to hold a weapon and when to bloody well use one. There's a time for words and a time for deeds and actions. Penda is a man of actions and deeds. I don't yet know what I'll b,e but I think I'll have to fight to hold whatever I get. For now, Penda is off doing what he does best, fermenting trouble.

As I say, a wise old man sits beside me. I think his express purpose is to bore me to tears with tales of this new God, this man who bled for his people, but to my ears, appears to have done little else of worth. Every time Edwin and I stop speaking, the old man manages to interject into our conversation.

Edwin, for all he says he'd like to call me an ally, seems to mean something else entirely. He wants to own me, possess my people, and that's not why I came here.

I plan to be his equal, not his subordinate.

I don't desire to marry into his royal family. I don't require anything more to do with him than I absolutely must.

Belatedly, I realise that Edwin has asked me a question. Quickly I replay the part of the conversation I can remember, trying to decide what he might have asked me. His eyes are fierce as they gaze at me, almost daring me to reveal my ignorance. I take a guess and assume he asks about my greatest victory to date.

"At Cirencester."

He turns to survey the assembled men and women before me, a reminder of how powerful he is.

"In the south?" he asks, "the lands of Cynegils and Cwichelm?"

I nod without speaking. Is Edwin testing me?

"I know of them, but I've never met them," Edwin qualifies, and I nod again, not liking where this conversation is going.

"My allies are in the kingdom of the East Angles and the Kentish lands."

Ah, I'm starting to understand now. He's boasting of his power.

"And the lands to the west and north of here. As you know, I banished Cadwallon to an island known as Priestholm, a tiny little peninsula off the great Island of Mon. I claimed Manx as well."

"I hear you went over the sea as well, towards the lands of the ancient Dal Riatans and the Picts."

Edwin sagely nods as I reveal my knowledge. He claims overlordship over many people. Yet I know that he doesn't hold all of them still. The moment he turns his back, the old war chiefs and kings reassert themselves or plot his destruction. He's already survived two attempts on his life, assassins sent from who knows where to rob him of his breath. I almost wish they'd succeeded.

I certainly think I shouldn't have come here. Not now.

"I have no problem taking men from the heartland of my kingdom. When I'm gone, my sons or my wife guard my kingdom."

Bishop Paulinus coughs into the conversation, and I'm confused until Edwin continues,

"And of course, I have the help of men of God. Bishop Paulinus has come directly from my God's representative on Earth. All the way from the ancient city of Rome, where great warriors heralded from, the men who built the roads and the great stone ruins, who ran rampant across our land to construct the mighty wall that sometimes separated our ancestors from the Picts and the Dal Riatans."

I've heard of this wall, and I'd like to visit it, but I don't know where it is. I'd thought it would run across the top of Edwin's kingdom, but I believe his borders are far in excess of it. I wonder if the tumbled down blocks of stone my men and I raced through is all that remains of it. I believe Edwin is being insulting to those who ruled before him.

Clearly, Edwin is a man who's overly proud of his accomplishments, even when they're not actually his.

I believe every word he says is double weighted. They appear simple enough, but if I take the time to decipher the actual intent, I'll be surprised and, more than likely, angry.

I've heard of Rome. It is a city with stone buildings and viaducts carrying water from the river to the city. Men who wore long tunics stretching to the floor once ruled there. They thought they owned the world. Just as Edwin does now. I consider whether he will fall to ruin as quickly as they did?

"Would you be interested in hearing my teachings?" the bishop asks me once more. I just about manage to suppress a shudder at the thought of it all. I love my Gods. Why would I want a new one?

Before I left to come here, I met with my brother to discuss our tactics. Since the success against Cynegils and Cwichelm, he feels as though we've gained too little. Penda says we could be great kings, should be great kings. Penda said he was disappointed and blamed our lack of success on the overreaching arms of Edwin. Penda also smirked and said that if I tried to ally with Edwin, he'd gut me like a pig. Just as much of a threat, Penda said that Edwin would try to convert me to his new God. It appears as though the second part has come true. I hope the first part doesn't.

My brother and I are uneasy enemies and even more distrustful allies. It could almost be amusing if it weren't so deadly.

I'd laughed at my brother. I'd told him that no newly converted king was going to sway me to his new God. Yet now, I find myself being offered that very thing. I speculate whether Penda can see the future before it happens. I consider if that's part of his power.

I curse myself for not thinking of this eventuality and for not devising an answer that's both non-committal and inoffensive.

"I thank you both for your offer. I'll think on it."

Bishop Paulinus sagely nods as he listens to my answer. King Edwin grins a little as though he already knows I'll change my mind. That annoys me.

"Your sons," and Edwin looks at me, a quizzical look on his face, "they have followed your faith?" I ask. I notice the faint grimace that flies across his face.

"My young son and my wife are, of course, of the new faith. It's because of our marriage that I discovered the error of my ways and turned to the correct God, the one God. My elder sons? Well, they still need a little more convincing. At the moment, they tell me one thing, and Bishop Paulinus another." Edwin tries to make light of his displeasure but does so poorly.

"They're impressed by the miracles our God can work," Bishop Paulinus clarifies. "The healing of the sick, the effect that the relics of our saints have on others. It's only a small matter of a little more time, and they'll be resplendent in their faith of God."

I nod as the two men speak, trying to show some interest, but really the only thing that makes me sit a little straighter is the strange allusion to relics and bones. Do they really mean to tell me that they worship the parts of dead people?

"Bones?" I enquire, and Edwin looks to Bishop Paulinus to answer my unspoken question.

"Yes, My Lord. The holy men and women we revere are made holier by their deaths. Our God works in mysterious ways, and their relics are taken to show to our people, to reinforce their faith."

I feel revolted by that but hold my tongue. My Gods call for rites that might seem strange to these Christians, followers of Christ, but we bury our dead with grave goods to help them in the afterlife. We don't bury them and then steal back parts of their body and take them on processions. It seems morbid even to me.

"I have some with me. Would you like to see?" Bishop Paulinus offers, hopefully. Now I don't know what to say. Surely it would show some good faith if I just looked at them?

I'm a man of my faith. I have to be. I'm the king of my people, the man who decides on matters of justice and belief. But I'm not closed to the faiths of others. I've heard that men and women devote their lives to all sorts of strange religious beliefs. Admittedly most of them are something that I can relate to, but I'm not about to alienate anyone by refusing to understand their views.

"My thanks, Bishop Paulinus. That would be most welcome. You could perhaps tell me the stories and miracles that have occurred around the relic as well. I know of many strange mysteries in my faith."

There, that's only half-grudgingly done. Bishop Paulinus is happy, and so is King Edwin. I only hope my Gods are as forgiving of my vacillating.

The feast continues long into the night. I'm pleased when a scop steps before us all and begins to recount tales of my Gods. I feel on safer ground here.

Bishop Paulinus looks uncomfortable at the stories and tales, but King Edwin smiles as he listens. His young wife looks furious, but I'm sure Edwin is playing to his strengths. No doubt there'll be a purpose to the tales I hear.

The words of the scop give me the excuse I need to draw my attention away from Edwin and his bishop. I take the time to study this hall. It's a huge, long thing, well-built and well-constructed. The wind, and the wind is harsh here in the north, only blows occasionally through some of the wooden sides, sending the smoke from the fire swirling through the smoke hole in the roof. I'm surprised by how warm it feels. It's not been a pleasant day outside. The men have hinted that snow might come. I hope it doesn't. I don't want to be stuck here, more a captive than ever in my life.

I rode first to the other royal site, on the coast, at Bamburgh, where King Edwin inferred he might be staying when he reached out to me. But he was already gone from the impressive site. It looked strongly defensible, with its wooden ramparts, deep trenches, and its difficult path to the summit, guarded by men and weapons.

I was pleased to turn away until I came here to Yeavering, or Ad Gefrin as some call it. I'm not sure of the correct terminology, as the men and women seem happy to roll both words around their mouths. I'm not going to show my ignorance and question it.

The place is constructed almost as well as the fortress at Bamburgh. I think Ad Gefrin owes much of its sleeping malice to the rolling hills and harsh weather. I've been here but half a day, and already I've seen sunshine, lashing rain from blackened clouds and even the odd piece of hail falling from a grey-rimmed sky.

It's bloody cold as well. I know I'd be shivering if it weren't for the great fire, fed with huge logs in the centre of the room. My huge fur cloak that I used when travelling here is soaked through from the rain, hail and general mizzle that afflicts these lands. It's drying by the heat of the fire. I miss its' comforting warmth, although its stink leaves much to be desired.

I hope it's returned to me before I have to spend the night here. I can't imagine it's warm at night if it isn't during the day.

The feast doesn't seem to be calming down. I wonder if I'll have to extradite myself from it because I'm growing too tired to sit still. The mead had deadened much of my exhaustion, but even that's worn off by now. It's been a long day.

At my side, King Edwin thankfully yawns widely and then turns apologetic eyes my way.

"It's been a long day. Come, I've been a poor host. I'll show you where you can rest, and then tomorrow, you and Bishop Paulinus can speak again about your faith. Then, of course, we can talk about an alliance."

Wonderful, I think. Just what I need. I came here to talk about men and battle, not my faith. I stifle my yawn as I follow King Edwin from the hall and out into the bleak night. A slave has helpfully brought my nearly warmed cloak to me. I shrug into it gratefully. It's bitterly cold.

Edwin stops just outside and looks up into the sky. It's clear he isn't going to come with me to the room where I'll be sleeping.

"Lord Eowa," he says, and I turn to glance at him, burrowing deeper into my cloak as I do so. I'd far rather have spoken inside the hall than out here.

"The old Gods tell us of our fates, that they watch us make the preordained steps that they decide we should follow. The only thing my new God promises me is that if I live a 'good life,' I'll go to his heaven when I die. I know what I'd rather know."

With that, he leaves me to the cold and the swirling snow and my thoughts.

Shit. Penda was bloody right. I'll make sure never to tell him.

8

AD630 - EANFRITH OF BERNICIA

The broch is smoky from the fire at its centre that struggles to poke its way out of the tightly woven roof that crests it. This is my home now. It has been for more years than it hasn't. My wife is here, my son, my adopted family. And yet, on nights such as this, when the fire is smoky, and the air is chill and damp, I find myself reminded of my past, of who I should have been and who I could yet be. Nights such as this remind me of my home in Bamburgh. My birthright. Stolen from me.

This king of Northumbria, Edwin, slew my father in battle, his brother by marriage, and sent my mother, his sister, and the rest of her children scampering into exile to keep our lives. I'm grateful to the people who saved me, who provided for me when I was no more than a youth. But sometimes, I'd like to reward their allegiance and prove to them all that I'm not just a dead king's son. I want to be a king in my own right, not just married to a royal line, but the head of one too.

My wife hates nights such as these. She long ago learned to stay away from me when my moods turn dark, and I despise everyone, including myself. On nights such as these, I'm no one's friend and everyone's enemy.

But this night is a little different to the ones I've had in the past. On this night, a stranger sits beside me, and he speaks softly and urgently to me of events taking place in my old homeland. Of the arrogance of King Edwin. Of his recent victory against Cadwallon and how Cadwallon is not about to accept the defeat without countering it.

His voice is strangely accented, and yet I understand his every word. I imagine that my years away from my people, speaking the language of the Picts, have changed my perceptions of how the men from beyond the borders sound.

I like what I'm hearing. Cadwallon is one of a handful of men who's strong enough to tackle Edwin. Cadwallon's defeat two years ago was a setback for me, but, well, now this stranger tells me of a new warrior, Penda. A man from the heartland of our island who plans on allying with Cadwallon and bringing Edwin to his knees. A man who's already skilled in warcraft and who works to carve out his reputation.

This is a man I think I've been waiting for my entire adult life.

This is the man I wish I could be but know to lack the skills and the wherewithal.

I thrill to hear of Penda's victory over two kings at a place called Cirencester, of his growing power within his heartland. Of his skill with sword and war-axe.

I wish I could fight as well as he does.

This man, Herebrod, says he's one of Penda's most proficient warriors and that he comes with a message of friendship. Penda wishes me to join the alliance, to pit myself against Edwin, my uncle, and steal his kingdom.

The man's words fill me with hope and fear in equal measure. The urge to join the alliance is great, far greater than anything I've considered in the past. I have my band of nearly fifty warriors; it would be nothing for me to take them to Penda, to join him when they decide to attack. In the past, there was only me who wished to exact vengeance. Me and my men alone wouldn't have been enough.

Fifty men would have been nothing more than an annoying insect sting to a man with the resources of Edwin.

Now, things have changed. Suddenly and unexpectedly.

For the first time in years, I feel a jolt of excitement.

I could have it all back—all of it.

"Tell me again the words of the message."

The man is very patient. I've already asked him to do this on three other occasions, but I want to be sure that I've heard everything. Not that the message has changed in the repeated retellings, not at all, but I want to be sure. Just one more time.

"Eanfrith of Bernicia," I like the beginning of the message already. Penda and King Cadwallon have read their history or know my history, for that's my title. My father might have claimed more for himself in his lifetime, but I would be happy with Bernicia and the royal sites at Bamburgh and Yeavering. My mother was Acha of Bernicia, and I would be Eanfrith of Bernicia if I were its king.

"Greetings from Penda, war-chief of the Hwicce and Cadwallon, King of Gwynedd and both enemies of Edwin, self-styled King of Northumbria, and usurper of your throne. We extend our sorrow for your great losses and hope that we might soon correct the wrongs done to you and your family. This messenger, Herebrod, will wait for a response."

"It doesn't really say what they plan to do?" I query because that's my worry. I don't want to endanger my family if I join an alliance. I might be unhappy here, but my wife is a princess, and my son is a prince of the royal family who rules the land of the Picts. He might be a king here one day, so why would he need my old kingdom? Neither do I want the Picts to pay for my disgruntlement. King Edwin is a menace on their southern border, always trying to push them further and further north.

"Well, they thought it best not to say too much until they had some token of your agreement to join them. I do know that they plan to attack him in the future."

"War?" I ask, my excitement mounting. Herebrod shares a conspiratorial grin with me and reaches for his weapons belt. I feel a stirring of unease, but I keep myself still. There's no reason for him to attack me. I'm no threat to anyone, not here and not now. I'm a man with warriors sleeping in their bed whilst I brood and moan.

Herebrod pulls from his belt a small ornamental hammer made from silver and gold and inlaid with a flashing jewel on the handle. He hands it to me.

"A small token," he says, bowing his head. With that movement, I believe every word he's said to me. Excitement stirs within me as I feel the weight of the small hammer. It's not a hollow emblem but a piece of precious solid metal, and it speaks louder than any spoken message mouthed by their messenger.

This is the intention behind sending the man to speak to me.

"My thanks," I mouth, running my thumb over the jewel-encrusted in the silver handle.

Suddenly the smoky broch and the bad temper leave me.

I'm going to be a king.

I'm going to join the alliance of King Cadwallon and Penda.

There was never really any choice.

9

AD630 - OSRIC OF DEIRA

The messenger arrives in a whirl of snow and wind, looking more like an angry bear than any man. I can tell he brings bad news before he opens his mouth. He might be King Edwin's messenger to me, and therefore effectively his man, but he has a grudging respect for me. He doesn't like the way that King Edwin treats me.

Edwin has little regard for me, his cousin, even though he relies on me to do unpleasant things that he can trust no one else to do.

I'm almost his toy to pick up and put down when he's fed up with all his other activities. I'm his final resort when any problems present themselves.

I could hate him for it, but I feel fiercely loyal to him.

He's my king and my cousin. He was my childhood friend. He brought me back from exile with him, and I'm grateful for that. He would have been well within his rights to leave me behind. After all, his experiences of family life weren't exactly to be commended, not after his banishment at the hands of his brother-by-marriage. Not that he seems to have held that against him. Oh no, not at all. That's why he personally killed him when they met in battle.

No, I think despite my unhappiness with the current situation that it's better to keep on the good side of Edwin. We were raised together before our banishment. Mighty warriors must still have some friends in later life. I hope he looks upon me as his friend.

I would certainly fight to the death for him. He has my respect, no matter what.

"Osric," the messenger, Liefbrun says, doing me the courtesy of only a small nod of the head to acknowledge that I'm his superior. We've talked about this before, and I'm tired of asking him not to do it. This small show of respect is our unspoken compromise.

"Liefbrun, you look as though you've brought half the winter with you," I comment sourly. The chill of frozen air has rushed through the hall, causing the great fire to gut a little. I don't like to be cold.

"My Lord, it's bitter out there, and yet Edwin was insistent that I come to you with a message."

We both roll our eyes at that. No matter how much we respect our king, we've both commented, when we're a little drunk and a lot warmer, that Edwin worries about things he shouldn't. As his representative sitting in his hall at Goodmanham, I often think he sends me details that I don't need to know.

"What's the message?" I ask. It'll be something mundane. He might want to tell me about a story of his new God that Bishop Paulinus has told him. Or he might want to tell me about a new ally. Either way, it really could have waited until the weather improved.

"He asks me to tell you that he's attempting to ally with Eowa of the Hwicce. He wants you to travel south, when the weather improves a little, his words not mine," Liefbrun says grumpily, "and ensure that his other allies are standing firmly behind him."

"Which other allies," I ask. Edwin changes his allies more often than I eat, or at least that's how it sometimes feels.

"Just all of them," he answers unhelpfully, a glint in his grey eyes. He knows that I'll need informing with whom Edwin is currently friendly. Since Edwin became king, he's ravaged Elmet, Lindsey and tried his hand amongst the tribes of the ancient Britons and the Dal Riatans. He's turned his young foster brother against him, a feat even I find amazing.

King Cadwallon was always in awe of Edwin. They were even closer than Edwin, and I were. When I journeyed to meet Edwin when he was in exile at the court of Cadwallon's father, I was amazed and also a little jealous of their close friendship even though Edwin was so much older than Cadwallon. It was clear their respect for each other was genuine.

Yet, Edwin sometimes lacks the skills he needs. He thinks men do what he says through love or loyalty. He doesn't realise how often honour and its satisfaction makes men do things they wouldn't normally consider doing.

An oath can mean more than anything else.

An oath is far too powerful amongst our people.

I glare at him, and he meets my gaze levelly before relenting.

"The king of Kent, the king of the East Angles and the king of the West Saxons, or Wessex, whatever they call it, are the only ones he mentioned for now."

Wonderful, I think. I'm not entirely a great supporter of any of these men. They, like Edwin, all have faults that make me consider why men and women support them as they do.

I've formed a list of attributes I think kings and war-leaders should and shouldn't have, and many of these attributes are lacking in the three men.

"He wants me to go now?" I ask.

"Yesterday would be better," he quips, and I glare at him again.

"Are you coming with me?" Edwin might well trust me to go and speak for him, but he likes to have other men in attendance just to ensure he hears everything, garners the opinions of all.

"Yes, as always, and not because King Edwin asked me to, but to watch your back. My sword is a little rusty of late."

"I doubt that," I say sourly, as Liefbrun grins at me once more.

"Any other news I need to know?"

Liefbrun turns more taciturn.

"Only things I've observed," he says, and I look at him meaningfully. Liefbrun's a good judge of a man's character if he can hold off killing them for long enough that they make an impression on him

"His sons are unhappy. His wife has too much sway. Bishop Paulinus is causing more problems than he should."

"Just a few things," I respond darkly. Edwin should know better than to alienate his sons, but as I said, there are some parts of the nature of men that Edwin simply doesn't understand.

"Who's the greater threat?" I query.

"His sons and his new son and his wife," Liefbrun responds quickly. He's been giving the matter a lot of thought.

"So his family is the problem, as always," I muse. "Why are men always so impervious to the discord they create in their families?" I ask, but it's not really a question, and Liefbrun stays silent. He's finally taken his great cloak off, and the snow is melting in his long hair. He looks less bear-like, but he could become that creature at a moment's notice.

"Did you speak to the sons?" I demand, and this time I do expect an answer.

"I always do. They don't say anything to me, but their disapproval of the alliance with Eowa is easy to see."

"The king of Mercia?" I ask. Men and women change places so often that it's all I can do to keep track.

"Yes, well, sort of. He styles himself king of the Hwicce, but he's growing in stature and land. Since Cearl's death, Mercia has disintegrated into a series of petty kingdoms."

"Is he a member of Osfrith and Eadfrith's extended family?" I muse. I will never forget that my cousin was first married to a pagan woman, the daughter of the king of Mercia. I think everyone else overlooks that small fact now that his new wife is such a huge presence at the Northumbrian court.

"No, another family."

"And that's why they resent him?"

Liefbrun shrugs his broad shoulders.

"I imagine so. The lads are loyal to the family of their mother. Probably more loyal than they are to their father."

"And Eowa threatens their mother's family."

"He does."

"Did you perhaps mention to Edwin that he should be assessing the risks of allying with Eowa before he worries about his other allies?"

Doing that is far above anything Liefbrun should be doing, and I know it. I'm asking him to do something that even I'd think twice about doing.

"No, it's not my place to say anything. But you can. Once you return and inform Edwin that the other men are still with him, I'm sure he'll do whatever you suggest."

Great, I think. Just what I don't need.

"Any other news?" I ask. I'm hoping for something good to hear, but I doubt I'm going to get it.

"King Cadwallon is amassing supporters. He has Penda now."

I'm not sure I know who Penda is. I'm searching my memory for the name, and then it comes to me.

"Eowa's brother?" I ask with disbelief. "The one who can kill with a look, or so the rumour goes."

"The very same."

"Why are they splitting sides?" I speculate. This smacks of something far more significant than a family rift. They've worked together in the past when they attacked the father and son kings of Wessex. Why aren't they anymore?

"I don't know, but I don't like it. As usual, Edwin doesn't see more than what he wants to see."

I sigh.

"You bring nothing but conspiracy and a threat of war," I complain, and Liefbrun is silent as he absorbs my complaint. When he doesn't try and justify his actions, I know that he sees troubled times ahead.

"Will we ever have peace?" I ask of no one in particular.

"Not whilst kings play at gods and gods play at kings," he mutters softly, and I glance at him sharply. I've never known Liefbrun to offer something quite so profound.

Damn the man. This will cause a lot of problems if even Liefbrun can see them.

10

AD631 - PENDA OF MERCIA

Herebrod returns with the better weather, his face tinged blue and wearing so many cloaks, at first, I think he's a hungry wolf come to ravage our force.

But his grin when he sees me is all I need to know.

Eanfrith of Bernicia is with us. He'll stand against the man who murdered his father and exiled him and his family. That's excellent. The coming battle needs to involve as many people as possible. King Edwin will call on all his allies. I plan on having as many lined up against him. And more than that, I hope that we'll turn some of his most loyal followers so that Edwin thinks they're with him until he meets his death on their sword or mine. Although King Cadwallon wants that honour for himself.

Foster brothers hate each other as much as brothers do.

The plan Cadwallon and I have made is simple. He'll use all his powers to persuade the small kingdoms of the ancient Britons to come against Edwin. Cadwallon says it'll be easy to convince the men who live in the kingdom of Powys because Edwin attacked them, leaving a swathe of death and destruction in his wake. The others might take more convincing.

I'll bring my warband and warriors from whatever parts of the central lands I currently hold sway over. For the time being, we're not counting on my brother's support. He's off, having his head swayed by Edwin. Eowa's fool enough that he'll believe whatever words King Edwin says rather than stand at my side.

Brothers can be hateful to each other, especially, and I'm not speaking out of immodesty when the younger brother is the better warrior than the older. Eowa needs to live in a more settled time than this. He can fight when he must, but he'd be more comfortable ruling a calmer land with designated borders and more congenial enemies. The bloodthirsty glut that runs through this island is not to his taste.

Luckily, it is to mine.

King Edwin will call his allies. Amongst their number, he'll count his grown sons and the kingdom of the East Angles and the kingdom of Kent, men who he can reach out to because they share their new God. He can also, possibly, rely on Wessex because I overwhelmed the king there and took the lands of the Hwicce from them. No matter that my brother now holds the kingdom, it's me who made it possible, and that will allow the kings in Wessex to side with Edwin.

But as I say, the land is not settled yet. Kingdoms come and go. Smaller peoples are absorbed into others, and nothing stays the same for long. Alliances are generally short-lived things. Men who think in terms of blood and death to gain what they want can rarely refrain from visiting the same on their allies when they become their enemies. And then, more often than not, they fall prey to the same fate themselves.

Men who become kings, rarely understand their weaknesses and always overestimate those of their enemies.

I've made an effort to examine what I know of my land, to decide what I want and how I'm going to achieve it. It's disappointing that my brother stands in my way so often, but I do love him, for all that we're often enemies. For now, that stops me from taking any action I might come to regret.

I almost welcome the coming battle because I'll finally know Eowa's mind. I'll know if he wishes to rule with me or to rule alone. Whether we'll be allies or enemies.

We went into battle together against the father and son kings in Cirencester, but I managed to come away the victor, not him. Even though he holds the land now. Men speak of my might and skills with a sword and war axe, never of his. I perceive he resents that, and I enjoy his unhappiness. He doesn't speak to me about it. I don't mention it to him. But it's a problem and always will be.

It's Eowa's problem, though, not mine.

"Tell me about him," I ask Herebrod when we're settled for the night. I want to know who my new ally is.

Herebrod, relaxed at last under our canvas home for the night, shrugs his broad shoulders.

"I thought he was no more than a foul-tempered beast when I first met him. The weather was cold and damp. He was huddled beside a meagre fire, his face black and his mood even darker. But as I spoke to him, I realised he might have a spark inside him that could be kindled. Just as when the fire burns too low because of a lack of interest in it. He can be contrary," Herebrod admits.

"He listened to my message, and he asked me questions. Then he made me speak it again and again. Each time, he seemed a little more hopeful, but when I gave him the jewelled hammer, his interest really spiked. Only then did he speak to me about what he'd like to do to King Edwin." Herebrod's eyes flash darkly at the memory of the revelation.

"He hates him, despises him. Although he's a prince in the land of the Picts, as King Cadwallon said, with a wife and a son, he dreams of being the king of Bernicia. Your advice to address him as such made him more open to my words. He grinned when I called him such." Herebrod speaks with relish now.

"I didn't see him fight, but he has a war band and the men who I did see training were highly skilled. They use different techniques to us, but that will be to our advantage."

"Don't you think King Edwin will know how the Picts fight?" I ask, and he shrugs again. He's not considered that. But his role wasn't to think. It was just to see what he thought of Eanfrith and whether he thought he'd be good for the alliance or not.

The fact that Herebrod's an excellent warrior was the other deciding factor. I didn't want to lose anyone in the northern lands. My men are all well-skilled, and I've trained them myself. It was a huge task I set myself when I was no more than a youth. I know they can all fight themselves out of even the most challenging situation. It's nothing for them to take on five men at once. Maybe even ten, and still be the victor.

I've taught them to fight with instinct, to listen to their movements and know what the enemy plan. To watch facial expressions and interpret the intent of their enemy. My men could fight in a darkened cave without even knowing how many opponents they faced and still prevail.

That's why King Cadwallon chose me and not my brother to be his main ally. I'm subordinate to him; I accept that because he's the acknowledged king. A king without all of his kingdom, but he's constantly pushing back Edwin's pretensions. It won't be long until the menace of their war two years ago is banished forever.

I might have met King Cadwallon on the tiny island of Priestholm, his last bastion just off the larger island of Mon, but I helped him take back Mon. I'm an excellent ally, and I showed him just that. I helped him regain a foothold on the mainland.

He was impressed. He can't deny it.

But my thoughts wander. I need to know more about this prince of the Picts.

"How old is his son?" It's essential to know. Is my ally likely to have a last moment change of heart because his son is too young, too old or about to marry?

"A lad, no more. Probably the same age you were when I met you?" Herebrod laughs at that, a deep sound that comes from the very centre of his body. We were bloody idiots when we were younger. We met with a fistfight, and we've not improved since. Not when we're together, and there's no one to make us see reason. No one can stop us from fighting when we start. Only exhaustion puts an end to our many and frequent bouts.

It keeps our skills keen. It's not because, with just one word, he can make me want to kill him there and then. Not at all.

"His wife?"

He shrugs once more.

"A thing of beauty that I'd happily help myself to if I were allowed."

I arch my eyebrows at that admission. That's a fine confession from him. He likes his women to be as beautiful as a Goddess before he considers dipping his cock. He has the tastes of a mighty king who can force everyone to do what he says, not those of a rough and ready warrior prepared to fight for every morsel of food he eats.

I like him. Shit, I probably love him more than my brother. But I shouldn't. I fear that eventually, one of us will end up killing the other, and I don't plan on dying. Not at his hand.

"His home?" I ask. Speaking to Herebrod can be a bit like having parts of your body pared off one tiny piece at a time. He sees and watches everything, but he keeps the information to himself unless you take the time to extract it from him.

"A strange place, built from stone and thatch, filled with curving slopes and odd little rooms. Surprisingly warm and comfortable."

"Is that how they all live?"

I've heard of stone halls and wooden buildings, even buildings made of animal muck and mud, but this thing he describes intrigues me the most.

"But they are men and women as we are?" I check.

He chuckles at my question.

"Apologies, Penda, I didn't mean to laugh. I thought the same myself when I first came across them, but I didn't want to admit it. But yes, they're men and women just like you and me. All the parts work the same," he adds as an afterthought, and it's my turn to laugh at him.

"You enjoyed your trip north more than you implied?" He chuckles and doesn't answer me with words. The women must be beautiful indeed.

The homes of the people on this island are strange and varied. The people who lived before us, who built with stone and fashioned roads out of stone, who used stone to make images of themselves, had skills that men and women no longer claim. Either that or no one is committed enough to take the time to learn. Or, I think darkly, no one can settle for long enough to learn the skills. Men and women who think themselves would-be-kings run in swathes across the land, taking what they can and murdering what they can't. The land is almost lawless. A mighty king must be everywhere at once to protect everyone who needs his sword to stay safe.

"I'd fight for one," he finally mutters. I laugh out loud at his revelation. I'm not used to seeing this side of him. Normally he gripes about everything and the lack of pretty women in particular.

"He'll be fine," Herebrod also adds. "Although, well, I think he'll only be your ally for as long as it's suitable for him. If you make him the King of Bernicia, or whatever the place is called, he'll turn on you soon enough. I'm warning you."

"I don't plan on being King of Bernicia, so why would he turn on me?"

"Cause he's mindful of what was taken from him. He won't want anyone else to steal it."

Once more, Herebrod's surprises me. Maybe I have taught him to think after all.

"I'll think on it," I say. Herebrod grunts at the admission and returns to his eating and drinking.

Outside, the night is chill and cold. The dark time of the year is passing but fitfully as though it's not quite sure it wants to give up on winter. We've met on the gentle slopes of a hill, and my men and I had hoped that the slope would temper the wind at our back. Clearly, we were wrong.

Now that Herebrod and his companion have returned to me, there are twenty of us all together. A small force, and intentionally so. We don't ride to bring war but to reconnoitre the land this far north. I've been here before, but that was before I trained myself to remember where every river, stream, farm and road ran. I carry a depiction of the land in my head, and still, I've not found the perfect spot to take on King Edwin.

But I will.

Herebrod and I will shelter within this tent for the night, most of the other men also managing to sleep, but four will stay awake all night. Ever alert and make sure that our enemies do not attack us.

Admittedly our reputation goes before us now, and any one who did try to attack us would die. But I sleep more soundly if I know someone else is watching my back.

"Have you spent the winter with King Cadwallon as you expected to?" Herebrod stirs me from my thoughts, and I nod to say I did.

"Were any other war leaders there?"

Now it's my turn to laugh. I don't worry when Cadwallon entertains other war leaders. I'm safe in my position. We've both made oaths to each other, and despite everything I've said about the fickle nature of men, I do believe him. More than that, I trust him as well.

A small part of me also knows that I'll kill him if he plays me false. He'll do the same to me.

"Yes, a few. Well, okay many. He didn't lie when he promised to entice more men into our alliance. The men of Powys almost fell over themselves, agreeing to it. He's even had warriors from Dumnonia and from across the sea, the land of Dal Riata. And, and I liked this one the most, a priest from their new God, the religion that Cadwallon already follows."

Herebrod grins in relief to hear that.

"Good, I'd feared I might be working for an alliance that no longer existed."

I roll my eyes at him.

"I didn't think you were a worrier?"

"I'm not," he responds quickly, "but well, it's been a long winter."

And it has. He's been gone many months, and I've missed him.

"I think the next few years might be long, but then, well, King Edwin will be dead, and you can go back to your woman."

"I might just like that," he lisps, and in no time at all, his snores fill the small space.

Fuck, I'd forgotten how noisy he was!

11

AD631 - CADWALLON OF GWYNEDD

The priest prattles to me. I listen with half an ear. He's come to preach peace, and I want to show him where he can stick his exhortations to his God. My God is the same as his, only older and wiser, more secure in his hold on my heart. He almost seems gentler to me. Yet, according to this priest, it is I who go against God's words and God's teachings with my thirst for vengeance.

I think, in a roundabout way, he's here to offer me the support of the Church in Kent. But it's so convoluted, I may have sharpened my sword to such a point by the time he gets to it that my sword will be embedded deep within his throat.

Penda has gone to meet the man he sent to treat with Eanfrith. I miss his presence in my hall. He's not a loudly spoken man, but even so, men and women listen to his words, even when he doesn't want them to.

It was a good decision of mine to entice him to my alliance. His brother, so I hear, isn't half as charismatic as Penda. I think it's magnetism that I need. My men are great warriors, yet they buckled under Edwin's onslaught. They had the skills, the weapons, the desire to win but Edwin, well, he did something, enacted some magical force over his men and then annihilated my carefully formed battle plan. Edwin says he fought with his God on his side, but his God is my God, so that argument holds no power over me.

To be victorious, I need that same power Edwin created, and I don't have it. But Penda does. If he weren't so firmly my follower, I'd fear him.

I wonder if Edwin yet knows what's coming for him.

I watch a commotion at the door with intrigue as someone I don't know walks towards me. He looks remarkably like my childhood foster brother, and I almost grab for my weapon, but reason stays my hand. I quickly appreciate that my good fortune just keeps growing. Surely, this must be one of Edwin's children, a nephew or a niece. Another one comes into my fold.

My seneschal is rushing towards me, trying to reach me before the hooded warrior does, but he only makes it by a few footsteps.

"Osfrith, My Lord," he manages to gasp before the man is in front of me. I nod and dismiss my seneschal in the same movement.

"My Lord Cadwallon," the man says, and I nod.

"And you might be?" I ask despite the words from my seneschal. He's a well-built man who looks well able to defend himself in the event of an attack. But he has hard eyes. I'm not sure I trust them.

"Osfrith of Northumbria," he answers. I appraise him carefully. I need to show disdain and no deference, even if his father soundly beat me in battle two years ago.

"Please sit and take food and mead," I respond. He does as he's told, the handful of men who must be his guards blending into the background. My seneschal will have ensured they're armed with nothing more than an eating knife. But I still run my eyes over them all, deciding who's the real threat. A few of the men bristle with their unhappiness. Still, I think the real power here is the man who sits beside me.

"What can I do for you?" I ask Osfrith, and he speaks without looking up from his food. He's ravenous. His men are watching him with some longing. Hungry men can be foul-tempered. I gesture for them to be seated and given food as well. A bench is brought so that they still protect their lord's back.

"I think it might be more what I can do for you?" he responds, his voice ominous.

"What can you do for me then?" I ask, trying to keep the flicker of annoyance from my words. He has a high opinion of himself. It's one I don't share, but, well, if he comes to ally with me, I'd be a bloody idiot not to jump on the opportunity.

"I can help you draw my father out and assist you in killing him in battle."

This raises my interest, but only a little bit. There is any number of ways to tempt Edwin to battle. Penda has thought of circumstances to enrage the king, some more outrageous than others. I think we should employ the most mundane of reasons. Penda believes the opposite. I'm curious to see what Osfrith thinks.

"How would you do that?" I ask

"Play to his weaknesses," his son says around a mouthful of food. I try not to watch in horror at the way he eats. Do they not feed their warriors in Northumbria?

"So, what are his weaknesses?" This is a painful conversation. It's quite upsetting my good mood.

"His new family, his new God, his new land."

Ah, I'm disappointed. He doesn't bring me anything I don't already know.

"What of his old family and his old Gods?" I push. I want some sort of reaction from this strange youth before me.

"Those things have no impact on him. He cares only for new things, not old things. It's almost as though the first forty years of his life didn't exist at all."

I hear the bitterness despite the affected tone that Osfrith uses. He's unhappy with his father. An unhappy son is a foolish enemy for a father to create. Especially a father who believes he should rule the entirety of this island; well, all of the Saxons, at least.

My people know themselves as the British or the Britons. We share similarities with others who live within the lands of the Britons, but each kingdom is a little different. Our laws and justice might be similar, but there are always slight disparities, little nuances that set us apart.

"That must make things difficult for you?" I ask, but Osfrith doesn't answer my question. He pretends not to hear, although I know he has because his shoulders slump a little. He's trying damn hard not to show his true feelings.

"Why come to me?" I ask, pressing him for more information. I want to know what he's heard? What Edwin knows? Penda warned me that his brother was going north to meet with Edwin at Yeavering. He assured me that his brother was ignorant of our alliance. But Eowa may know anyway.

I'm always amazed by how quickly word reaches my enemy. I sometimes fancy that the rocks talk to each other, or perhaps the streams whisper to one another. Either way, it pisses me off how my most secretive of secrets are spread to my enemies and amazed that it takes allies far longer to become aware of the self-same facts.

I'm still waiting for an answer.

"You're almost my family. I feel as though I can come to you with my problems."

I laugh at that. I can't help myself, and Osfrith scowls at me around his food. Not the best way to make an ally.

"Apologies, Osfrith. It's just that you can claim familial ties with almost every war chief on our island. So why choose me?"

"My father always said you were too clever for your own good," he says, his mouth almost turned up in humour. "I came to you because of your defeat two years ago," he finally says. "I assumed you'd be keen to exact your revenge on him."

At last, a bit of honesty that rings true.

"That's right," I say. "I'm already firmly back in control of just as much land as I used to have. Your father has been pushed back from the land of the Britons. Why would I intend to do more than that?"

Osfrith's eyes narrow further. He knows I'm playing a game with him, but he's come to me. He's made his intentions far too apparent. I could almost call him a fool. But I believe he comes to test the waters, to see whether he can exact the greater promises from his father or me.

"You and my father are allies turned enemies. I assumed, and correct me if I'm wrong, that you want to stamp out his pretensions to the lands of the Middle Angles, the Mercians as they call themselves. That you want to box him back into the lands of the Northumbrians, and maybe even just the land of Deira, his birthright."

"I'd quite like to see him suffer as much as I did," I say slowly and without malice. Osfrith's words fill me with excitement and also fear. I plan to do those things, but I don't want my intentions so easily uncovered. I hope, as he says that his understanding of me comes from my one-time friendship with his father.

I knew Osfrith as a boy before his father was the king of anywhere. When Edwin was still reliant on Rædwald of East Anglia for every morsel that came his way. When Edwin had exhausted the good graces of the king of Mercia and made use of the Mercian king's daughter to whelp sons.

"As would I," he replies, his eyebrows raised. I almost blurt out my goal to him, so swept up with the possibilities before me. But I stop myself before I do anything that will compromise my plans.

"What do you propose?" I ask, intrigued to see what his reaction will be. He doesn't disappoint, tensing immediately. He must have thought I'd tell him first and then be able to weave his way into it somehow. I'm disappointed. I believe his father's sent him to discover what's happening after all.

Finally, after long, drawn-out moments, Osfrith speaks.

"I would stay with my father's court but work for you whilst I'm there. Sow a few seeds of doubt. Make men question my father's intentions when he calls for a war against you. Again. A war he should have already won."

I can't alienate this angry young man, so I pretend to consider his words. It would be intriguing to see what would happen if I sent him away with the understanding that he was working towards a shared goal. What damage could he cause in Edwin's court? Would he be able to undermine his father as he suggests?

"What do you propose?" Osfrith counters. I quirk a smile at him. His tone is pleading; suddenly, he's lost the little bit of guile upon he's managed to draw.

"An alliance and a war."

Osfrith watches me for a long moment to see if I'm going to offer more, but I don't.

"You don't trust me?" he asks, his voice aggrieved whereas before it was pleading.

"I don't trust anyone, not anymore," I qualify. He looks out at my hall full of men and then back towards the few he has in the warband.

"I've shown I trust you," he interjects angrily. I can't deny that.

"Then you've not been disappointed often enough. You're too trusting."

"And you'll drive men from your side if you show no good faith," Osfrith retorts.

"You've done little but make a show of coming here, announcing your visit to everyone. If you wanted me to confide in you, you should have come secretly, sent someone to speak for you first."

Osfrith laughs at that, an unexpected response.

"My father sent me to take your oath of allegiance. I had no choice but to come with as much pomp and ceremony as I could. He expects it of me. I simply hoped to use it as an excuse to plot against him."

My anger surges at his original intent. How dare Edwin expect me to do him any sort of homage after he attacked me?

Osfrith watches me closely as I fight with my emotions.

"Your father needs to reconsider his attitude towards me."

"My father thinks, and he's right to do so, that he was the victor in battle and that you owe him your fealty."

"Is your father ignorant that I've reversed his gains against me? That I think of him as my enemy, not my overking?"

"I don't know what my father thinks," Osfrith answers languidly. Suddenly he's more in control of the conversation than I wanted. "As I told you, he doesn't tell me anything. He commands me as he would any man who's a member of his warband. He shows no special treatment to me."

"And you expect him to?" I ask. Osfrith is deeply unhappy with his father.

He stands abruptly, his men rushing to attention with a creak of wood on wood as the bench tumbles backwards, but he waves them down, and they retake their seats just as noisily.

"Walk with me. I've been riding all day, but now I need to move around and not sit and drink and talk."

I follow him outside, surprised to find the sun still shining. I thought the day more advanced than this.

I point to show Osfrith the best track to take, the one that leads between my hall and the outer gate and ditch. I know two of my men follow at our back and two of Osfrith's own. Yet, in all honesty, the eyes of everyone within the enclosure follow our every move. I wonder what would happen if Osfrith or his men made an attempt on my life. Who would intervene first? His men or mine?

The weather has been dry, and the track is firm beneath my feet, although the smell of animal manure and cooking meat stalks us.

When we're out of earshot of everyone else, Osfrith stops walking and turns to meet my intrigued eyes.

"My father treats me with little or no respect. He'd rather ask any other their opinion than hear mine. It's clear to see his intentions to set me aside and have one of his new Christian children become king in his place. I hope to prevent that from happening by ensuring he meets his death long before his other children reach adulthood. Edwin is an old man now. He's a grandfather. My son is older than his new children. He's playing a game for young men. I intend to ensure he stops. And soon as well."

"You speak very openly of his death. Is he unaware of your disillusionment?"

"My father would need to speak to me to know that I'm unhappy. And he doesn't. He doesn't even have an inkling of my real intentions."

"You'll stay the night?" I ask, and he grunts in agreement. "We'll talk more in the morning."

"What's there to talk about?" he mutters, but I leave him to his thoughts. I need to think about all the implications of this traitor in the midst of King Edwin's northern court. I must decipher if it's likely to be a ploy of Edwin's or a genuine outpouring of distrust from his son before I make any decisions.

12

AD631 - EDWIN OF NORTHUMBRIA

My stronghold at Bebbanburh, or Bamburgh as some call it, is very different to Yeavering. It has its good points and its bad. It's more compact and far more defensible. At its side, the sea rushes against the cliffs making it feel as though I live on an island. That it's the stronghold of my predecessor only adds to my enjoyment of it whenever I visit. That it's the fortress his family take their name from fuels my annoyance and unease.

The family of Bamburgh, all apart from its head, King Æthelfrith, lives and is a constant cross to be borne. I wish I'd killed them all, even my sister, his wife. It would have made my tenure at Bamburgh far more secure. Knowing that I have men who wish to take my place almost the length and breadth of this land makes it difficult to sleep at night. I've already endured two attempts on my life. I don't intend to suffer anymore. I've changed my God to prevent another from killing me. It better bloody work. I don't like bargains where I seem to receive nothing in return.

Gazing out from Bamburgh, out to sea, on clear days and on those that are more atmospheric, I can see the islands that harbour more birdlife and sea life than the coast around me. The men and women who fish the waters are filled with tales of wonder and magic about the sights they see. I can well believe every single one of them.

The settlement at Yeavering can be eerie, but its open nature doesn't lend itself to the same tales. The men and women tell of haunting songs and eerie whispers when the mountains and trees speak to them as they hunt, fish, or farm. The men and women of the sea believe in a God of the sea who sends them good catches and poor as well, depending on how well they've prayed to them before they fish. Bishop Paulinus despairs of the stories he hears. But I imagine he'll somehow turn them to his own good, substitute one God for another. I might be a Christian, but even I understand how the Church twists and manipulates the people's beliefs and would-be-kings.

My wife is pious. I am …. I am opportunistic.

I understand that Bishop Paulinus already eyes the islands off the coast and coverts them for his monks to own and farm. He says they like the seclusion; only he calls it aestheticism. That's a long word for quiet and tranquillity. I wish he spoke with words that all men and women could understand. It might help him convert people away from the old faith and towards the new.

I've sent my oldest son to ensure the compliance and support of King Cadwallon. I know it'll piss Cadwallon off, but I don't much care. I've given him two years to come to me and make his submission, and he's refused.

In that time, he and Penda, the man Bishop Paulinus sneeringly terms a pagan, have clawed back much of the land I took from him. That I don't much mind. If he demands the allegiance of those men and women, then he must exact tribute from them in my name, and he must accept my overlordship. There's no compromise.

On his journey south, my son will visit with more of my allies and more of my would-be allies. Eowa, Penda's brother, will be one of those he meets. I can't say Eowa's visit at Yeavering was an overwhelming success. Even so, I hope he'll stand against my enemies whenever they make their intentions clear.

I appreciate that King Cadwallon is planning something; I hope my preemptive strike will force him to decide whether to make himself my irreplaceable enemy or my ally. We were foster-brothers once, admittedly I was the elder, but we could be rulers together.

Perhaps.

Whilst my son meets with Lord Eowa and King Cadwallon, I plan on visiting the new king of the East Angles, Sigeberht. I might also travel as far south as Kent to see how Bishop Paulinus fares as he reinforces the claim as the premier religious man on our island. I wish him luck. I'm certainly pleased that, for the time being, I don't have to listen to his sermonizing and earnest words. I've heard it all too many times for them to have any impact on me. Yet I still have to nod my way through them.

Osric has preceded me south. His reports assure me that my allies are firmly with me. I'll be walking into a congenial atmosphere, not one where I have to barter for their support. I thought changing Gods would give me more freedom, not less.

"My Lord?" a voice at my side, and I turn to meet the eyes of one of my noblemen. He's a good man. Sometimes, he is a little slow because he thinks with his sword and spear, not his mind. He presides over the far northern borders for me. His presence here is worrying.

"Yes, Ahlred, what can I do for you?"

He looks unhappy, standing before me, obstructing my view of the scenery and generally being a nuisance. I know he has to share something that I don't want to hear. I wait patiently, listening to the stray sounds of a wave crashing far below me, the noise disjointed with the distance and the direction of the wind. Finally, Ahlred speaks.

"Lord Penda has been to visit with Eanfrith."

That immediately has my attention. How strange that I was only just thinking of the house of Bamburgh and the old kings of Bernicia.

"When was this?" What I want to know is, did he do so with the support of Cadwallon or is it merely a coincidence?

"Last year," Ahlred responds quickly.

So it was with the support of King Cadwallon. I doubt my son will gain his allegiance after all.

"Penda went himself?" I ask, but Ahlred shrugs and shakes his head. He only has part of the story.

"Find out more. This might be the start of something."

He bows his way out of my presence as my mood darkens. It's never done. I thought making myself king would end war and battles, but really, they've just changed their name. Before, I was a war leader in a skirmish, and now I'm a king in a battle.

If I weren't so righteous about my kingship, I might find the whole thing tiring.

A final look out to sea, and I return to my great hall. I have another war to plan, and I want it to be on my terms, not King Cadwallon's.

I call my son to me, Eadfrith, the one I've not sent to meet with Cadwallon. I want him to ride north, treat with the Picts and see if, once and for all, they'll give up their honoured guest, the man who's my enemy; my nephew and his children.

I'll send Eadfrith first, an Eadfrith to bring me back an Eanfrith, and then I'll dispatch a more considerable force as well, to enforce my son's claim. I need to start being proactive if I'm to keep my place as over-king of the Saxons. The thought fills me with renewed vigour.

Perhaps, after all, I need constant action. Maybe, after all, I'm not happy unless I have an enemy I need to conquer.

13

AD631 - EADFRITH OF NORTHUMBRIA

I like to ride north with my men. The land is wild, even more so than in central Bernicia, and the people are wild as well.

There's a sure chance of encountering someone who wants to fight if you ride north. Only this time, my father is sending me with no more than the intention of a battle. If King Edwin doesn't get his own way, then there'll be a battle, and that dampens my enthusiasm for the task.

Why the Pictish king would decide that now is the perfect opportunity to stop giving his protection to the son of my father's predecessor, I'll never know, but my father hopes to hold some sway with the man.

I'm dismissive of the idea, and that cheers me a little. At least I know there'll be a battle in the future, and sooner than that if I get my way.

My father has sent my older brother south to gain the allegiance of King Cadwallon, but I think my brother is as unhappy with his task as I am. It'll be interesting to see with what stories we return.

I always know when my brother is being truthful and when he's not, a trick my father has never learnt. I'll know what my brother thinks, and for a price, well, I'll tell the other.

There's no need for loyalty in my family. The past has taught me that. My father killed his brother-in-law to become king of Northumbria. He's tried to kill his foster-brother as well and claim his people and land. I imagine I could do well for myself if I turned on my father, my brother, my step-mother and the new sons my father has. I imagine I could be king over everything, just as he is, but I'd trust no one, and no one would trust me.

That's not the way to be a king. Kings need to make men keen to do their bidding, even when they're family. My father is making his life far more complicated than it needs to be. He appears to be enjoying it as well. I'm almost starting to believe Edwin wants to *fight* for his kingship. I wonder if his staid, Christian life has become too much for him.

The Picts don't know that I'm coming to visit them, but that doesn't mean that I'm not being watched from the moment I come close to their kingdom. My father claims the land far past the first Roman wall that runs below Yeavering and Bamburgh. It's turning to rubble and sinking away, back into the landscape, leaving a clear scar across the landscape.

The Picts dispute my father's claim to the land, but he arrogantly maintains the assertion anyway. Edwin even claims the land up to the second, more northern Roman wall. Only small parts of it remain. It's his way of ensuring that the Picts know they're being punished for their persistence in harbouring his enemy, his nephews.

Every year, Edwin sends a warband this way to harass the borders, to keep everyone alert. The king of Alt Clut, the other kingdom that shares a border with my father so far north, tolerates my father's violence because his border is too vast to militarize adequately. If he had a choice, I think he'd attack and kill my father in a heartbeat.

I've followed the sea for most of my journey, luxuriating in the better weather and gentle sunshine. When the land starts to curve ever inwards, I know it's time to find the Pictish outriders, to seek out the king and his court. I almost wish that wasn't my task.

I have fifty men with me, half from my warband and half from my father's. My father didn't send Osfrith south with any of his men, and if I were a less astute son, it would probably bother me, but actually, I'm the one on the more dangerous path. My brother walks amongst men my father's already beaten, subjugated. I'm visiting men who stand against my father and have done for the last fifteen years. Amongst them live my cousin, his wife and his son.

I remember him vaguely from our childhood together. But his face is no more than a blur of hair and eyes, mouth and nose. I appreciate that he would be unrecognizable if I met him without an introduction now. We used to joke and tease each other because our names were so similar. I once saw my future clearly, with him as my king and my brother and I serving him as we do our father.

I didn't anticipate my father's naked need and intense greed for renown and warriors, land and wealth. He's even abandoned his Gods to become king of all Deira and Bernicia, Mercia and even Gwynedd. I disagree with his choices.

"My Lord?" one of my outriders has returned, some concern on his sun-reddened face. The winter has been fierce, and the summer has been warm so far. I know my face is just as pink from the sun.

"Yes, what is it?"

"We've been sighted, and we're being watched."

I almost roll my eyes at him. It's such an obvious statement. I've felt the eyes of men and women on us for much of the morning.

"Has anyone approached you yet?" I ask, and he nods then. Good.

"Yes, My Lord, apologies. There are twenty men, there," and he points close to where I know the sea flows around the headland. "They say they'll escort you, but only if you leave many of your warriors behind."

Hum, I'd thought the numbers I rode with might be a problem. My father is sometimes over-cautious, and other times he's simply misguided in his attempts at playing the mighty Christian king.

"Tell them I'll leave half the men here, provided they leave at least five of their men with my own."

I doubt they have anyone important enough within their ranks to act as a solitary hostage for their good behaviour in our land. If there had been a son or an uncle of the current king, I might have considered lowering the number, but five will do me fine. That will mean that five of my men can watch one of theirs. Likewise, it means that there will only be fifteen of their men to twenty-five of mine. The odds are good all around.

I've not been into the Pictish kingdom before, but my father says they're much the same as the Saxons and the Britons. I wish I didn't have to find out.

And then a surprise.

"They say there's no need to venture onto their land. Lord Eanfrith is here, waiting for you."

Now, this is unwelcome news. Eanfrith has foreseen my father's actions and is attempting to blunt them. If I cannot speak to the king of the Picts, how can I threaten him? How can I know that anyone will give an accurate account of the conversation about to take place between Eanfrith and myself?

"Fuck," is all I say, and the man nods unhappily.

"My apologies," he offers, but I know it's not his fault.

"Come, take me to him. Tell me, is he on horseback?"

"He is, My Lord, yes."

That's good then. It means I can take my horse with me, and then if I fear any sort of treachery, I can attempt a quick escape.

I can see now where the small party of twenty men waits. The great swathe of sea narrows perceptively, almost allowing the two clefts of land to touch, but not quite. It's here that the Picts linger. I try to determine how they've come to be here. There's no bridge over the water that I can see, and neither can I see ships. Can they have ridden all the way round to where the sea becomes little more than a river rushing the wrong way inland?

I've split my force of fifty men, but only a little. Five of the men wait, almost out of sight. They have the task of rushing for home should the worse happen here. The other forty-five men surround me. We make a good show, all bristling with weapons and bedecked in byrnies of mail. We've placed our helms on our heads so that the Picts will struggle to determine who leads them. I think anonymity is a good disguise. I expect the Picts to have employed the same tactic, but they haven't.

Eanfrith sits astride his horse, slightly in front of his men, apart from his standard-bearer who holds aloft a small banner depicting the House of Bamburgh, upon which a clear imprint of the rock the fortress sits. It flickers in the gentle breeze. It would be better if it hung limp and impotent. His intention is evident even before I open my mouth to speak.

I signal to my bannerman then. He holds a similar banner; only this one depicts the royal houses of both Deira and Bernicia, representing my father's ancestry. It doesn't show a rocky cliff but rather the emblems of Deira and Bernicia combined on a bleached white background.

I also have another banner, this one for the royal house of Mercia, showing her eagle standard. People often forget that my mother was a Mercian princess. Even my father does so on occasion.

As Eanfrith's so proudly displays his intentions, I decide I may as well do the same. The time for subtlety has passed.

"Cousin," he calls to me across the gap that divides us. I grimace. His voice is rough. It sounds as though he struggles to say the word.

"Cousin," I respond. His mother was my aunt, no matter how much my father tries to forget that fact.

"You look like your father," Eanfrith says, with no sound of rancour. I resent it all the same. He's older than me. I don't remember what his mother or father looked like, so I can't repay the compliment.

"So I'm told," I respond, hoping to move away from a discussion about family. It won't end well.

"He sent you?" Eanfrith asks without any preamble. I feel caught off guard. I wish I'd considered an alternative meeting to the one my father envisioned. He told me I'd simply walk up, demand Eanfrith's return to me in the name of my father, and be either given him or threaten war and then receive him.

"I've come to speak with your king," I say, looking behind him in the hope that there might be another party of horsemen racing towards us.

"My king is dead," Eanfrith intones says. I wish I'd chosen a better phrase. "The king of the Picts doesn't wish to speak with you either," he offers. I think he's enjoying this far too much.

"You can speak with me here, but you may not come onto into the Pictish kingdom. If you do, he'll interpret it as a declaration of war and will raise his warbands and ravage the border and much further south as well."

Wonderful. This isn't going how my father described it to me at all.

"Can I come and speak with your king alone?" I know he'll deny all of my requests. I try to reason, but Eanfrith's eyes are filled with joy, shimmering beneath the blaze of the sun.

"No, as I say, you can speak with me, or you can initiate war. There isn't an alternative."

"Does the king even know you're here?" I ask. I want to do something to make him feel as uncomfortable as I am.

"I can only act with the aid of the king," he responds. "I'm a guest within his lands and within his home. Nothing more."

I bite back my initial reply.

"You're married to his daughter and the father of his grandson."

He smirks then.

"My grandson, a youth of fifteen years, has the ear of the king. Not I."

"And yet he sends you to meet with me and speak on his behalf." I've finally managed to determine what's bothering me about this conversation.

His grin of triumph is all the answer I need. He has far more influence over the king than he's trying to pretend. It's even more apparent that he has no intention of speaking to the king on my behalf. I think my father needs to accept that the Picts aren't going to be turning over their adopted son anytime soon.

This was a bad decision by my father. It isn't the first, and it won't be the last.

"The king, my father-by-marriage, allows me some freedoms, but not all of them. I will, of course, tell him of our meeting and that you wished to speak with him and that I denied you the possibility. If he decides that he wants to see you, then we can send a messenger."

I'm still trying to find a way to get to the Pictish Court, and if not me, then maybe another.

"Would it be allowable to send one of my priests with you? He has a hankering to visit the holy site on Iona."

I'm trying to decide who could play the penitent monk, but Eanfrith is already smirking.

"Show me your monk? I'm curious as to which one of these men speaks directly to your God."

I look behind me a little desperately. Is there someone here who can pretend to be a monk and who's clever enough to just do it without being coaxed?

"I'm afraid he's not yet caught up with the rest of the men. I think he stopped a while ago in order to ... pray at ..." I let my words trail away. Eanfrith suspects my ruse and is unwilling to play along. I almost wish I did have a monk amongst my men so that he could appear over the horizon any moment now and prevent me from the heat of embarrassment that floods my face.

"Eadfrith, cousin, your father needs someone to stand up to him, and if the first person is me, then so be it. He's not going to convince anyone amongst the Picts that I'm their enemy and should be handed over to him as though I'm a sack of wool. I suggest you turn yourself around and go and tell him that."

"He sent me to barter for you and threaten war if your king wouldn't give you up."

"Then," Eanfrith says, and he arrogantly turns his back on me as he speaks, "I'll ready the warbands for your coming warriors. Good-bye, cousin," he calls as he canters away, his men watching me menacingly, their hands on their weapons.

I stare after him, feeling impotent and useless.

Perhaps I should have gone south in place of my brother.

14

AD631 - EOWA OF MERCIA – THE LANDS OF THE HWICCE

This is it. My brother watches me with an open expression. By the end of today, we'll either be enemies or allies. I really don't know which way the conversation will turn.

We are within my hall in the kingdom of the Hwicce, and I'm the king here, not him. Not that Penda doesn't want to be. I know he wants it. I could share it with him, make him my sub-king, a prince of the Hwicce as opposed to its king, but I don't know if I want to do that. Penda's a powerful man in his own right. He's made himself invaluable to King Cadwallon of Gwynedd as opposed to myself.

I have a fledgling alliance with King Edwin of Northumbria. He's made it clear to me, by sending his son Osfrith to me, that if I intend to keep the alliance, I have to turn Penda away from Cadwallon. Either that or my brother and I must become enemies. If I weren't already so unsure of him, I might be offended, but as I'm uneasy about Penda's intentions, I can understand Edwin's desires.

Neither is Penda doing himself any favours. He's swaggered into my hall, filthy and dirty from wherever he's been, and he's not instructed his men to leave their weapons at the doorway. Neither has he led by example.

He's wearing war clothing of byrnie and helm, his weapons belt filled with blades and edges. He stinks of sweat and metal.

Penda bristles with aggression and anger. I could almost laugh at him if he weren't so bloody dangerous.

I wish I had half his skill in battle.

"Brother, speak your mind to me," Penda demands, leaning toward me and helping himself to a decent piece of beef from the table. I try not to notice that it's the piece I'd been considering eating. He's always known to take what I want.

"Brother," I respond, rolling the word around my mouth.

He meets my eyes, waiting for me to say something further, but I still haven't decided what I want to say.

"Tell me about King Cadwallon," I finally mouth, and he quirks a smile at me.

"Tell me about King Edwin," his immediate response. He's blunt. His weapons are sharp, his mind is sharp, but he's blunt. He's bloody deadly.

"King Edwin is a Christian king, keen to share his experiences."

Penda roars with laughter at my response. His eyes sparkle with delight.

"Don't tell me. He did *actually* try to convert you, didn't he?"

I feel a grin tugging my lips. And that's the other thing about Penda. He makes men happy.

"He asked Bishop Paulinus to speak to me. I agreed to listen to his words, but I didn't take it any further than that," I response defensively.

He's still smirking.

"Is this the great Bishop Paulinus that all new Christians speak about?" His tone is anything but respectful. The use of the word 'great' slides from it easily, but it's not what he means when he says it.

"Yes, it is," I retort. I wish I could tell him everything about my trip, say to him that King Edwin is as smug as Penda believes, that he does think more of himself than he should, and that his elder sons all hate him and want him dead. But I can't. My brother is my enemy, not my friend. At least not yet.

"Tell me of him?" Penda demands, but I shake my head.

"No, you tell me of your travels. Rumour has it you've been far and wide."

He chuckles again. He expects me to keep track of him. It's arrogant of him, and yet I do, so he's correct.

"I've been surveying the land, yes. But not for any great purpose."

Now it's my turn to splutter with amusement as I help myself to the second tastiest piece of beef from before us both.

"You need to work on that," I say, and he growls as he eats. It's hard to keep secrets from brothers.

I take a mouthful. He does the same. I'm trying to decide what to say next, but he's first to speak, as always.

"King Cadwallon says that King Edwin isn't to be trusted. Ever."

"King Edwin says King Cadwallon's not to be trusted," I respond.

"I told King Cadwallon not to trust you," Penda replies. I arch an eyebrow at him, unsure how to interpret his tone.

"I told King Edwin the same about you."

"So no one is to trust anyone else, even brothers." Again, Penda beats me to the heart of the matter.

"No, not even brothers," I agree, a little sadly. That's what it comes down to with us. He is my brother. I'd happily split the known world with him if I could, but it's not just him and I. And we don't yet govern the world. If I want to get to that point, then I'm going to have to make some difficult decisions first, and they'll be to the detriment of my brother.

"So we're not going to call on our family alliance?" he asks. He's far too accepting of this.

"You don't seem surprised?" I demand. Did he come to tell me this, or have I forced his hand? Was he thinking along the same lines as me?

"We both want the same thing. We can't both have it. At some point, we have to acknowledge that and deal with the consequences."

"And that's alright with you?" I query. I know we're no longer close, but I had expected something more from him.

He's still eating and drinking the food from my table as I watch him suspiciously.

"None of this is acceptable to me, but until you acknowledge that I'm the superior warrior and war leader and that I should be king here, there's little you or I can do."

I'm spitting at his audacity. He simply winks and reaches for more of my best beef. I put my hand out to clamp down on his questing fingers. He glares at me with his deep blue eyes. Gods, I'd forgotten how strong he is. Even with all my strength, he's still able to move forward and claim my beef. I can't stop him. I hope it's not a portent of things to come. I don't want him always to be the tougher one.

I wonder how much of what he says he means. Does he genuinely think that he's the better man than me? Does he just toy with my nervousness?

"When I leave here tomorrow, we'll officially be working apart, not enemies, but not allies. We'll be family, nothing more. We'll not be honour bound to do anything other than enforce our familial bonds. If King Edwin," and Penda grins at this showing me his strong, white teeth. "Kills you, then I'll be able to kill him in retaliation or take your blood price."

I deeply breathe before I respond. How does he know to get under my skin so quickly?

"Likewise, if King Cadwallon kills you, I'll be able to do the same."

Penda chuckles. "You can try. King Cadwallon won't take too kindly to your accusations."

"I'm not going to argue about that. The point remains. We won't be working towards a common goal, but we can still avenge each other, should the need arise."

The smug bastard is still grinning at me. Not for a moment does he think he'll be dying anytime soon. Clearly, Penda believes I might be.

"What do you want, Penda?" I ask him. I'm curious to uncover what drives him. I've always thought that I knew, but now I'm not sure.

"I want everything," he says, still chuckling. "From one side of the island to the other. I want it to be mine, but for now, I'll be happy to be King Cadwallon's ally and see where that takes me. Now, brother, what is it that you want?"

I wish I could downplay my heart's desire as well as he does.

"I want Mercia," I say roughly. There, I've said it. His eyes dangerously flash as they scan the hall before him. He grew up here. This was his home. Beneath the blackened rafters, we played as children and dreamed of our future together. He's distanced himself from the place because I'm the older brother. I'm its king and war leader.

"And I want you to have it," Penda says flatly, his humour fled. I think he does mean it.

I wish I understood my bloody brother better.

15

AD631 - EANFRITH OF BERNICIA, THE PICTISH KINGDOM

My meeting with Lord Eadfrith has been the topic of a great deal of conversation. The men I took with me have regaled anyone who'll listen with tales of our war with words. None of them thinks that there's any substance to his threat to return with the warriors of Northumbria. Not one of them believes that King Edwin of Northumbria has any right to demand anything from their king, the King of the Picts, and none of them considers that I should just give myself up and walk back into Northumbria. It's reassuring to know.

There's always a fear in the back of my mind that at some point, my adopted family will be put in a situation so untenable they'll decide it's just easier and more politic to no longer support me.

At the moment, and for the last fifteen years of my life, I've had very, very little to give in return for the assistance I've received. Hopefully, I'll soon be the victor against King Edwin and finally have more than empty words to offer in return for their unfailing support.

Since meeting with Penda's representative, I've fluctuated between excitement and deep fear. After so long of dreaming that someone will champion my cause, I'm now worried that the words spoken will dissipate like fog on a warm day. I've been training and honing my skills during the early summer sun, keen to do away with the lethargy that afflicts me every winter, but sometimes it still tries to weigh me down.

My wife smiles at me now, pleased with my change in mood. I'm trying hard to keep her happy.

My young son is happier as well. I think I smile more easily now.

But I'm impatient to be getting on with the next part of my life. I'm a king, and I want to be one now.

"My Lord," a voice calls to me as I stand and watch my men train on the slopes of a gentle green hill. I squint into the sunlight, trying to determine who beckons me. I don't recognize the voice, not quite, but it has to be someone I know, or they wouldn't understand where to find me.

A grin covers my face at seeing Herebrod emerge from the fog of too bright sunlight. He's smiling and wearing his weapons, but he does so in a friendly way, his body loose and relaxed. I don't think I'd like to meet him in battle. He's too formidable. He's returned to me from Penda far sooner than I thought he would.

"Herebrod," I call, and he strides over to me. This time he has men with him, which excites me as well.

"My Lord Eanfrith, you look better," his words mirror my thoughts so closely that I laugh out loud. He looks at me quizzically, but I wave my humour away with an apologetic grunt.

"You have news?" I ask, and he smirks again.

"I hear you've had visitors." I'd take the time to work out how he knows this, but I decide that I've been on the periphery for too long, and maybe everyone knows what everyone else on our island is doing.

"Yes, but they went away again. Why? What do you know?" It's always best to identify what others know before saying something you might regret.

Herebrod watches me for a moment as though weighing up what to say.

"We heard that you won without any bloodshed and that Lord Eadfrith went away unhappily. King Edwin is scurrying around trying to find supporters who might have any leverage with your king."

I hadn't expected that. I didn't think King Edwin was so desperate to remove me from the Pictish kingdoms.

"Does he have anyone?" The Pictish kings don't make good allies. None of the people this far north do. They never have. They're even more jealous of their land than they are in Northumbria.

"No, he doesn't. King Edwin doesn't have many friends. He makes enemies far too easily."

"Good, I'm pleased," I say, and I am relieved. Again, it's nice to have some proof that not everyone hates me and that they might share my opinions of King Edwin.

"There's been a slight development," Herebrod continues. His tone doesn't imply whether it's good or bad. "Lines are being drawn, and Lord Penda wanted you to know that he and his brother, Eowa, are now on opposite sides."

"Is that what Penda wanted?" I demand. I've learned all I can about the kingdoms in the south from every travelling merchant and anyone who has even the slightest knowledge about what happens there. But there are many people of note, and I find it a little challenging to work out who likes whom and who doesn't. With King Edwin and King Cadwallon and their shifting allegiances, it makes it impossible to keep the alliances and kingdoms clear in my mind.

"Lord Penda wants to be king of Mercia. His brother is currently king of the Hwicce and moves to make himself king of Mercia. It wasn't going to go any other way," Herebrod says with a chuckle, as though he doesn't speak of brothers becoming mortal enemies.

"The brothers are enemies?" I ask. My brothers and I were mostly friendly towards each other. When we last saw one another.

"They're brothers," Herebrod's reply is simple.

I don't know what he means by that, but he seems to think it's self-evidentiary, so I let it go.

"Families," I mutter and he grins. Obviously, that's the response for which he was looking. "So, should I be worried?"

"What about Penda and Eowa? No, not at all. Eowa is not the

warrior that Penda is. At the moment, he seems to have chosen King Edwin as his ally, not his brother."

Now that does worry me slightly. I don't like the thought of anyone being an ally of Edwin.

"Don't let that alarm you. Eowa is looking for an easy way to get what he wants, and Edwin is using everything he can to turn Eowa to him."

"So it has nothing to do with me then?"

"I doubt it. Eowa does not quarrel with you. Well, not yet he doesn't."

"So why have you come?"

Herebrod grins at my abrupt question.

"I thought I should come and visit your land when it wasn't so bloody cold." I think he might be speaking the truth. I believe Herebrod and I could one day be friends. When all this is over, and I'm King of Bernicia, with something with which to reward him.

"Really?" I probe, but he just keeps grinning.

"Come, you should feed me," he says, "and my men. We're starving, and you know how much I love the food."

His cheer is almost infectious. I lead the man away from the training ground, and we weave our way through the collection of circular, stone brochs that make up my home. Herebrod mutters as he walks. I know that he's contrasting what my home looks like in the summer compared to the winter. Even I accept that the place can look unwelcoming during the winter when there are no bright colours, and people only move when they have no choice.

During the summer months, the broch is a hive of activity. Men and women fish, boys and girls run about playing, and hounds and other animals make their noises and nests as best they can. It's a homely place in the summer. In the winter, it's a bastion against the cold and the winds, the rain and the snows.

Inside the broch, there's a hive of activity. Herebrod watches with amazed eyes as people worry at their designated tasks, somehow never colliding with anyone else, but even I admit that it looks as though they should, in the confined space.

Within the hall, I ask for food and mead for Herebrod and his five men. My wife smiles at me and comes to speak with Herebrod. She also likes the southern warrior, not just because he gave me back my hope.

"My Lady," he begins, and then it's he and my wife who converse as I watch them with half a smile on my face. My wife is a charming conversationalist. I can see she has Herebrod under her spell.

"Tell me of Lord Penda," she asks, and Herebrod begins to speak.

"Penda is a warrior. He can fight and kill with his sword, war-axe, shield, spear, and bare hands. He always acts concisely and efficiently. He thinks before he attacks, and he always seems to be a step in front of any enemy. None of his men can better him in battle. None of them. He smiles easily. He rouses to anger easily, and despite the current rift, he's fiercely loyal to his family. If he were the older brother and Eowa his younger, he'd gift him with riches and gold, position and trust."

"His brother is not so open?" she asks. I listen on with interest. Herebrod almost sounds as though he approves of Eowa.

"His brother is jealous of his position. Because he lacks the skills and natural agility that his brother has, he worries and because he worries, he overthinks everything. He won't give his brother the very things that would make him a greater ally than anyone else."

"Ah," my wife says, nodding as she listens, as though Herebrod's words are easy to understand.

"Eowa is everything a war leader and king should be. He would be great, but he lives in the shadow of Penda, and Penda casts a huge shadow that Eowa would do anything to step aside from him. Sadly, it won't happen."

"So this war, if it splits Penda and Eowa, will only be the beginning of a larger attack?"

"If this war splits Penda and Eowa, it'll be the beginning of something between the brothers, yes, but, provided that King Edwin is dead, the brothers will, at some point in the future, resolve their problems. They're family. Almost anything can be forgiven. Well, so I tell myself."

"You like both brothers?" she presses.

"Penda is the man I've sworn to protect and defend. He holds my oath, and he can do with me what he wants. Eowa, he doesn't command me in the same way, but if I could work for both brothers', I would probably be a slightly happier man. No disrespect to Penda, but he can learn from his brother, temper his ways a little. He could be thought of as a little ... wild, for all that he does think about the impact of his actions. He never sees any problem that can't be countered. He's stubborn and determined."

"Not bad attributes for a man," she offers. Herebrod is grinning again.

"Not at all. Now, tell me about your husband."

She turns to look at me then, her eyes open and honest, a small smile on her face. I don't know what she thinks of me. I've never thought to ask.

"Eanfrith is a better man than he thinks. He commands respect from all his men, and my father thinks him invaluable. But he's scared by what happened to his father, and he's fed up with feeling impotent. He needs to realize that many amongst my people will fight for him and die for him if those are his commands. I would die for him if it made him the king of Bernicia."

Herebrod is watching the interplay with interest. I gasp with surprise at my wife's assessment of me. She's right. I do think too little of myself. I try not to be too outspoken, too much at the centre of events. I don't think I've earned my place within the Picts. I've been fortunate to be gifted it.

"My husband will make a mighty king, tempered by his experiences and keen to rule well." Here she leans conspiratorially towards Herebrod.

"Make him king for me. Give him back what was stolen from him, and even I will reward you as well as I can."

He looks between the two of us, seeing if I'll contradict anything she says, but I know better than to speak against my wife. She's a quiet woman, used to being listened to when she does speak. As much as her words have surprised me, I'm not going to challenge them.

"And I'll make you a mighty queen," he offers, and my wife is laughing with delight.

"Herebrod, please tell Penda that he's like a summer's breeze, come to clear away the cobwebs of winter. His alliance with my husband is a wonderful thing. The Pictish people will do all they can to support the endeavour against bloody King Edwin."

"The king says the same?" Herebrod queries, and she nods, looking towards the seat where her father would sit if he weren't out hunting with his men.

"The king of the Picts agrees with everything I've said. Everything."

Herebrod reaches forward then and snags himself a piece of delicately cooked fish. It's a speciality of my wife's, and one of my favourites.

His eyes blaze with delight when the warm food touches his tongue.

"I like it here in the summer," he announces expansively. "I think I'll visit next year as well."

Somehow my wife has just turned the messenger into our loyal man. I wonder how she's done it, but I'm no less grateful to her for speaking as she has. This time next year, I hope to be a king. She'll be my queen. And Herebrod. Well, he'll be standing at my side as well, able to steer me through the difficult situation that persists in the Saxon and British kingdoms to the south.

Impatience pulls at me. I wish the time for words were done.

16

AD631 - PENDA OF MERCIA – GWYNEDD

Cadwallon and I stare at each other across the wide piece of wood before us that's serving as a table. We both wear slightly smug expressions, which worries me a little. We need to be keen and less sure of ourselves if we're to win the coming battle.

"King Edwin is trying his hardest to bring together all his allies," King Cadwallon offers. We both look meaningfully at the wooden pieces that represent the allies upon which King Edwin can call. On the opposite side, there are tiny representations of our allies. It's fairly evenly balanced, and that's not the way I want it to be. I think we need to wait before we attack, although King Cadwallon is eager to get on with it.

"Next year," I offer again, my voice firm. I've been saying it for much of the day, but Cadwallon has yet to be convinced. He wants to push for an earlier resolution.

"Why?" he demands once more, his keen eyes taking in the vast array of support we have arranged against King Edwin. "Why give him another year to prepare?"

"Because we need to turn more of his supposed allies against him. We need to have him isolated. We want to kill the bastard, remember," I say with a growl, and Cadwallon glares at me. "We want him unsure of himself. We want him on the defensive."

"Once more, Penda, who else can we turn against him? We have one of his sons."

"We think we have his son," I qualify. Cadwallon waves my concerns aside.

"We have his son. I know the youth better than you do. He's made his move; he's spoken against his father. When the battle comes, he'll stand with us."

"Provided he never discovers that we've given the kingdom of Northumbria away twice," I offer, and now Cadwallon's getting angry.

"Lord Eanfrith can have Bernicia. That's his home. Lord Osfrith can have Deira. That's what their families can both rightfully claim through the accident of their births."

"I don't think either of them will be happy with that. We'll have to kill one of them," I say. I'm pragmatic. I can foresee the outcomes of our alliances in the coming years. I don't want to kill King Edwin just to have more problematic kings in his place.

"Penda, we can't kill our ally. And how would we choose anyway?"

This is what I wanted. At last. It's taken much of the day. To begin with, Cadwallon was totally against my plan to kill one of the cousins during the battle. I admit that killing an ally might send out the wrong message to our other allies, but in trying to isolate King Edwin, we've ended up with one too many allies with their eye on Northumbria. It's something we need to acknowledge and work around. If we don't plan now, everything we hope to do could fall apart, and, even worse, it would be our fault! We'd not be able to blame King Edwin for our troubles, and that would be awkward for everyone involved.

"It'll have to be done on their abilities," I initially say, but then I change my mind because I have an idea that Cadwallon will decry. I'm not about to share it with him yet. I'll wait for nearer the time. Maybe I'll even do it without telling him.

"No, I've reconsidered. Leave that decision to me, and that way, you can treat with both men without worrying about it and giving anything away."

I can see Cadwallon wants to be outraged at my words, but he sees the truth in them and subsides quickly, beckoning for some of his other allies to join us now. Good, this part of the discussion is finally over. Without anyone noticing, I grab the piece of wood that represents Lord Osfrith, son of King Edwin. As much as I want everyone to know of Cadwallon's coup in securing his support, I also want it to be a secret from everyone but us. It'll keep Lord Osfrith safe at Edwin's court until the time of the battle, and that, if I have my way, will be next year, not this.

These men Cadwallon has as his allies aren't yet my allies. I don't want them to know of our associate amongst the enemy. Cadwallon has, at last, agreed with my decision on that. I also grab the wooden counter that represents Lord Eanfrith. He's a secret weapon and one about which the other associates don't yet need to know.

"Penda," Cadwallon says congenially, our disagreement forgotten about, "I'll introduce you to the rest of our allies."

The men are a strange collection, and some of them I'd think were the lad tasked with minding the sheep, not with running a prosperous kingdom. Some look kingly, but others certainly do not. I wonder if they think the same of me when they see me.

The first man is Eiludd, the King of Powys. He's much the same as Cadwallon in appearance, and I wonder what ancestry they share but know better than to ask about it. If they knew they were related, it would be common knowledge. Still, as they don't, it must be a secret from many years ago, probably a grandfather who couldn't help himself, or perhaps even a grandmother desperate to get pregnant and provide an heir. I amuse myself with little scenarios before realising the men are both looking at me.

"Well met," I manage to stumble. I allow half a smile to touch my face because I want to be friendly but not too open. I want the man to trust me but not think of me as a friend. I need Cadwallon's allies to believe me their equal, and then, when I prove myself in battle, I'll be their master.

"Well met, Lord Penda," Eiludd replies, his yellow teeth flashing in a smile. His eyes alight on the arsenal of weapons I carry around my waist even though I'm an honoured guest at Cadwallon's court.

"I've heard a lot about you," he continues, and I grin more widely. Good, I like it when my reputation precedes me.

"I wish I could return the compliment," I say, seeing if his smile will falter or if he'll brave his belittling with some aplomb.

"Well, you'll have been too busy in the Saxon lands to pay more than a passing glance towards the kingdoms of the Britons. I understand that."

Good. He's a player in this charade, and my respect for him grows already.

"I understand your men already have an issue with King Edwin," I press, pleased when his eyes narrow in anger.

"King Edwin is a traitorous bastard," he offers in a hiss. "And yes, the men of the kingdom of Powys have a score to settle with him. One that's so big only his death will satisfy their honour."

"It would be my honour to help you," I say. I place as much force into those words as I can. I mean them. I can imagine what it feels like to have been almost annihilated by an enemy.

Eiludd meets my gaze as though he's weighing my words, and whatever he finds in my face, he's satisfied because he nods and walks away decisively.

Cadwallon winks at me, his face crinkling in delight.

"Well, he likes you. That's good. Now, for a more difficult ally."

A younger man walks towards us. I think he must be another of the Britons because he looks similar to Cadwallon and the King of Powys. There's little difference between the men who inhabit this island, but the ancient ones, the ones who claim an ancestry none of the Saxons can hope to imitate, have something about them. I don't know if it's hardness or just an outlook on life, but it infects their very being. I like it. I always have. But it marks them as different to me, even with my uncompromising ways.

"Cloten," Cadwallon says as he greets the tall man, his green eyes flashing intelligently in the firelight.

"Cadwallon," the man lisps back, much to my surprise. His voice is too quiet for a man of such stature. "I'm impressed by this," Cloten states, gesturing at the great hall and the men within it.

Cadwallon watches him as though he doesn't believe a word he says. As though he's waiting for some other words to follow, words he won't like and that will purposefully upset him. He doesn't speak.

"Well met," I offer into the silence, and the man glances to my open hand before grudgingly taking it in his and clasping my forearm. He's strong. I expected him to be strong.

"You're Lord Penda," Cloten says as though he's setting the name in his mind. It's not intended as a greeting. "I know your brother. He's a great strategist," Cloten half grins, and I feel that this man means things with his words that are contrary to the terms he employs.

"He is, yes. But I'm better," I simply say. I don't know if I want to engage with the man. I can see why Cadwallon said it would be more difficult to speak to him.

That brings a grudging cough of respect from the great man, and he stops glancing around the room with acquisitive eyes and looks at me.

"You might be," Cloten admits slowly, as though he's still trying to decide for himself. "But I'll reserve judgment until I know you better."

"And I you," I say and turn to walk away. A giant hand on my shoulder stops me. I only just manage not to lash out angrily. I don't like to be touched without being the one to initiate the contact.

"I'm not your enemy," Cloten menaces, a dangerous gleam to his eyes. "I hate the bastard more than you can imagine."

I give him a moment to elucidate, and he does.

"My voice, it wasn't always like this." And then he does an obscure thing and sticks his tongue out at me. That's when I see it. His tongue, a large portion of it, is shorn away.

"King Edwin?" I ask with surprise. I've not heard of this.

"Yes, Edwin and his men. They held me down when I tried to submit in battle, and they cut enough of my tongue that now I speak with a soft voice. He laughed as he did it." The large man trembles with anger. I feel it in the weight of his hand on my shoulder.

"My apologies," I offer, and I mean it. Great warriors shouldn't be demeaned in such a way. "We'll kill him," I boom, and he nods once in agreement.

"We will, and we'll strip his bollocks from him and make him as female in his death as he has me." With that, the giant walks away to mingle with the other guests. I turn to Cadwallon, but he's watching me with a strange half-smile on his lips.

"He doesn't tell anyone that story," Cadwallon informs me. "I didn't know it, and I thought I knew everything about my fellow kings."

I stay silent as he continues to appraise me. There's something on his mind.

"You're a fucking scary individual," Cadwallon finally announces. I don't know what he means by that. Is it a compliment or a complaint? I have no idea, and he offers nothing further, instead walking towards another of the British kings.

"Penda," Cadwallon calls to me when I don't immediately follow. I walk towards the two men, a half-smile of interest on my face. I don't like being wrong-footed by my ally. I don't know what just happened.

"Clydog, this is Penda, from the Hwiccan lands."

Clydog is a young man. I imagine he's the same age as me, and immediately I feel competitive. Not the best frame of mind to meet a new ally in, but I can't help myself. I want to win renown as a young warrior, a man who accomplished much with few years to him, a man wise beyond his years who crams three lives into only one.

I do my part and reach out and shake the hand of a man who might steal my claims to renown.

His handclasp is firm and assured. Damn, he will have to become a strong ally of mine. I can't allow him not to be associated with me.

"You're bigger than I thought you'd be," Clydog offers with a hint of amusement.

"No one here is bigger than Cloten," I simply say. He arches an eyebrow at my attempt at politic.

"No, but you need to grow your reputation to match your physique," Clydog replies testily. I suddenly realise he's as nonplussed by our meeting as I am.

"We should be good friends," I say quickly. I want to make my feelings known immediately. "Join me. We'll drink and feast."

For a moment, I think he's going to say no, but then his shoulders relax, and he flings his long arm around my neck.

"I didn't want to like you," Clydog explains, "but I do already. Come, Cadwallon and you and I will get well and truly pissed and forget all about this battle for the evening. Tomorrow will be soon enough to talk about gelding a man."

Cadwallon laughs loudly at his speech, signalling for more mead and food to be brought. He directs us all to a large table where some of the other men already sit. I've not met everyone yet. Cadwallon has at least three other allies within the hall, but he seems almost to have forgotten about them.

As I make myself comfortable beside Clydog, I quickly survey the room, pleased when I notice that everyone is talking in small groups. No one looks angry or concerned; indeed, everyone looks keen and pleased to be meeting. Perhaps I owe Cadwallon more respect than I've so far given him. He's done a great thing here. Eight men within this room all want to kill King Edwin of Northumbria, whilst hiding away amongst Edwin's faithful followers, we have his son Osfrith, and in the far north and ready to attack his borders, we have Eanfrith, son of a man Edwin killed.

I muse on that. Edwin has killed many men and made many enemies in the same way. I wonder if I should learn a valuable lesson from that revelation.

Maybe not.

When men stand in your way, they have to be removed, and really, death is the only sure way of doing that. If you let them leave, as Edwin will soon realise, and seek sanctuary elsewhere, they'll simply come back when you least expect it.

Edwin has many enemies. I'm just one of many, but I want his death just as much as all those he's wounded.

I almost feel the desire to ride to war now, to kill Edwin in the morning with the sharpened edge of my war-axe.

I breathe deeply.

We have ten men and their war leaders ready to attack King Edwin. But and this I firmly believe we can get more yet.

17

AD631 - CADWALLON OF GWYNEDD – GWYNEDD

The morning had been long and tedious, talking of tactics and alliances with Penda, but I have to grudgingly accept that his ideas are good. I've managed to gather many, many men to our cause, but in appealing to so many men, I might just have gained myself one ally too many.

I'll not let Penda think that I agree with his decision to kill one of them on the battlefield. I'll happily let him do it, though. I'll ensure neither of us is held accountable for that murder. It'll have to be a thing of deception and subtlety. Something Penda should do alone. He's the kind of man who would lie easily about it.

I've watched him with interest mingling with the other kings. He's supposed to be the most junior of us all here. He has no kingdom to call his own because his brother holds the Hwiccan lands firmly in his hands, and yet it's Penda's inclusion in the group that's making these men flock to our side. It's a strange situation.

I'm the king here, yet these men want Penda and his pent-up rage and fighting potential to be the guiding force. Having witnessed first-hand how Penda wages war, I don't blame them. It's probably better to be his ally now than his enemy later. I don't think King Edwin has the slightest indication of just what's about to be unleashed against him.

Good, I want Edwin to be caught out. It'll make the battle easier if he doesn't know the size of our support.

I'm also pleased that Clydog and Penda have decided to be friendly allies rather than grudging allies. It would make our alliance very difficult if both men decided to be the youngest, the bravest and the most reckless. That position needs to be taken by Penda.

I excuse myself from their conversation and thread my way through the crowded hallway to an ally I've not seen for many years. Clemen is an old man, his beard almost to his knees, his face creased and wrinkled from the glorious weather he and his people enjoy. I've been to Dumnonia on many occasions, especially in my youth. The mild weather and gentle winters very much meet with my approval. The wine made with the grapes that love the mild climate is delicious.

Clemen greets me with his low gravelly voice. I feel a pang of remorse. He's an old man. I shouldn't have dragged him into this. Something in his stance makes me realise he knows my thoughts.

"Far better to die in battle than pissing yourself with old age," he mutters into my ear, his beard prickling my ear where I've inclined it to speak with him.

"I've fought many battles. I've bedded many women, and I've many children to rule when I'm gone. I'm happy," he says without me even speaking. I fling my arm around his shoulders with welcome. It's good to see him, no matter my worry about his advancing years.

"How are your children and grandchildren?" I ask, and he shrugs his shoulders.

"I love them all, but they're all happily plotting to kill each other. And I, well, I don't care anymore. Provided one of them remains alive to be king on my death, I leave them to their tricks."

It's not the response I was expecting, but then Clemen never says what I hope to hear.

"And whilst you're away?"

"Oh, they'll probably announce my death and try and to be king in my place. It's not a problem," he says when he notices me start as though to move and call my men to battle. "By the time I return, another one might be dead. But I have so many, it little matters. And they always give me my kingdom back, eventually."

I wish I could be as little concerned as he is by the thought of men trying to steal my place and my kingdom.

"I'm the king. That's what they always forget. I'm the one my people support, not them. I'm the one who taxes them lightly and protects them. One day I hope that my elder son will realise that. In the meantime, he thinks to govern in my stead. My advisors almost let him. But as soon as I return, they'll drop him and come to do my bidding. Families are funny things," he offers as an afterthought. I laugh at that. Families certainly are.

"Penda is a powerful warrior," Clemen muses. "If my sons were like him, then I might worry, but they don't have his raw edge, his desire to succeed."

I seek out Penda, noting with amusement that he and Clydog are engaged in a drinking game. I wouldn't bet on who'll win.

"Penda is better as an ally than an enemy," I amend.

"He'll be a great king if he ever gains any land to govern," Clemen offers. I know he's right. Penda has something about him, something that average men don't possess. I wish I knew what it was.

"Go, speak to the others," he says, shooing me away with his hand. "I need to sit for a bit and think about nothing at all."

I walk away from him, and Clemen shuffles towards a wooden bench placed before the fire. It's a warm and pleasant day outside, for my kingdom. I wonder if it's a bit cold for Clemen after his sea voyage. I almost worry he won't be alive to fight our coming battle, but he'll be stubborn. He wants to die in battle, and he's decided that will be as my ally. I'm honoured and grateful.

My next two allies are deep in conversation and might well resent my intrusion, but there's nothing for it but to intrude. I have to get between them and ensure that they at least pretend to have the same objectives that I do.

"Domnall, Beli," I announce, reaching out to grasp both men's arms at the same time. They look at me with fleeting expressions of annoyance. I believe I'm right to suppose they talk of other things than the coming battle.

"Cadwallon," Domnall replies, his eyes dark and hooded for all that the hall is brightly lit. I often think of him as a creature of the winter, plucked from a nightmare of stark contrasts. He's not an easy man to like, but I admire him. He holds away over vast lands, divided by a sea. I think his blunt demeanour is a necessity.

"For the first time in many years, I feel as though I'm not a king." His comment is a little barbed. He's looking around the hall as he speaks and what I think he means is that in a hall full of kings, being a king is almost irrelevant.

"We're all equals here," I offer.

At his side, a fleeting grin jumps across Beli's face. Beli is far more assured in his position as king of Alt Clut, and that means he's always more relaxed than Domnall as the King of Dal Riata. They're neighbours and enemies all at the same time. The kingdoms in the north are as complex as those that surround Gwynedd. They contract and expand with the will of their rulers. I assume some sort of peace is currently in place to see them talking so closely. But I could be very wrong.

"We're all kings," Beli replies. I could almost punch him for his comment, the implication being that we're not equals. That's not how you make friends and allies.

"We are," I jump in before Domnall can say anything else. "Apart from Penda," I clarify, hoping to distract both men.

"But he will be," Beli says with an assurance I find amusing. He approves of Penda; he made that very clear when I approached him.

"He will be. He has a brother," I say as though that explains everything. Domnall hasn't yet spoken, and I consider if he will.

"Better to have allies than brothers," Domnall announces, and his words so clearly match Penda's words that I look at him in surprise. Has Penda spoken to him already? I didn't think any of the men knew Penda, but perhaps I'm wrong.

At that point, Penda himself joins the conversation, Clydog trailing him across the hall.

"A fine feast," Penda shouts to me when he's still some distance away. I believe he might be quite drunk. I smile and accept his thanks until he's close enough that I can speak to him more quietly. His wink as he leans toward me tells me everything I need to know. He's a little drunk, but he knows what he's doing. His ability to change and mould his behaviour to what others think he should be is something that makes him so difficult to read. I think I have a fair measure on him.

I summoned him to me, offered him my alliance and not vice-versa, but he pretends to be something he's not for the other men. He's not a drinker or a stupid warrior; he's an intelligent man who's always at least ten steps in front of other conspiracies. His words about Northumbria have shown me that.

I only hope he doesn't kill me when he realises that I've played him for a fool. I want Northumbria. The other two men will both be dead by the time our battle is played out.

I'm an ambitious man, and with all these other allies, I'll get what I want.

In the process, all I need to do is keep Penda by my side. If I lose him, I'll lose everything.

18

AD631 - EDWIN OF NORTHUMBRIA

Osfrith worries me. There's something about him that's changed whilst he's been away. I wonder what King Cadwallon said to him? Has he made him doubt his own father? Cadwallon knows me well. He knows things I'm not proud of, but would he really turn my son against me? I don't think so. He would think it dishonourable, and yet? Well, there's something not right with Osfrith.

Osfrith has been gone for much of the summer. He's missed the summer raids, and that might be the source of his changed behaviour for my men, and I have had an outstanding raiding season. The enclave at Yeavering is filled to capacity with cattle that belong to other men. Bamburgh is locked up tight for the coming extreme weather.

My people and I will feast well come the dark times of the year.

The news that Osfrith carries with him is a mixed bag of good, bad and quite good and only confirms what Osric has uncovered for me and what I've seen with my own eyes. Sigeberht, the new Christian king of the East Angles and Essex, is no stranger to me. I know he'll support me. He doesn't like the growing power of the war leaders within the kingdom that stands between us, the kingdom that

Eowa hopes to rule with my help, Mercia. Sigeberht's an exile like I was, who's forced his way back into power. Since Rædwald's death, the kingdom of the East Angles has been unsettled, but Sigeberht has calmed it.

And further south, Penda has ensured that King Cynegils of Wessex will never side with any alliance that claims him as a member. The defeat of Cynegils at the hands of Penda and Eowa is a source of great anger and frustration for him. Luckily, one that Cynegils has helpfully forgotten involved Eowa.

Bishop Paulinus has guaranteed that King Eadbald of Kent will support me. We share an important link, our faith, and Paulinus ensures that everyone is aware that Penda remains a pagan. He has no problem forgetting that Cadwallon and many of their allies already ascribe to his Christian God because, so he says, their God is a mangled interpretation of the true Christ.

Provided I have the man's support, I don't much mind how it's come into being. Still, I might send Bishop Paulinus, or some of his monks, to speak to others who are like-minded. There are many kingdoms I could yet turn away from Cadwallon. After all, and this I do find amusing, I won our last battle. Not him. I think he forgets that I'm already a victor and he's a loser. A great loser who's spent the last two years gaining back land that he should already have held and which I took from him.

I should have ensured he died there and then. My weakness against someone I thought of as a brother has left me vulnerable and exposed. I don't like it.

Eadfrith, I sent north, to seek out his like-named cousin, Lord Eanfrith, and he returned with disappointing news. Eanfrith has more power within the Pictish kingdom than I thought he'd have. He has the ear of the king, and that means he can direct the king as he wills. He can shield the king from information that will harm him. Unless I send a spy into the kingdom, I'll never be able to present my arguments to the Pictish king as to why Eanfrith should be banished from their realm and sent home to me, to his death.

Again, weakness. I should have ferreted out and killed the spawn that King Æthelfrith produced, but they were so like my own sons I could never bring myself to destroy the entire family. I loved my sister as fiercely as I despised her husband. I let her children live as a sign of my love. I should have had her and the boys killed. It would have made my kingship more secure.

My cousin Osric is the only one I don't doubt. He's always been loyal to me. Perhaps too loyal, but it is to be rewarded even when it feels cloying. When I'm in the part of my kingdom known as Bernicia, he governs in Deira for me and vice versa. I give more power to him than I do to my sons because I have faith in him. If he ever played me false, I'd think the end times had come. Then it wouldn't matter anyway, for God would be sundering the land, and everyone's deaths would be imminent.

I know that Cadwallon is building an army to defeat me and deprive me of all the land I've gained. He no doubt means to take my life, but that doesn't concern me too much. Not now. They won't attack before next year, allowing me time to manipulate events. I will try and gain more allies whilst at the same time keeping those that I already have close. It allows me to choose the place of the battle.

Maybe I've been too aggressive since becoming king? Perhaps I deserve to have my expansionist plans curtailed? But maybe not? The kingdom of Elmet is mine, and so too is Lindsey to the south of Deira.

Their kings have been killed or sent into exile. I doubt that either kingdom will ever reassert itself; the dynasties of the ruling clan were weak. In taking them, I've shown other kingdoms how aggressive I can be, how single-minded. I wanted to scare them into submission, but with some of them, especially Cadwallon, I seem to have created the opposite effect. I've made them want to attack me, kill me, remove me from my place as king of Northumbria.

If only they understood how firmly I hold my position, I believe they'd all realize their venture will be unsuccessful. I'm king now, over a vast swathe of land. I have sons who will rule in my place and the name of God as my supporter. And perhaps more.

My fate is no longer tied to the old Gods, to those who had control over my actions and where I was merely a plaything for them. I can determine my own future now, thanks to my new God. Cadwallon and his allies have mostly shared my beliefs, believing as they do in the same God, but the Saxons, the men who follow Eowa and Penda, have a different viewpoint. They're happy to meet their death. On the other hand, I want to accomplish much in life first.

"Father," Eadfrith sits beside me, calling my attention to a man who's been shown into my hall. He brings the wind and rain that shroud the palace at Yeavering, protecting it and making it an almost mythical place.

"Who is he?" I demand. I don't recognize him at all.

"I don't know, but he wears the clothes of the Dal Riatans," Eadfrith confirms. Suddenly I'm vigilant; my meandering thoughts are entirely forgotten. Although I try not to, I hope this man brings news that will make up for my disappointment with Eadfrith's journey to the north earlier in the year.

I signal to my servants that the man should be brought before me. As he walks closer, he removes his soaking wet cloak and his layers of furs. He's come from the north; there can be no denying it. The men there know how to dress to keep warm.

I squint at his face. Something about him is familiar. At my side, Eadfrith gasps in recognition. I turn to him, waiting for him to say something. Only he doesn't, his face turning quizzical again.

"My Lord Edwin," the man says, his voice lilting and soft, his face reminding me so vividly of someone that I feel uncomfortable not knowing the man's name or how I know him.

"Eanfrith," Eadfrith says beside me, but the man turns his hazel eyes on him and shakes his head.

"No, My lord. But he is my brother."

And now I know who this man might be, another of my nephews, son of my sister. He looks like her. It's almost uncanny to see her face on the body of a man.

"Oswald, my Lord Edwin, or should I say, Uncle Edwin." He says the phrase with no animosity, and I'm surprised. He's come here unarmed. Yet I killed his father and banished him to the north. As I understand it, he lives not with the Picts but within the kingdom of Dal Riata, the realm separated by the sea.

"Well met," I say, standing and reaching out to offer him an arm clasp of friendship. I've not seen the man since he was fourteen or fifteen, another fifteen years have elapsed since then, and he's a man now, not a child.

He returns the greeting, his hand firm and steady on my arm. Close up; he looks even more like my sister.

"Your mother?" I ask. I've often wondered how she survived what happened. It was King Rædwald of the East Angles who insisted on their exile; at least, that's what I tell myself to assuage my grief at some of my actions. It was probably for the best. I might have had to kill her myself if she'd stayed.

"Dead, My Lord," he says without flinching. "She succumbed to a contagion about five years ago."

I close my eyes briefly in grief, an image of her as a young girl flashing before my eyes. She was a pretty thing, although as her younger brother, she tortured me as only sisters can do to their brothers.

"My sympathies," I offer, but he shrugs them aside.

"She heard of your great victories. I think she hated you a little, but she spoke well of you at the end."

That doesn't entirely fill me with remorse for her death, but at least it's honest.

"Did you come to tell me of this?" I ask. I'm trying to understand why the man is here after all this time.

"No, My Lord. I've come to call on your family honour and ask you to reinstate me to the family. To give me land that I can control and with which I can support myself and my warriors."

Ah, he doesn't come alone, after all. As he speaks, a steady stream of fierce-looking men begins to make their way into my hall. I try to count, but a movement before me distracts me as Oswald flicks his wrist towards me. I tense, waiting for some sort of blow, but he's simply removing fabric that wraps his arms. He sees my undertaking and glances at me with interest. I assume he doesn't know of the attempt on my life five years ago because he offers no words of apology but does show me the length of fabric he's undoing.

"A device to keep the rain from going up my sleeves," he offers as he works on the other wrist.

I've not yet offered him food or drink, but Eadfrith must have done so because a servant appears and hands him warmed mead. He drinks deeply from the hollowed-out drinking horn. No doubt it came from a stolen Pictish cow.

"A chill day," Oswald confirms. "Although nothing to what I'm become used to in the north."

Silence descends. I don't want to say anything further whilst I consider the implications of his words. I can almost hear my cousin Osric telling me to let this man into our family once more, to give him the power of my word and the ability to act in my name. Osric badgers me, saying I need more allies who are tied to me personally and through fear of what I might do if they err.

"I'd be honoured to welcome you into my family," I finally say and realize I might mean it. "I could gift you some land, some small part of your patrimony. You could use it to support your men and fight on my behalf."

A chair has appeared behind him, and he sinks to it gratefully, the fire now at his back so that I feel cold whilst he must be warm. I shake my head with irritation at the blast of cold air over my body. He must witness my action because he shuffles along a little, the scrape of wood on wood.

"What would you give me in return?" I ask. I don't tend to do anything unless there's some gain involved.

"Details of King Cadwallon's plans and the alliance forming against you," Oswald offers, and when I don't immediately jump at the opportunity, he adds something further. "Who your enemies are and who your allies really are. There are traitors everywhere," he says ominously, and I know there and then that I'll have to give him what I promised. I need to know what he knows. Although, I pause for a moment.

"How do you know about the alliance?" Suspicion mars my

words, but there's no hope for it now. His face clouds a little with annoyance. I've disappointed him already.

"It's always best to keep some secrets," he says slowly. "But when the king of Dal Riata takes you to one side and informs you that you need to fight against your family because the whole of this island is uniting against you, it's time to make some tough decisions."

"The king said this to you openly?" I'm surprised, but then, I'd always assumed that my nephews would be accorded little respect in their adopted kingdoms. I might well have had the support of the King of Gwynedd when I was in exile, but I'm a better man, a man who was always going to claim back his land from a brother-in-law who'd simply grown too mighty to be contained. That was why King Rædwald took me in. I spent my youth making myself a king. King Æthelfrith of Northumbria wasn't allowed any time to enjoy his spoils because rumours of what I was plotting and whom I was plotting it with were always in circulation. I made sure of it.

"The king, Domnall, has grown to rely on me in recent years. I'm a child no more, uncle. You'd do well to remember that."

I watch him carefully. Eadfrith is still at my side. He's probably wondering why I'm letting his cousin speak to me this way. I keep him under much firmer control. He might have his war band and his warriors, but he's my son, and he'll do as told, no matter what.

"Yet it appears as though his trust in you was misguided," I taunt, trying to regain the upper hand here. This is my hall, my kingdom, not his. He might have lived here as a boy, but it's not his anymore, and it never will be.

"No, he wasn't misguided. He asked me what I wanted to do. He respects me enough to know that his decisions might contradict my desires. He told me all he could and then told me to do as I must. He plans on aiding King Cadwallon, but as little as possible. It's better for him when every other kingdom is in upheaval. It makes the lands of the Dal Riatans easier to control."

I smirk at that. King Domnall and I have long been enemies. After I took Elmet and Lindsey, I also tried to gain a foothold in his kingdom, the one across the sea. The men of Dal Riata expected me to engage with them on our island. I took them by surprise, but my gains were too small and few. I have some fine jewellery from my raid and a small goat that I took a fancy to, but nothing more. Ad Gefrin, Yeavering as I know it, always has room for another goat. Why else would it have a name such as it does?

"I would expect nothing less from him. They still view us as interlopers, men who stole their land from under their unsuspecting feet. I'm not surprised that he sides with Cadwallon. But you? You want to fight for me even after everything that I've done to you?"

"I hear rumours," Oswald intones again. I consider what these rumours concern. "And they tell me that you need your allies more than you think you do. Your position is less secure than at any time in your long reign."

I laugh at that with delight. I don't know what this mirror image of my sister has heard, but I'm the bretwalda of this island. I hold sway over many kingdoms. The Saxons, the men of Kent, and even the West Saxons pay me to protect them and keep their lands safe. It might be in a lesser degree the further south I go, but every single one of them knows that they have to act with my permission, or they face an invasion on a scale such as that which enveloped the kingdoms of Elmet and Lindsey. They fear my power. All of them. Even Lord Eowa of the Hwicce. He knows he needs me to rule Mercia without fear of attack. Only King Cadwallon seems to think that my rule is a transient thing.

I'll show Cadwallon how wrong he is once more. I'll ensure he's killed this time.

My nephew watches me carefully, his familiar face neutral.

"It's that attitude that makes men realize how deluded you are," he offers. I feel my rage build. How dare he insult me in such a way within my hall?

My son clamps his hand on my arm. I try to calm myself, but I'm outraged and about a breath away from having my warriors attack Oswald. He surprises me by laughing openly in my face.

"You don't listen to anyone else because you think you're the only person who knows best. That alienates people, and your fury makes them change their words when they try to speak to you about it. A good ruler needs people who disagree with them, as well as agree."

"I take it you've come to disagree then?" I ask bitingly, but he laughs again.

"Of course, Uncle, why else would I be here?"

His words have unnerved me, and suddenly I wonder if what he's saying could be true. Bishop Paulinus is always appreciative of what I do. My wife is filled with wonder for the success I've had converting the men and women of Northumbria to the true faith, and my older sons, well, they're sullen creatures who simply nod and do as I say. Have I, after all, surrounded myself with people who only say what I want to hear? Or have I made them into people who only say what I want to hear?

A sudden doubt clouds my mind, growing in intensity as Oswald continues to smirk in my direction.

I think I hate him.

But he might have a very valid point.

"I'll give you land and wealth if you become oath sworn to me, and with the oath, you'll be promising only ever to tell me the truth and not what I want to hear."

Eadfrith is incredulous at my side. I can tell from his gasp of dismay, no matter how he tries to mask it with a hasty cough. I wonder if he's angry with me for offering this oath to a stranger when he could have done the same for me, or whether he's just outraged on my behalf to think that anyone says I act incorrectly.

"I'll take my inheritance," Oswald responds slowly, emphasizing the word inheritance. "And I'll always promise to speak my mind provided I have an assurance and a similar oath from yourself that I'm not to be punished for so doing."

I nod to show I agree and then wave him away. He goes grudgingly and with much scraping of wood over wood. I believe he sought an invitation to eat with me, but I don't want him near me. His words haunt me. Suddenly, I feel vulnerable, whereas only moments ago, I was self-satisfied and smug, thinking of my joy at killing King Cadwallon.

I turn to Eadfrith.

"Does he speak the truth?" I ask. I don't need to say anything further. He knows what I mean.

"Yes," is his simple reply. I appreciate then that I've strained the bond that should exist between my sons and me.

"I'll give you more power, you and your brother. I'll give you your own land and your own halls, and you can rule in my name, as my cousin does in Deira. My apologies." I stand abruptly; my good cheer in the day all dissipated. My son tries to call me back, but I ignore his voice and head for the doorway. I need to feel the chill of the air on my face; the damp rain needs to suck my boots from my feet as I walk over the soggy, muddy ground.

I need a moment alone, with nature as my only witness.

A servant rushes from the hall behind me and flings a cloak around my shoulders. I settle it around me but don't thank the woman for her concern. That, after all, is her role at my court.

Outside, the clouds are as dark and menacing as my black mood. Have I been a bloody idiot, have I only myself to blame for the men who want to see me dead?

I stamp beyond the animal pens, the joy at seeing the stolen cattle dissipating. Have I imperilled my kingdom? Have I injured myself with my raiding more than if I'd made allies?

At the wooden staging erected so that Bishop Paulinus can preach to my people, I stop and glance upwards and upwards, wondering why so many people come to hear his words, are taken in by his stories of this new God as opposed to our old ones. And my gaze continues ever upwards, to see the vista of the imagined hills, shrouded now in thick grey clouds, the rain so big I can see it before it hits the wooden steps. Up and up until I'm looking at the sky, the place my new God supposedly calls his home. I feel my rage growing and growing, dragging me down, forcing me to my knees, as my tears of anger and grief mingle with the great fat raindrops.

What the fuck have I done?

19

AD631 - OSFRITH OF NORTHUMBRIA

I watch my father and the man who looks like him, with interest. Apparently, he's a relative of ours, but my father hasn't asked me to sit beside him, so my curiosity can't be sated. Since I returned from visiting his client kings, he's accorded me little respect, and my wrath grows daily.

I hate him. I wish him dead.

When the stranger leaves, my father asks my brother a sharp question, somehow high in his favour despite his shortcomings with the Pictish kingdom. Then he abruptly leaves, and I find myself following him with interest.

What has the man said to my father to send him rushing into the damp, gloomy day?

What have I missed now?

I watch my father stumble his way to his strange grandstand for the bloody Christian bishop. I see him walk to its top and then tumble to his knees. I even hear his cry of anger, a blasphemy so loud I wonder if his new God will forgive him for his doubts. I'm sheltered within one of the buildings used for storing grain. It's warm and dry inside, and through the slightly open doorway, I can watch what my father's doing.

I wish I knew what the stranger had said, but I don't want to move and find out from my brother. I want to spy on my father, let my anger pool and grow as I observe my weak king, who thinks too much of himself and too little of his children. The man who hears the words of the false Bishop Paulinus and believes them. Fervently.

I hear the squelch of footsteps coming from the hall. I peer into the gloom, questioning who else follows the king. When I decipher my brother's shape before me, I hiss for his attention and beckon for him to join me. He does so without speaking, and we both stand and stare at our father.

Whatever's going on, it seems very important.

"Who was that?" I finally ask, and Eadfrith tells me of the king's visit from our cousin. I almost smirk when Eadfrith repeats the words that have upset the king so much. But the truth of them can't be denied. It sobers me to realise I'm not the only man to doubt the king.

"Will it make a difference?" I ask Eadfrith. I've not discussed my change of alliance with him. I can't. He might tell the king, and then I'll never have the opportunity to kill the man I've grown to hate.

"God alone knows," Eadfrith jokes. I do love my brother. He's irreverent at the right moments. "I imagine he'll summon Bishop Paulinus back to him to discuss his fears and his worries."

"No doubt," I say with annoyance. "He could just bloody ask us, but clearly, he's not going to do that."

"What would you say to him if you could?" Eadfrith asks, and so many phrases rush through my head that I have to stop them from pouring out of my mouth unheeded.

"I'd tell him that this Oswald's right. He's made more enemies than he has friends. He's alienated his sons. Why, what would you tell him?"

"That his religion is a farce, and he needs to call on the Old Gods if he wants to remain king. He needs to rule with the force of the Old Gods, not this weak new one."

My brother makes an excellent point. None of the men who've changed their beliefs has succeeded. King Rædwald of the East Angles is dead and gone, his son reverting to paganism on his death.

And when he did rediscover his God, giving up the throne, thinking himself unworthy of his position. The bloody fool.

Whilst a man of the new religion now rules the kingdom of the East Angles, he's from the continent, just as Bishop Paulinus was. Neither man fully understands what's happening within the land of the East Angles.

The Kentish kingdom of my stepmother's birth also pretends to its Christianity. King Æthelberht might have been the first to be converted to Christianity, but his son reverted to paganism on his death. Only recently has he returned to Christianity. A pity, he could have stayed a pagan and then my father would never have been prevailed upon to convert to Christianity. Neither would he have taken his second wife, my stepmother and sister of the current king of Kent.

It remains to be seen how successful Eadbald will prove to be. He's been king for nearly sixteen years, and all he seems to have done is drive out his fellow rulers and brothers and convert to Christianity. I hope to be remembered for more wondrous deeds than that.

We lapse into silence then. I can feel the weight of my traitorous alliance trying to push itself through my lips. But I won't. I can't. I love my brother. I trust him, but not with this, never with this.

Outside, the day grows slowly darker, the hills that surround Yeavering shrinking away into the mist of the rain clouds. I feel the stirring of the ancient Gods. If the king can't feel their power here, the site he's tried to make as Christian as possible, then I believe he's gone too far in his new religion.

I hear whispers and the moaning of dead men and women in this place. I feel as though monsters from the ancient stories inhabit the land. I shiver a little with the thought. We are but men, nothing more. The king needs to realise that he's no God and never likely to be.

My father needs to appreciate that he needs men and women to help him rule just as much as other kings do. His conversion hasn't made him *more* than anyone else.

"Our father needs our support," my brother says softly. I stare at him in surprise. Has he heard something?

"He needs the support of everyone within Northumbria, or the kingdom will dissipate and return to its two sovereign states. I don't want to rule half a kingdom," he says a little sullenly. I could almost laugh at his tone. He thinks the king will let him rule on his death. I'm incredulous.

"He has the support of the men and women of this kingdom, but he needs to hold it. He needs to stop making men question their consciences and let them do what needs to be done; build houses, grow crops, keep the animals safe. Anything else is irrelevant." I mutter angrily. I believe my words. If the king let me do what I need to do, then I'd be a far happier man, and I know I'm not alone with my thoughts.

"He's the king," Eadfrith hisses louder.

"Yes, he is, but only with the support of his warriors."

"His warriors are loyal," Eadfrith states, his concern making it a question, not a statement.

"His warriors *want* to be loyal. That's a huge difference," I clarify, and now he is looking at me with concern.

"What have *you* heard," he demands, his voice rising slightly, causing me to silence him so that the noise of our conversation doesn't reach our father.

"Men grumble, and women moan in bed and without," I respond. I'm not telling him I speak mainly of myself, and in all honesty, I don't. I've heard many, many complaints, and it's those that made me question the king's ideas more closely, made me seek an alternative to him.

"So nothing then," he growls, and I feel my frustration build. Like the king, my brother is quick to hear what he wants to hear and slow to hear anything he doesn't.

"If that's what you think," I say just as furiously as he's been hissing at me.

I know I'll never be able to speak openly to him of my deep unease and unhappiness and certainly not of my betrayal.

I thought he'd finished asking me questions, but suddenly, another rushes from his mouth, and I don't know how to answer it.

"You plan to oppose our father?" he asks in disgust.

A deep silence falls between us, broken only by the sound of the rain falling on the grass roof. I phrase the answer in my head. Should I act angrily or with disappointment? I watch the king in the rain for a long moment yet, hating him with every breath.

"I do not. I wouldn't imperil my claims," I say levelly. Then I leave, walking into the freezing rain, the sound of the wind and my rapidly beating heart roaring in my ears.

Shit.

Now my brother suspects me, and that'll make life very difficult.

20

AD631 - EADFRITH OF NORTHUMBRIA

I watch my brother leave with apprehension. His words were well-spoken. They sounded true to my ears, but in this place of rain and wind, I hear portents and the whispers of the dead warning me of difficult times ahead. I don't know if they speak the truth or just taunt me with the possibilities.

A howl of wind has me closing the still open door on the grain storage. Just as my brother did, I came out here to watch the king. What I don't need is to witness him doubt himself, shouting his anger and frustrations at his new God. I need him to be my father, the man who's fought for everything he's ever gained throughout his life. The man who evaded Uncle Æthelfrith's attempts to kill him found favour at the royal court of first King Cadwallon's father and then at the Mercian court of King Cearl and then the East Anglian court of Rædwald.

I don't need to see that the king can be weak and feeble, torn apart by the same worries that plague me.

I want to hide away and pretend that the king isn't bellowing his rage to his new heaven and that my brother hasn't just told me what I want to hear as opposed to the truth that I seek.

But I don't. Wrenching the door open, water pools into my eyes as

I pull my cloak tightly against my face. I can barely see one step in front of me, but I walk to where I know the king was a few moments ago. Even he's now shrouded in the rain-soaked mist. No one will see us together. No one who didn't know where the king was will even know that we've had this conversation.

"Father," I call against the wind and rain as I climb up the rain-slicked steps of his grandstand.

"Eadfrith," he says in response, his voice thick with emotion. "Go away," he calls, his voice breaking as he does so, but I ignore him.

"We need to talk," is all I say, finding a damp seat on the wooden steps and taking it. If I have to sit here and shiver the night away before my father speaks to me, then that's what I'll do.

Silence falls between us, but I can hear his ragged breathing even over the sound of rain on wood, of the howling wind and my erratic heartbeat. I'm fearful of the king's reaction, but I need to speak with him and now, whilst he's feeling so unsure of himself.

Water pools down my nose, and I lick the moisture from my lips, luxuriating in the clean taste, the fresh feeling, whilst forcing myself not to shiver with the cold. My cloak is a great thing that entirely covers me, but this weather is remorseless. It might well rain for a week without letting up. It's happened before.

"What do you want to talk about?" his voice drifts down to me from above, and I flinch at the anger there.

"What Oswald said," I say. He growls.

"You didn't need to listen to his words."

I think for a moment, I don't want to cause more bad feelings.

"I don't mean his actual words. I mean what he implied."

"I don't understand," Edwin says, his voice a little muffled. I'm wondering if he's turning his head or if he too is wiping the moisture from his face with his hand.

"They're only his words and his thoughts," I offer, trying to change tact. I don't know how to phrase what I'm trying to say.

"You mean he's lying?" he asks in confusion.

"No, I mean he wants you to trust and support him, have him as a member of your household, and he's thought of a way to do just that.

By being the only man who allegedly tells you the truth, he could be doing quite the opposite."

"You *do* think he's lying," Edwin says again. I suppose I am saying that.

"I'm saying he's presented a version of events that's different to yours, but still only his interpretation."

"Ah, sod off, Eadfrith. Speak your mind or just leave me to my thoughts," Edwin growls violently. Without thinking, I jump up and bound the last few steps to where he sits, his clothing sodden, his hair and beard and moustache heavy with rain.

I stop myself from grabbing him forcefully but only because a skirmish up here, in the rain, will probably result in the death of both of us. The wood is slick and slippery. I don't want to die yet.

"Oswald's words have only wounded because you already believe them. Deal with it, don't worry about it, and then you'll devise a way to regain the upper hand. And father, do it fucking quickly. You're losing men all over the place. Men you can't afford to lose."

With that, I turn and walk away. I'm breathing so fast, and it's so warm from my superheated body that my breath pools before me on every exhalation, adding to the mist and fog that surrounds me.

A noise behind me has me turning abruptly, fear deadening my legs. Surely my father wouldn't attack me now?

I feel the swish of empty air as he comes close to me as I try to determine how far down the grandstand I still have to go. Could I jump it? Get out of his way that way?

A hand grabs my arm, and I tense myself for whatever retribution he plans, stunned when Edwin embraces me and pulls me tight to his soaking wet chest.

"Thank you, son," he coughs, the strength back in his voice. "I needed to hear that," he continues and then he's gone, striding back into his hall to sit by his fire and eat his food.

I don't know what I've done here. Should I have reawakened his flagging spirit, or should I have left him to mither and grow scared of every step he takes?

As my foot impacts the muddy floor at the bottom of the grandstand, a figure steps out of the gloom.

"Well done, brother," Osfrith calls. "You've rekindled the beast. Now let's see what he does."

Osfrith says nothing more but walks before me into the hall where the king has just gone. I wait for a few heartbeats more.

Did Osfrith mean what he said?

Did my father?

21

AD631 WINTER - EOWA OF MERCIA

My men and I sit around a huge blazing fire at the centre of my huge wooden hall, nursing our mead and bragging about past exploits.
Most of us are young enough that our histories only reach back two handfuls of years. But there are a few, my father's chief ally amongst them, who can tell much older tales, of King Æthelfrith of Northumbria, and his quests against the men and women of Mercia which still raise ire amongst us.

I sit and listen, a little worried about how my recent actions will be interpreted. Will these men turn against me because of my alliance with King Æthelfrith's successor, or will they remember that a combined force of King Rædwald of the East Angles and his allies killed Æthelfrith, Edwin amongst them?

Or will they remember that Edwin was married to the old king of Mercia's daughter and had two children with her before her death; that King Cearl was the grandfather of those children. Some of these men will remember King Cearl, my father's ally amongst them.

Will they see the alliance as a good thing, something that needs to be done to prevent King Edwin from swallowing up another kingdom? He's already removed the royal lines of the kingdoms of both

Elmet and Lindsey. Mercia lies next in his path, and I'd rather ally with him to prevent him from taking it forcefully. I still need to grow my power base. I have the land of the Hwicce and some of the Mercian heartland, but I need to be stronger to gain more of it.

I hope my men agree with my decision to ally with Edwin as the means to achieving a united Mercia once more. As of yet, only the rift with my brother has become common knowledge.

Aldfrith is busy regaling us all with the story of an attack on King Æthelfrith, and I almost think that he can decipher my thoughts. There's little other reason for him to be telling this particular story, of Æthelfrith's victory against a far superior Mercian force and how he put to death any who yet lived once the battle was done. I meet his old eyes above the rim of his horn of mead. I consider if he knows and works to undermine me. And if he knows, who else knows? It's a conundrum.

I don't wish to tell my men yet about King Edwin. When the weather turns once more, then it will be time to inform them of the coming battle, but right now, it's too soon, far too early. They'll think there's time to question my decision if they disagree with it if I tell them too soon.

There is a flurry of activity at the door, and I look in bleary-eyed surprise to see a winter-clad warrior making his way into my cheerily lit hall. I don't recognize him, and yet he gains easy admittance past my warriors on guard there. Whoever he is, they know him.

He walks towards me, tearing his cloak from his back as he does. I finally recognize my brother from beneath the layers of fur. Why is he here? We've made our peace with each other and decided we must be enemies for the time being.

"Brother," Penda calls, and my men cry greetings to him, all of them too sodden with mead to realize that he shouldn't be here.

Penda's face is grim as he reaches out to grasp my offered forearm in greeting.

"What news?" I ask, fearful of what he might know that I don't.

"The other men of Edwin's alliance. They're doing all they can to distance themselves from it. You must be careful, brother," Penda informs me without pause.

"Why, what have you heard?" I ask, suddenly sober, my plans in pieces.

"A man from the north, another of Edwin's lost relatives, has made himself a regular fixture at his fire and his side. He works to poison the king against everyone he used to count as an ally and to remind the king that he has sons who should hold positions of honour and respect."

The news is alarming but not enough to bring my brother to seek me out on a grim winter's night.

"And what else?" I demand. My brother's face is pinched from the cold. His hand was cold on my arm. Yet he seems to shun the heat from the fire, sitting with his back to it so that his face stays dark and hooded to my vision.

"He plans on converting Mercia to his new religion," Penda finally blurts out. I could almost laugh at him for his concern.

"You said men and women were free to choose their religion."

"I did, brother, yes," he answers frankly, never one to shy away from the truth. "But King Edwin intends to use force. That's not allowing men and women to choose. That's forcing them to do as he wants." Penda growls as he speaks.

I consider his words. There's truth in them, after all.

"How did you hear all this?" I exact, suddenly as riled as him. I would have thought that my spies amongst the court would have told me of such monumental developments. Perhaps King Edwin has purchased their silence. I might have to send a new man to watch Edwin. One he won't suspect of being my spy.

"You don't need to know how, but you do need to know that your alliance is a poisoned blade. If you remain as his ally, your people will suffer, and remember, brother, those people are also mine."

Penda's voice has grown low and menacing as he speaks. Whether he really acts out of worry for the men and women of the Hwicce and Mercia as a whole, I don't know, but he'll gain the support of everyone within this hall if he makes those views known.

"Why tell me?" I enquire. He could use this to claim the kingdom himself, to have me removed from my place as war leader and would-be king.

"You're my brother," he simply says, his eyes finally turning to meet mine. There's raw emotion in those winter-glazed eyes. We might be enemies, but he loves me still.

"My thanks," I simply say, noting that he already holds a drinking horn of mead in his hand. I didn't see anyone give it to him.

"From where have you come?" I query, and now a grin touches his chilled face.

"That, I can't tell you, brother."

His smirk annoys me, and I wonder why I should listen to anything he has to say. Then he leans into me, his face almost touching mine, as though he might kiss my lips rather than speak, but then he does speak, moving his mouth to my ear so that his hairy face tickles my exposed ear.

"My words are true. I wouldn't lie to you, brother."

He moves away. I feel unsettled by his close touch. I wish I could learn to anticipate his movements and actions better.

"Penda," the old warrior shouts joyfully, his hand raised in greeting. Penda chuckles to see him.

"Aldfrith," Penda calls, real joy in his voice. He loves the old man, really truly loves him. I blame Aldfrith for all of Penda's battle joy and skill with his weapons. Aldfrith was his hero when he was no more than a sword's length tall. Our father used to laugh about it. Penda will perhaps mourn Aldfrith more than he ever did our father. And both men knew it when my father died.

"Where've you been?" Aldfrith asks bluntly. Penda almost answers him but just manages to stop himself with a rueful look my way. I should probably speak to Aldfrith and prime him to extract as much information as he can from Penda. After all, Aldfrith warms his arse at my fire, not Penda's.

"Busy old man, very busy. Where've you been?" Penda asks, trying to deflect the conversation away from his secrets.

"Not too far, boy," Aldfrith answers breezily, the use of the word 'boy' intentional. Penda lets it go with an amused grin. He loves the hoary old warrior who refuses to acknowledge that the sons are now his war chiefs. I think the old man still sees our father leading us.

Sometimes I almost share his wish.

Aldfrith has deep blue eyes and long, long hair that was once blond but now sits grey upon his head. He says he's never cut his hair, not once throughout his long life. I can well believe it. He says his hair is sacred, that the Gods have told him so, that when he dies, we must all take a piece of his hair and weave it into our own.

I might just do so. He's lived a long time for a warrior. I'd like some of his good fortune.

"In fact, really, I've only travelled through women," he coughs and smirks at the same time. Penda and I are laughing with delight at his outrageous comments. The women in the hall know to stay away from Aldfrith's roaming hands. He has his sons by many women, but they don't share in their father's incredible luck in battle and life.

"I wish I had your handsomeness and charming ways," Penda jibes.

"You learnt all your best tricks from me, and you know it," Aldfrith responds, calling for the slave girl to refill his drinking horn. She's a mere slip of a girl, and Aldfrith leaves her well alone. Everyone knows he likes his women older and well-seasoned. The girl briefly bobs as she fills all the drinking horns and ducks away quickly before she can be tasked with something else to do. She's a bright thing. I wish that her mother and father hadn't been forced into slavery to keep themselves. She'd have made someone a fine wife one day. I suppose she might still do if I can help in any way.

"I learnt how not to do things," Penda continues to tease the man. I feel myself relaxing. Penda has come here with his fears and his worries and stolen my good cheer, but Aldfrith is working to restore it, to put Penda's worries into some sort of context. If he won't tell me how he knows what he knows, I don't feel that I should pay too much attention to him.

"Why are you here?" Aldfrith asks his good humour gone immediately. "I know that you two are no longer working together. What do you suspect?" He's so blunt with his questions that I flinch in shock, but Penda, as I said, loves the old man and listens attentively.

He sighs deeply and then begins to speak.

"King Edwin has lost the support of men he relied upon. The kings of Wessex, of the East Angles and even Kent, are tired of his overmighty ways. They've sent word to King Cadwallon that they wish to ally with him."

Why the fuck my brother couldn't just tell me that, I don't know. He's too fond of games and takes pleasure in knowing more than I do. Damn him.

"And within his kingdom?" Aldfrith presses. I look at him in surprise. What else does he know?

Aldfrith turns his drooping eyes my way.

"I knew Edwin when he was sheltering in the Mercian kingdom before he married his wife. Before he became king. I know how his mind works." Once more, I think the old man can read my mind. Perhaps it's his hair, after all. Now I'm cursing myself. I should have thought of this and taken Aldfrith into my confidence. Penda has.

"Talk to me about Edwin," I demand. It might be a little late to be asking him, but Penda nods in approval at my words.

"Edwin was a young man when I knew him, wounded by King Æthelfrith driving his family out of Deira and claiming it as his to rule. Edwin was wary of everyone and trusted few men, apart from King Cadwallon and his father. Those two, he always esteemed, and that's probably why Edwin is so angry now. He never expected Cadwallon, his young foster brother, to turn on him. He never expects that from anyone. If you're right, Penda, your news that his allies are massing against him will wound him, deeply."

Penda is nodding as though he knows as much. I suddenly consider how often the two of them have spoken about Edwin and why they've not included me in their discussions.

"Back then, he tried to make men like him by being generous with his gifts. Then, when he thought they were loyal to him, his demands would become imperious, and he'd stop asking them for their opinion. He tried to rule before he had anything to rule."

Aldfrith sounds disgusted. He has clear rules on how warriors and their leaders should treat one another. Not that he abides by his rules all the time. As the trusted advisor to my father, he thinks that he has a prior claim on the affections of Penda and me. Both of us have always let him get away with his slight irreverence. None of the other men shares that luxury.

"When he married and left Mercia, wife in tow, to gain the support of King Rædwald of the East Angles, he had to begin all over again. But in Rædwald, he found someone keen to have a protégé at his heels. He didn't see Edwin's faults, only the possibilities, and that possibility was that with Edwin, he could replace King Æthelfrith and gain control over the combined kingdoms of Deira and Bernicia. It did no good for Edwin's skills with men. And, of course, when he began to win, men just followed him regardless of his abilities. He never needed to learn anything."

"So he's a king by default?" I query.

Aldfrith fixes me with his gaze, his eyes suddenly sharp and bright. The years have sloughed from him as though he's a sheep being shorn of its winter cloak.

"Yes, he has little or no skills. He uses religion as his crux now that Rædwald is dead and gone. He's easily manipulated. It's just that someone needs to realize how easily it can be done, and so far, no one has."

"They have now," Penda offers and Aldfrith chuckles darkly.

"It took bloody long enough."

"Who?" I ask, and Penda drinks deeply, staring into the fire as he considers his answer. Damn, he said he was my brother and that he loved me. Surely, he'll tell me this. It's vital to the future of the Hwicce and Mercia as a whole.

"Oswald," he responds.

"Who?" I say. I've never heard the name before, but once more, Aldfrith seems to know who it is.

"Really?" he says in wonder. "That little dick has worked his cousin out? I'm almost speechless with surprise."

"It's taken him long enough," Penda laughs darkly. He reads men with a flick of his eyes, a moment of scrutiny, nothing more. He's always disappointed when other men don't see quite so clearly, quite so quickly.

"What's he doing?" I demand to know.

"He's making his sons adore him, and that, in turn, makes their warriors adore him as well. He's given Oswald land to farm and men to command, and he's directing his eyes towards the north and the south. He wants to make his position stronger."

"I can't believe it of Oswald," Aldfrith muses and Penda smirks at the old man, affection in his eyes.

"Men are contrary beasts," he offers, setting Aldfrith to cackling again. I almost worry he'll fall from his stool, but Penda hauls him upright, flinging his arm around Aldfrith's neck and keeping him upright. Aldfrith nods drunkenly, and then his head lolls to one side, and he's snoring loudly, right there and then, in the middle of my hall.

Penda grins at me. This isn't the first time Aldfrith has done this. He is, after all, a bloody old man, well into his fiftieth year. Our father didn't live so long, dying nearly ten years ago, during one of Edwin and Rædwald's many skirmishes along the border.

"Why do you tell him things you don't tell me?" I ask petulantly. I want my brother to treat me like other men, not as his brother.

"He asks the right bloody questions," is his logical and straightforward response.

"What do you think I should do?" I query. He looks at me in surprise. We rarely decide to act together, but if we happen to want to do the same thing simultaneously, we can agree to work together. Even more rarely do I seek his opinion.

"I think you should join with Cadwallon and me. More than half the kingdoms will be arranged against King Edwin."

His words make sense to me, yet I'm not sure I believe him, not yet.

"Wouldn't that spoil your plans?" I press. He flinches as though I've punched him.

Damn, I wish I understood my brother better.

"Brother," he says, using our family connection, not my name. I'm paying attention no matter how drunk I am.

"Me and you are just the eldest of our father's children. Coenwahl stays with you, and you have his hall and his men. My plans fall outside of the accepted norm. I want to be king, I can't deny that, but I need to carve out a kingdom of my own. You have this one here. When Coenwahl realizes he needs to get off his arse and forge a powerbase, he'll do the same as me. For now, we need to keep our lands whole. You claim the kingdom of the Hwicce, but you need to hold Mercia. If I happen to win the land of the Maegonsaete or the Middle Angles, then that's all to the good of our family."

"King Cearl was too much a friend of Edwin, and Mercia has crumbled at his death because of that. He left no one behind him with enough power to hold the kingdom together. We need to set that right."

That answer sounds so reasoned, I'm nodding and agreeing before I realize the underlying threat.

Either I do it, or he bloody will.

I raise my drinking horn to him. He mirrors my actions, still grinning over the noisy snores of Aldfrith.

"To Mercia," he says, and I almost spit my drink out in shock at his audacious comment.

But I simply shrug in the end, meet his eyes, my voice as menacing as I can make it.

"To the kingdom of Mercia," I respond, and we clunk horns and drink deeply.

Have I just reneged on my alliance with Edwin?

I have no idea.

22

AD631 WINTER - EANFRITH OF BERNICIA

Herebrod has stayed with me all winter, filling my head with stories of Penda and Eowa, King Cadwallon and the rest of the men from the south. I wish I could leave this place and meet them all before the impending battle, but it won't be possible.

I'm a weapon to be kept safe and secure until the coming engagement. A weapon about which the other men of the alliance are ignorant.

Not that we're oblivious to events in the south. No, Penda sends men at regular intervals, uncaring of the terrible weather and their grumbling. I think it's mostly good-natured. Certainly, Herebrod never does more than tease the unfortunate man a little and then offer food and drink and have him seated before the roaring fire at the centre of our home. He makes our frequent visitors welcome and then extracts every tiny piece of new information from them that he can before letting them leave once more.

Events seem to move apace in the southern lands. It's all I can do to keep up with the shifting alliances. I'm relieved to hear that Eowa has returned to the coalition with Penda and Cadwallon, but Herebrod doesn't share my joy.

"It's better if they're enemies," he grumbles late one night, drink in one hand and the other resting on the thigh of the woman he lives with as though they were permanently joined. I've worried about the union, but my wife told me to bite my tongue and assured me that the woman knows it might only be a temporary thing. She doesn't seem to mind. She thinks it's an honour even to be the concubine of Herebrod. I wonder how she'll feel when she grows bloated with his child. But that's not my concern.

"Why? They're family. They should be together?"

Herebrod laughs and hiccups at the same time at my words, all traces of his warrior bearing gone in the haze of alcohol that we're consuming.

"I don't recall you sending for your brothers," he goads me. I watch him unhappily. He has a good point. Me and my brothers are very different. I do hold myself aloft from them. I suppose I could reach out to them, at least to Oswald and Oswiu, the older two. But I shake the thought away for now.

"But you said Eowa and Penda are good allies," I argue, just as drunk as he is.

"I said they make good enemies, not allies," he mouths back. "They're too different to be able to rule together. Penda knows that as. It's Eowa who doesn't realise."

His words give me pause for thought. Family is so important to my people, and yet, more often than that, it makes for the most bitter quarrels, the most violent deaths.

"Who would win if they faced off against each other?" I ask, my thoughts meandering all over the place.

"Penda," Herebrod says without even pausing for thought. "He knows how to kill men."

That's a sobering thought.

"Do you?" I query, my two words slurring together.

Herebrod sits upright at that, his eyes creasing into a smile.

"Of course I bloody do. You don't get to be so close to Penda without learning how to slice the head clean off a man."

"How many?" I ask. I've been in battle. I fought for my father when he lost his life. I ran from the battlefield when the outraged shrieks of our warriors reached my ears. There was a long moment of uncertainty when my father was killed. Men looked my way for leadership, and I almost gave it. I almost had the support of my men, but then King Rædwald realised that my father was dead. His men rushed across the divide between us, their resolve redoubled. I immediately knew there was no way our force would reform itself in time. My father was a man who liked to govern personally, through the selected men he most trusted and as with most fathers and sons, that didn't include me.

Instead, I ran, taking as many men as possible with me. Firstly, we went to Yeavering and then, when it became clear that Edwin still wanted the deaths of all the men in my family, we slipped away, one at a time, me and my brothers, my mother, and we sought sanctuary where we could and with whom we could.

I was lucky. As the eldest son, I was accorded far more respect than my younger brothers. I was impotent to demand more for them, too scared of my shadow and too worried that at any moment Rædwald or even Edwin would come to claim my life. I was fearful that my temporary salvation at the Pictish court would be a transitory thing. I worried that the king of the Picts would see me as a liability and hand me over to the grasping hands of Edwin. I'm grateful he didn't, but I still don't know *why* he didn't.

"Fifty," the man says, and I'd almost forgotten that I'd even asked him a question. Fifty, that's a lot of men for one still only in his twenties.

"How long have you been a warrior?" I ask, intrigued now. At his age, I'd killed about ten men. Most of them fell during the battle that killed my father, which saw me running away from my homeland. Away from the fortress my father built for his first wife, the one who died too young, birthing a child that didn't survive. In my father's rage and anger, he built a fortress as a memorial.

I always thought it a strange thing to do, but my mother respected him for acting so publicly in the face of his loss. I think she hoped to receive her own fortress at her death. Sadly she didn't, and neither will she ever. Being the wife of a slain king is uncomfortable for a woman.

"I've always been a warrior," Herebrod responds, a self-satisfied grin on his face. I could almost believe him. "My father used to tell me I slew a dog before I could even walk. The bloody thing had been trying to help himself to my dinner." He roars with laughter when he sees the look of horror on my face. But he can't help himself.

"My father found me sheeted in blood, with my hand in the dead dog's head, trying to work out why the bloody thing wasn't moving anymore."

I swallow a little bile at the thought of that. I wouldn't want my children to do anything quite so garish.

"And you?" Herebrod asks. I've forgotten the topic of our conversation.

"How many men have you killed," he prompts slowly, enunciating each word to ensure I know what he's talking about in our drunken state.

"Oh ten," I offer without even thinking to inflate the number.

His eyebrows rise in disbelief. I almost think he's going to deride me for so few kills.

"In battle with your father?" he prompts, and I nod.

"Yes, against sodding Rædwald and Edwin at the battle where my father was killed."

"You must fight like a warrior from the old days," Herebrod announces, his reaction utterly opposite to what I thought it would be.

"You find that impressive," I press. He nods, his head seemingly unable to stop the up and down movement once it's started.

"I do, yes. You've been here for most of your adult life. How many battles have you fought in whilst you've lived with the Picts?"

I want to say many, but actually, I haven't fought in any. The Picts have accepted me as a suitable consort for their king's daughter, but they don't necessarily think I'll represent them in battle as well as they can do it themselves. I've always trained, always maintained my small band of men. But we've rarely been used in any capacity other than for guarding my home and my wife and son.

"None," I say unhappily, and Herebrod glares at me.

"No wonder you were so keen to join with King Cadwallon and Lord Penda then," he announces. "A man should fight to protect in what he believes."

"A man should only fight if he has no choice," I caution. Herebrod looks at me a little strangely.

"So what drives you then," he goads with a snarl and a slur. I don't know if he means to be offensive or not.

"To gain back what was stolen from me."

"Is it that simple?" he demands. I feel a small knot of annoyance beginning to mar my pleasantly drunk state.

"Yes, oh, and it helps that Edwin is a bastard, and I want him dead."

Herebrod chokes on his just taken mouthful at that statement. I have to reach over and pat him on the back to help him regain his speech. His eyes are sparkling with enjoyment, no matter his discomfort.

"Shit, I like you, Eanfrith," he chuckles when able to speak once more.

"Is that a problem?" I demand. He shakes his head again.

"Provided you stay loyal to Penda, I have no problem with it at all."

Damn, I thought he was my man, but he's not. He still looks to Penda as his war chief. I need to meet Penda, learn how he encourages such loyalty.

My young son barrels up to me then, all arms and legs into which he's yet to grow. He should have been in his bed, but we probably woke him with our loud laughter and conversation.

"Who's that man," Talorcan asks, pointing to the doorway. He's a lad of fifteen years, my oldest son and my pride and joy. For him, I'd kill thousands of men if it meant he was able to live the life that's been deprived me.

Herebrod and I both sit up immediately, squinting into the dim light, but neither he nor I know the man's identity. My wife looks at me uncertainly, and my man on guard duty looks unhappy as well. Shrugging to myself, I stagger to my feet and make my way over to the little pairing, Herebrod at my side.

"King Eanfrith," the man says, setting Herebrod to chuckling again. I look at him in annoyance, and he stops it immediately, his excellent humour disappearing.

"And who might you be?" I ask, all my good manners evaporating with the mead running through my body.

"My name is Centwine," he says, "I come from King Cynegils, in Wessex," he clarifies at my blank expression. As I said, I still don't know who everyone is.

"How did you make your way across the border?" I ask, immediately suspicious. It's winter and not the time of year for friendly visits.

"I followed another man," he admits without embarrassment. Herebrod looks around with annoyance. It can only be his man from Penda that Centwine could have followed.

"What can I do for you?" I ask, and he looks around nervously.

"King Cynegils wants to ally with you."

Herebrod is immediately tense at my side.

"What sort of alliance?" I press.

"One where he supports your claim to the throne of Bernicia," he states simply. I feel the room sway around me. After so many years of nothing, to have not one but two men offer to make me a king is a strange experience. Herebrod is alert and rigid at my side; the mead drained from him as though the jug has spilt onto the floor.

Abruptly, I'm far more important than I ever have been. Suddenly I don't need to be in an alliance with Penda and Cadwallon because another promises me the same.

I start to laugh, my wife and Herebrod looking at me in disbelief.

Fuck it all. This might just be the best night of my life. Ever.

23

AD632 EARLY SUMMER - PENDA OF MERCIA – GWYNEDD

In a replay of this time last year, I find myself at Cadwallon's court, surrounded by men who say they stand with us against King Edwin. But there have been many changes, and I'm questioning what drives men and why they change their minds when everything is in place.

Chief is the knowledge that Osfrith of Northumbria, the man who approached Cadwallon last year and offered to be the snake in the grass, has turned away from our alliance. For now, at least. And to make matters worse, the king of the West Saxons has made overtures of friendship to my secret ally, Eanfrith of Bernicia. Herebrod was quick to inform me of the possible betrayal, but I've heard nothing since then. I don't know if Eanfrith is still my ally or not. I take comfort from Herebrod's failure to return, but it could just be that Herebrod has grown to support Eanfrith instead of me.

Neither are they the only two missing from our great wooden board of pieces. Last year we had all the kings of the Britons and the King of Dumnonia. Now we are missing a Cloten of Deheubarth, and Beli, King of Alt Clut, has not yet made an appearance. Yet, Cynegils of the West Saxons, a man who has every reason to hate my me and brother, is here, asking to be allowed into our alliance. I almost don't trust him, but it's he who's approached Eanfrith separately and tried to make him his ally. He must be thinking along the same lines as Cadwallon and me. I find the situation ironic.

It's all becoming extremely complicated. Whilst I want to be angry that some plans are in tatters, I find myself thriving on the confusion. Cadwallon and I can play this to our advantage. If no one knows who is allied with whom, if enemies and allies are intermingled like good and sour grapes, then we can win the coming battle with hardly any need to raise a weapon against an enemy. Or an ally, I think a little slyly.

Cadwallon doesn't share my enthusiasm for resetting what he thought was already set.

"What the fuck's happened?" he keeps muttering to himself. I have to stop myself from laughing at him and enjoying his confusion.

"Eowa has allied with us. King Cynegils wants to ally with us. We still have my weapon in the north, but we've lost yours. Cloten is undecided, and Beli is not here." I say as patiently as I can, counting off everyone on my fingers.

"So, how many do we have now?" Cadwallon whines. I don't think he can reasonably determine whether we're better off or worse.

"We have me and you, Eowa, the man from the north, Clydog, Eiludd, Clemen and probably Cynegils."

"That makes seven," he says petulantly.

"Edwin has his two sons, Sigeberht from the East Angles, his cousin Osric and Eadbald, his wife's brother. That makes six."

"And two undecided," he says. He's not to be mollified no matter what I say.

"And two undecided, yes."

"You forgot Domnall and Oswald," Eowa interjects. I find myself going back over the names. But he's right; I've forgotten Domnall and Oswald.

"Thanks, brother," I say, managing to keep the temper from my voice. "We have eight then. Edwin has seven, of which only half have their own kingdoms as opposed to our side, where five have kingdoms. And there are two undecideds."

"So we have the superior force," Cadwallon surmises, his eyes gazing into the fire and seeing whatever it is that haunts him.

"We have the superior force. We'll destroy him, claim his land and set up our kings in his place."

"We can go ahead then?" Cadwallon clarifies. If he doesn't stop asking me for reassurance, I might leave here. After all, he's the mighty king, not me. I'm only a king in waiting. A king who can only be king if his brother dies or supports the wrong side, but even that slight possibility has been denied me now.

Damn my brother. If I didn't love him so much, I swear I could kill him, challenge him to some sort of battle and kill him.

But I love my brother and his small children. I'll not deprive them of a father. That's the best way to make enemies for life amongst our people. Sons will do all they can to avenge their dead fathers, and my brother already has two young children.

"We should send men to Beli and Cloten, find out their intentions. I can't for a moment understand why Cloten would want to ally with King Edwin. They share no borders or boundaries, and he'll have to march through our land to get to Edwin if he ever calls on him to fulfil his duties as his ally. As to Beli. Well, it has to be hoped that he's simply been delayed."

"Or overrun already," Eowa adds in a bored tone. I look at him sharply. Is he trying to tell me something? He winks at me, and I think he is. Damn, did King Edwin plan on laying waste Beli's land and forcing another royal family from their people?

Cadwallon watches the interplay between us with amusement on his lips. A moment ago, he was worried and considering blaming me for the failure of his alliance. Suddenly, he's all relaxed in the face of family intrigue.

I suppose Eowa has to be good for something. I'll have to ask him for more details when we're alone. If he's kept this from me, I'll be less than pleased. Not quite murderous but exceedingly angry.

"Have you an idea of where you want to lay the ambush?" Cadwallon queries, still watching Eowa and me. I'm pleased he's decided to put his worries aside.

"I have several sites in mind," I offer, purposefully not looking at my brother. I know I should trust him, but something stops me from divulging all my secrets just yet. I don't want to give too much information away.

Cadwallon retains the image of a grin on his face as he tries not to look between the two of us. I can't meet my brother's eyes. Then I think I should.

"Eowa, do you know of any good places to meet Edwin?"

His eyes take on a faraway look for a moment, and then he grins.

"Have you ever heard of our people being called the Southumbrians?" he asks. I wonder where he's going with his strange-sounding words, and I shake my head.

"The what?" I ask again.

"The southumbrians," he says again, more slowly this time. "As opposed to the Northumbrians," he explains, and I'm beginning to decipher what he means.

"Who calls us that?" I ask.

"The sodding Northumbrians," he says, grinning around his mead.

"What's it got to do with a battle site?"

"We should use the Humber River," he elaborates. "We should use their name for us to bring about their demise."

Cadwallon shakes his head from side to side. I think he'll say no, but he grins as well.

"It's a good idea. It's as good a place as any, and it'll upset Edwin."

I nod along with Cadwallon, I don't necessarily agree, but I don't automatically trust that my brother is genuinely my ally.

"When will we strike?" I press. I've been wondering this for some time now. I made Cadwallon delay the attack last year because I didn't believe we had the time to gather the men and resources pledged to us. But now, I'm worried that I might have contributed to the men shearing away from the alliance with my delaying tactics.

I think we should attack sooner rather than later and as close to the borders of Northumbria as possible. Initially, Cadwallon and I had wanted to draw Edwin from his lands, but we've since changed our minds. It'll be far more significant if we beat Edwin inside his kingdom.

This time it's Cadwallon who gives me a cautioning gaze. He, like me, can't be truly comfortable sharing all our secrets with Eowa.

"I think early summer," he says, but his voice catches. I know he's lying. It's a good attempt at tricking Eowa, but Eowa, contrary to what Cadwallon seems to think, is not a fool. He knows the time to attack is later in the year, when the harvests are ready to be brought in and when men are distracted by thoughts of surviving the winter.

"I agree," I say, without pausing for thought. I'd rather have my men in their battle gear and ready for half the summer than risk it not happening this year. It's already been too long since Cadwallon's defeat. Too long, the seeds of anger have lain dormant. I don't want Cadwallon to lose the support of Powys or his men, and it's becoming a real possibility.

Eowa watches me with half a smile on his face. He doesn't believe any of this. He stands abruptly and turns to view the rest of the men in Cadwallon's fine hall. I don't know what he sees there, but he casts me one more look before walking away to mingle with the others. That's almost worse than having him listen to our conversation.

Cadwallon is instantly at my side, his broad face, expansive and aggrieved, his black eyes never leaving Eowa as he moves amongst the other men, stopping here and there to clasp the forearm of a man he's never met before.

"Do you trust him?" Cadwallon demands, his voice quiet and insistent in my ear.

"Yes and no, and you should understand that better than any man here," I gripe. I don't know why he has to mention my cagey comments.

"Then why welcome him?" he hisses again. I turn to glare at him, my rage burning beneath my skin. Why does he always have to labour the point?

"It's far better to have him with us than with Edwin," I say as evenly as I can through my gritted teeth.

"What if he runs to Edwin?"

"Then he'll tell him a long list of misinformation. We're not going to attack at the Humber, and it'll be far later in the year, even though I think it should be earlier than we might normally consider. Anyway, you agreed, not me. You could have taken it under advisement instead of consenting quite so easily."

"He's your damn brother. I thought he was to be trusted and that we could speak openly in front of him."

"So why did *you* lie to him?" I press, but he turns away from me to walk back to his seat on the raised dais.

"I lied to him because I thought you were lying to him," is his response. I do think I could happily walk away from the alliance as well. If I didn't hate Edwin quite so much and crave his death, I'd not ally with Cadwallon. He, like many of his fellow Britons, is unable to scheme."

"So, where are we going to attack?" I ask, trying to steer the conversation away from this acrimonious subject.

"We're going to meet on the northern borders of Mercia, where Lindsey used to be, and we're simply going to keep going until we meet Edwin's force."

"So we're not going to plan any of it?" I ask, annoyed once more/ I've spent much of the last year trying to find suitable places to mount an attack.

"Well, yes, we are, and I've planned that much anyway. It's going to be difficult enough to get everyone in the same place at the same time as it is. I don't want to risk more specific information being floated on the wind like a leaf in a winter storm."

I suppose he has a valid point, but still, he could share such plans with me at least. I'm his firmest supporter and longest-held ally.

I meet his eyes again, holding them for long moments. Does he distrust me as well?

"When?" I ask, and he smirks now.

"Near to the dark times," he says with pleasure. "Let's have him think that battle won't come this year, have him halfway back to Yeavering or Bamburgh. Have him deep within the Northumbrian lands so that we win much of what we want with little further effort.

But first, we'll simply disappear, hide from him, so that he doesn't know where we are or what we plan."

Now, that I do like, and I almost smile back at him.

Perhaps, after all, Cadwallon is worthy of being the most respected King of the Britons.

24

AD632 SUMMER - CADWALLON OF GWYNEDD

I sit upon my official chair before the fire that spits and coughs in the breeze through the open doorway. My mind has been preoccupied of late, but it seems empty of all thoughts right now. I'm enjoying the silence. No doubt at any moment, some new calamity will befall me, but until then, I might just close my eyes, dream of nothing and wake feeling refreshed.

Slowly and unbidden stray words of conversation percolate through my thoughts, drifting through the open doorway. I speculate about who speaks of weapons and war, betrayal and murder. I stay still, as still as it's possible to be when a man is pretending to sleep.

I don't know who speaks. I don't recognize the voice. I consider if it's one of my servants who's been turned to the side of King Edwin or any other of my enemies.

"The, Humber, Edwin, Osfrith, Osric and Eowa." I hear every other word. I'm almost frantic with curiosity. Who the hell is outside?

The doorway darkens imperceptibly, and a man strides through the door. I squint at his outline and then relax. It's only Penda. I've been expecting him. I rise in greeting and then slow my actions. Was it Penda outside speaking to someone about the battle? Surely of all my allies, Penda is the one I trust the most. I fervently hope that he's not betraying me.

He grins on seeing me, not seeming to notice when my smile falters a little. He walks up to me and grabs my arm, pulling me tight to his mouth.

"Have you heard that little prick out there? He thinks he knows things he shouldn't. Edwin will have heard the same story from so many of his supposed informants by now that he'll be certain it's what we plan."

My good cheer in the day returns, and I nod at Penda.

"I did hear his words, yes," I say. I need to know whom he was talking about, but I can't now because I've acted as though I know who it is. I'll have to try and extract the information from Penda later.

"Edwin has sent one of his son's to treat with me," Penda announces without any preamble. My good cheer disappears again. "I thought I should let you know before someone else does."

"Which one?" I ask with annoyance. Bloody Edwin. Why can't he accept that he's going to lose this without trying to steal my most loyal follower?

"Osfrith," he says with a gleam in his eye.

"Ah," is all I can manage. I need to let Penda speak when he wants. I beckon for mead and food, and whilst Penda avails himself of my food and drink, I watch him. Since I've known him, he's grown in stature. He was always a mighty man, with huge bulging muscles and a menacing posture, but now he's more. If it's possible, he appears even more powerful, and his eyes have lost their acquisitive glare. He appreciates what he's about to gain. He's confident enough to wear his victory already.

"Osfrith might, or might not, be working for his father again. He gave little away and seemed keen to pressure me, but I'm not convinced. I think his father has acted too late and offered too little. Osfrith is, as far as I can tell, still firmly supporting you."

"Ah," I say once more. I'm thrilled to hear Penda's words. I was so disappointed when I thought I'd lost Osfrith. It would boost my sense of confidence if I knew Osfrith was still with me.

"Did you give him an indication that the alliance is still in place?" Penda winks at me.

"I gave him a few winks and nudges, being my normal, good-natured self. He was with that Oswald man. He's an ugly brute, but nothing to fear. He thinks he's clever with his speech, and that's his ultimate downfall. I can't imagine I gave him any fodder with which to return to Edwin."

"Where were they going?" I query, and then I rephrase my question. "Did he come to meet with you or with Eowa?" After our last meeting, Penda decided he needed to spend more time with Eowa at their family home. It's just possible Penda wasn't the intended recipient of the visit.

"I don't know, Cadwallon," he says, voice slowing as he thinks. "I'd not even considered the possibility."

Honestly, Penda is a true piece of deviousness. Of course, he's considered the possibility. Does he think me a fool?

"Truly," Penda continues, "I think he came for Eowa but was pleasantly surprised to find me there. Oswald wasn't. He fared much the worse when trying to hide his true feelings."

"And Eowa?" I ask.

"He played his part well. Oswald thinks he's still nominally supporting Edwin and that he's trying to turn me to his side of the alliance as well."

"This is becoming increasingly complicated," I moan a little, but Penda grins, the smile covering his entire face.

"It's bloody exciting," he says. "Anyone could do anything. We should trust no one, apart from each other."

"Does that include your brother?" I press.

"Of course it does. He's the one I'm least sure of, but that's no doubt because he's my brother, and I know him the best. He's not done anything to make me think he regrets joining us."

"Good. We need to act soon, though. I've spoken enough about the battle."

His grin, if possible, grows even bigger.

"I thought you'd say that. As soon as Osfrith and Oswald left,

Eowa and I began preparing. He'll meet us on the way back. Call your men, and send word to our allies that we march."

I jump to my feet, invigorated by Penda's words. I feel instantly more relaxed than when I was sitting and trying not to think. This is what I need to do. I'm a man of action. Not a man to think and plot his way through things. That's Edwin's role, and possibly also Penda's.

I beckon my most steadfast men to me and offer instructions as to the messages they're to carry and where they're to take them. They listen, most alert and excited at the promise of the coming altercation. The man who doesn't react at all, Walaram, is not known for being much of a talker anyway. It doesn't mean he's not keen. I have only to watch his hand as it caresses his seax to know that. He likes killing. Only in battle does his face even remotely rise in a smile.

Penda watches my actions. It's then that I note he has a new mail byrnie. It almost blinds me with its high polish. Penda notices me looking.

"It's only for show. The old one is far more comfortable."

"It's beautifully made," I offer, and he nods firmly.

"It is. I'm having one made for you as well."

That's a high honour from him, and I'm taken aback. A gift from a man such as Penda is a real gift.

"I just hope you live long enough to bloody receive it," he adds, any thoughts of thanks evaporating from my mind with his insolent tone.

"Oh, I'm going to live long enough to make even your life enjoyable," I retaliate, and suddenly Penda has grasped me in his huge embrace.

"I'm going to relish this," he promises. Then he leaves, almost as though he's never been there at all. But everything is changed. Battle is coming, and at last, my nemesis, my foster brother Edwin, will meet his death, and the land of the Britons will be restored to its former self.

Penda's right. This is going to be gratifying.

25

AD632 EARLY OCTOBER - EDWIN OF NORTHUMBRIA

The summer has been wasted. I felt sure that battle would come at its height, but no. Me and my men were battle-ready and waiting at the Humber River, but nothing happened. Then Eowa stopped responding to my messengers, and then the final messenger, sent when any decent men were busy harvesting, didn't return at all. I wonder if Eowa killed him or if the man deserted me for a better life in the south?

I look like an idiot and a fool. Most of my allies have deserted me. I must face my people at Yeavering, Bamburgh and Carlisle, tell them that I was mistaken and shouldn't have taken their men from them.

I've sent other messengers south to find out all they can, but they report the land is calm, that no warbands have been seen.

I don't know if they lie or if it's the truth.

Has King Cadwallon decided he can't beat me? Has he changed his mind? Will I receive a request for a peace soon, or does he intend to attack me with the bad weather, or even early next year? The not knowing is too much for one man to tolerate, especially when so many look to me for leadership.

This fake alliance by my enemies has made me appear weak and has done more damage than if we'd met in battle and shed blood.

Now I look as though I believe every false rumour and will call my men to arms only on whispers and possibilities.

I wish King Cadwallon would just bloody attack.

I'm at Goodmanham, a royal site of Deira, the home of my childhood, within easy distance of the Humber River, where I understood the attack would originate. But so far, no one has seen anything. My sons have ridden out and carried out daily reconnaissance missions, but they've encountered nothing more than a frightened farmer or an annoyed cow.

I would almost think that Cadwallon has become a mythical creature, able to move without detection because there's one thing I know for sure; Cadwallon hasn't been in Gwynedd since high summer, and neither has Penda.

The men are somewhere, plotting something. I'm powerless to know what that thing is.

I know they're coming for me.

I just wish they'd get on with it.

Oswald watches me closely. He's said many words to me that I don't want to hear, but I don't think they're necessarily wrong. He sees me for what I am. That's not a nice thing for a man to have thrown in his face.

He predicted this, and I ignored him.

He's also forecast the betrayal of my oldest son, but I don't see it, and I've looked. I've pushed and prodded, almost so much that I've turned him away from me again anyway, the work of the past year undone before any good could come from it. My son is loyal, of that Oswald is entirely wrong, and I, despite all my other doubts, am right.

As the weather turns decidedly colder, my men have grown more morose, all five hundred of them. They want to be home, by their warm hearths, not here, with me at Goodmanham, a site that, despite my best intentions, is simply not big enough to house them all. Whilst the weather was warm and mild, men didn't mind sleeping on rough ground. Now they're grumbling and aching. They've lost their desire to fight for me, I need something to happen to claim back their loyalty.

Simply put, I need Cadwallon to attack finally.

I have five hundred men who'll fight to the death in my name. Cadwallon must give them that opportunity. If I have to disband the men, send them home, then even more damage will be done to my reputation.

I have three choices. I can wait here longer until the first snows come. I can let my men go home. I can take the battle to Cadwallon. Only to do that, I need to know where the bastard is in hiding.

I've been having the same internal conversation with myself for more than four weeks. If I do this, then that will happen. If I do nothing, then this will happen. I'm not a man who finds it hard to make decisions, but until I know where Cadwallon is, I'm impotent to act. It might well be that he's in hiding, and as soon as he hears that my men and I have retreated to Bamburgh and Yeavering for the winter, he'll attack. No doubt when I'm too far away to meet their advance and stop it before it swallows up the land of the Deirans, the southern part of Northumbria.

"My Lord," my priest, Cofi, calls to me. He's been in the small church saying his prayers. The church is his pride and joy. He smashed the ancient shrine to the pagan god, Woden, that sat on this site until only five years ago. It's he who the local people resent for his work that day. I'm not unconvinced that his actions haven't angered the old God and made him work against me. Perhaps I should have stayed at my other palace site, Sancton. Maybe my enterprise would have been blessed with success then.

"Cofi," I respond, meeting his slightly wild-looking eyes. If the new God hadn't come, he'd have been one of the blessed of the old Gods. He'd have mothered the shrine here and allowed no one else to defile it. He has the look of many men who are God-touched. He sees only God's grace and favour.

"They're coming," Cofi simply says before slumping forward onto his knees. As I rush to his aid, I consider whether he's had some sort of vision? I hasten to catch him before his face slumps to the wooden floor.

Oswald quickly joins me at Cofi's side.

"What did he say?" he demands. So I tell him. Oswald absorbs the information silently as we manoeuvre the priest to a position where he can sit upright. He still breathes, but his eyes are firmly closed, his body limps. I think he's been touched with a vision.

"You should ride out," Oswald says to me when Cofi is settled. "You have an eye for battle that your sons don't. Ride out. At least half a day to the south and see if you can find Cadwallon."

It's a good idea, but I'm suspicious of it all the same. I thought to scout anyway, but why would Oswald push me?

Oswald looks annoyed at my less than complimentary response. I detect his sister's haughty expression on his face.

"You're my uncle," he says slowly and with care. "I have nothing to gain from undermining you. I have few men to call mine."

He's right, but still, his forthrightness doesn't sit well with me.

"You go," I say. I speculate if he'll force me to make it a command.

"Me?" he asks in surprise.

"Yes, you, go to the Humber River, go round the Humber River. Find King Cadwallon for me. I'll reward your loyalty. Would you like this palace?" I ask. I'm goading him, but I want to see how far he'll take the offer.

His blue eyes challenge mine as he stares at me.

"I will and now, cousin. I'll send word when I find them."

Oswald marches from my presence, his anger settling itself around his shoulders. I've riled the man who said he wouldn't be upset by my commands or reaction to his statements. It's strange how men change when they're pushed to the limit.

Cofi doesn't yet move, so I follow Oswald out of the door, pulling my cloak tightly around my shoulders. It's still morning, and it's cold, the sun shining only as a dull, half shielded candle in the day. I shiver with the chill of outside. I'm unsurprised that the men are aggrieved with having to sleep outside. I wouldn't want to if I were in their position.

"Where's Oswald going?" Osfrith calls as he walks towards me, his young son swinging on his arms. The pair are similar in appearance and personality.

"To search for Cadwallon," I simply state, reaching over to tussle the hair of Yffi's head. He's a beguiling child. I've always had more time for him than my children.

"Why, is there news?" Osfrith asks in excitement, but I shake my head. "Cofi had a vision," I inform him, and now Osfrith looks intrigued.

"Here, on the site of the old shrine?" he presses, and I nod. I don't want to hear his words again about the ill-treatment Cofi visited upon the shrine. It's an old argument, and I can do nothing about it now. I didn't expect my conversion by Bishop Paulinus to have such a profound effect on my people. That it did has worked to the bishop's favour but not necessarily to mine. I now govern people who are divided by faith. It would be easier if they were split by their loyalty towards the old royal family or mine. It would be simpler to sway them to me. Matters of the heart and the mind are no place for a king to meddle.

"It must mean something important," Osfrith presses. I let him consider the implications out loud. He seems more animated than all summer long. Maybe he needs the battle as much as I do.

"Go with him?" I fling. He looks from me to his son with hunger on his face. It's clear he wants to go. "Yffi will be safe here with me. Now go," I command. He runs to do as I bid, rushing back to hug his son before he does so. He's not about to defect, I think, as I watch him ride away. He loves his son too much.

I spend the rest of my day with my young grandson. We engage in mock battles with his tiny wooden shield and seax. Then, when he's too tired to fight on, in long winding tales of my childhood before I receive the news I've been waiting for all summer. It's Osfrith who rushes to me, so reminiscent of Yffi during the day that I feel a moment of sorrow for his youth that I missed, too caught up in my quest for a kingdom.

"Cadwallon is massing with his allies," he simply says. "They're close to the border with Elmet."

I try to determine how far away that is.

"How fast did you ride?" I ask, but he shakes the question aside.

"They have at least a thousand men," he simply says. I understand his rush to inform me. They have twice as many men as I do.

"When will they be here?"

"I don't think they're coming here. They have a camp in the forest. I couldn't see it all."

Various scenarios are running through my head, foremost of which is 'who can I call upon to reinforce my men?'

"King Sigeberht?" Osfrith queries. He thinks as I do.

"Yes, can you go?" I ask, but he's shaking his head. "Send Eadfrith. He and King Sigeberht are more alike than him and me. Eadfrith will convince him to return. How long has it been since he left?"

King Sigeberht of the East Angles had been with me until only ten days ago. It was then decided he and his men could be put to better use, ensuring the harvest was taken in.

"They might be home by now. I don't know," I confirm. Osfrith is thinking and talking.

"I'll tell Eadfrith. He has that horse of his that can ride faster than the wind."

He does. My son has trained the best horse in my kingdom. Many men eye the beast with covetous eyes.

Quickly I call my men together, wondering when Oswald will arrive back.

"The enemy is in Elmet," I share with them. The warriors before me both growl and raise their voices in joy.

"We march in the morning, at first light."

Cofi has finally woken. His strange eyes stare at me.

"You should pray, My Lord," he softly says, standing unsteadily and making ready to leave my hall. "Come with me, and I'll pray with you."

It's hardly the most reassuring statement he's ever made, but if Bishop Paulinus has taught me anything, it's that his God only listens when you shout at him.

I follow the priest outside into the frigid evening air. I'll pray all night, and tomorrow I'll ride to war against my enemy and the men he's assembled against me. It shouldn't matter with God at my side that the odds are so heavily against us. But, I think this is an ancient site of the Old Gods. Maybe, I'm praying to them and they're contrary bastards.

Tonight I'll pray to whichever Gods will listen.

Tomorrow I ride to war.

26

AD632 OCTOBER - OSFRITH OF NORTHUMBRIA

When my father converted to Christianity five years ago, the priest, Cofi, destroyed the ancient shrine at Goodmanham. I warned my father that he shouldn't have allowed the defilement to go unpunished, but all he did was make Cofi the shrine's caretaker and earn himself the enmity of the local people. This shrine is far too important for its apparent destruction by Cofi not to be taken seriously. People here know that the Old Gods still visit the site. They're not fools to think a moment of madness undoes centuries of religious observance.

And I know that if Cofi has heard any sort of warning today, it must be the Old Gods that speak, for the new one is a silent man who shows himself in strange ways. Normally around dead people, and usually in circumstances that can be just as easily ascribed to the Old Gods as the new.

Here, in this place, I know the only power is from the Old Gods. Priest Cofi can pretend all he wants, but he's a deluded man, driven half-mad with his talk of what his God wants.

With those thoughts foremost in my mind, I seek out the shrine, fearful of what I'll see. I know what Cofi did. I've been here often, but it always shocks me to see the great white stone altar toppled and a small wooden church almost upon it. Even in the deepening dusk of winter, back-lit only by some lights that spill from my father's hall, I can see everything before me, the stone shrine and the wooden one. I don't believe I need to think more about the permanence or fleetingness of Gods: wood and stone. I know which one I'd rather follow.

The old stone has been worn smooth by the passage of many hands over the years, and at its base, small offerings are left every day by the local people. Cofi has been ill today, so he's not yet had the time to remove them all.

I know he does so every day. He picks them up and takes them inside his tiny wooden church, and lays them before the wooden altar there. I wonder if he'll ever stop trying to ignore the faith he once professed to and the one that the people of Deira still ascribe to, no matter the words of my father or his pet bishop.

In the deep black of night, I stand beside the worn old stone, unheeding of its poor state, and I hold myself quiet, trying to listen for those voices that Cofi heard. I need some guidance to know for sure what I'm supposed to do in the coming battle.

From the small church, I can hear the elaborate prayers of Cofi and the deep responses my father makes in reply to those exhortations to his God. I find it bizarre that father and son have both had the same thoughts. Yet, we're apart, as always, separated by an inability to reconcile and see things in the same way, even in something as fundamental as our faith.

Does that mean that I should turn my back on my father? Follow through with my alliance with King Cadwallon? Last year and following Oswald's intervention on behalf of my brother and me, I had decided that I should stand with my father. But now I feel Oswald's work unravelling as quickly as a callously dropped spool of wool. What Oswald says and what he does are two separate things. Whatever his words, Oswald has his eye just as firmly on my father's throne as I do.

After I saw my father weak and bawling like a newborn child, I decided that he didn't deserve to be a king, shouldn't be a king. But I slowly relaxed my fierce opposition until suddenly I was no longer his enemy. Well, until I met with Eowa on behalf of my father, and Penda was with him. Then I remembered my hatred for my father and that I wanted to be the one to kill him. As much as I hate the truth, I know that still is my intention. If another man kills my father, I'll never forgive myself. Never.

There are far too many men who want to be king, and there's only really one option for me. Cadwallon and Penda. They don't want to be king of Northumbria. They simply don't wish Edwin to be its king.

And more, Penda wants the lands of the Middle Angles, he wants to reconstruct Mercia, and I think he'll do it. With the aid of his brother.

If Eowa can see that the future doesn't lie with my father, then I should do the same.

Penda ensured that I knew he and King Cadwallon would still have me back. All I need to do is present them with my dead father's head. A grim thought, and yet really, all they ask me to do is what my heart most desires.

If I kill my father, I'll be carrying out my most sincere wishes. It's just fortunate that they coincide with Cadwallon's as well.

Slowly, the outside air cools, and I know I should be shivering, but the heat from the stone altar increases, my hand staying warm and keeping me temperate, despite the chill breeze and the increasingly desperate cries of prayer from within the church.

And that is all the answer I need.

27

AD632 OCTOBER - EADFRITH OF NORTHUMBRIA

It takes me only a little over a day to catch up to King Sigeberht and his men. I see them first as a mass of moving black on the horizon, and only as I rush towards them do they coalesce into men and animals. I think they must be taking the most roundabout way home possible.

When King Sigeberht sees me riding briskly towards him, he stops his horse with what looks to me a lot like relief, his face clearing from the scowl that had covered it. I don't think he wanted to leave my father, but neither could he keep his men from their homes any longer.

"You have news?" he calls. I nudge my horse through the press of men and beasts that surround him. I do have news. Great news.

"The battle will be within a day or two. King Cadwallon is amassing on the border with Elmet."

"Excellent, I've been fervently praying for an opportunity to kill the heathens," King Sigeberht announces, satisfaction settling over him like a cloak. Then he raises his voice.

"Men, we must support King Edwin, as we decided to do. His kingdom is now under attack, and we have a duty to aid him. Quick, turn back north." With no grumbling and without even a pause for thought, King Sigeberht of the East Angles and his array of men are suddenly racing back the way they came.

"I dawdled as much as I could," he calls to me above the sound of hooves on turf and the heavy breathing of men and beasts. "I was sure King Cadwallon would come, eventually. Damn the man for waiting until the snows are almost upon us."

I'm surprised by King Sigeberht's admission. I hadn't thought he was quite as war thirsty as that. But then, he's a strange combination of a man. He looks like a priest, but he's been a pagan for most of his life. His conversion and military prowess were gained on the Continent when he was in exile there. I imagine him as a monk, not as a warrior with blood dripping from his hands, as he separates men's heads from their necks.

"It'll have been done to cause the most disruption to the kingdom. He'll hope that the harvests have been destroyed and that the people of Northumbria will starve throughout the winter."

"You've probably got a good point there," Sigeberht says after some consideration. "War is always about more than who has the biggest army. Do you know how many men he has?" Sigeberht asks.

"My brother says at least a thousand."

Sigeberht looks behind him at his men. He has over two hundred with him. Abruptly he reins his horse in tightly and signals for one of the men to come to him. The man's animated face immediately falls as though he knows what he's about to be instructed.

"Go to my palace. Issue a command for the household troop to join me on the border with Elmet. Tell them it's urgent. Take this as proof that you come at my orders." He hands the man a small ring that flashes with a heavy red stone. It's a stunning piece of jewellery just to hand over so nonchalantly. It's obvious he trusts the man implicitly.

The man nods and turns his horse around without further thought, but his disappointment is clear to see in the droop of his shoulders.

"Hopefully, they'll join us before we make battle."

"How many more men do you have?" I ask, intrigued by his actions.

"Another fifty, not enough to make us equal with King Cadwallon, but enough all the same. Each man is worth two normal warriors because they were all trained on the Continent. They know how to kill a man in many more ways than the rest of the men do."

The news sends a slight shiver down my back. Men who are more deadly than our force? It makes me worry for a fleeting moment that Sigeberht will turn traitor on us, as well as so many others. Hopefully, I'm wrong. After all, he and my father share their faith now. They also have shared experiences from their youth when they were both sent into exile.

The fact that Sigeberht seems to have fared far better than my father ever did is of little concern. He was still sent into exile by a previous king so that he wouldn't be an alternative to Rædwald's son. It didn't work, and Sigeberht fought his way back to the kingdom and made himself king. A fine Christian king. I'm not sure my father wishes to be remembered as such, but I could be wrong. King Sigeberht doesn't hide his hopes.

After that, we ride in silence, everyone considering the coming battle and little more. However we look at it, we'll be outnumbered. I trust my father has considered this and found a site that will advantage us. We need to use every piece of guile to undermine the alliance of Cadwallon and Penda and their advantage.

Not for the first time, I think about Eowa's place in the coming battle. He was an ally of my father's, and he changed his mind, went back to his brother. But I've always held a sneaky hope that it's all been a double-bluff, one about which only my father knows. But if it was a ruse, why didn't he send word of the battle site?

I reconsider that thought as soon as I've had it. He did send word. He told Osfrith that the attack would take place by the River Humber, and it will. It gives me pause for thought. Eowa must command a substantial part of the force ranging itself against us. What if he changes sides halfway through the fight? Or before it? The thought of an extra few hundred men is cheering. I urge my horse ever faster. I want to get back to my father before the attack begins.

AFTER RIDING ALL NIGHT, I smell cook fires in the distance and turn my grinning face to King Sigeberht's silent one. We've made it back in time. My father's men have marched, but not too far. They're still on the northern side of the River Humber. Men on guard duty note the force arriving and make way for them to join my father. I assume the king will march further south, but suddenly I'm not sure. Surely, it's better for us to have the river before us, not behind us. The river could trap us if we march too far south. It's a great cleft in the land, with few passing places, and in the panic of battle, it would be very easy for the enemy to cut off any retreat.

King Sigeberht sees the king before me and rides to greet him, sitting upon his horse, surveying the changeable countryside. The king's stern face breaks into a smile when he sees Sigeberht. Keeping the king company, my brother nods to show he approves of my swift flight to rein in the departing Sigeberht.

"Well met," Edwin calls to Sigeberht. His voice is solid and steady, giving no hint of worry about the coming attack.

"King Edwin, I understand our enemy has finally shown its face," Sigeberht responds, his voice high with excitement. He feels no need to hide his joy at the coming battle. For him, it's a case of fighting for his religion, and he's conveniently forgotten that only Penda is the pagan and that Cadwallon has held his faith for far longer than Sigeberht has his.

"Yes, they're hiding and seem to have been in concealment for some time in the great wood that covers the old kingdom of Elmet. I never thought conquering that land would cause me so many problems," Edwin growls, but Sigeberht shakes his head at the recrimination.

"You took what you conquered, don't doubt the righteousness of that action."

King Sigeberht is in awe of Edwin's military accomplishments. I think it's good that Sigeberht is his ally and not his enemy. Like Penda, Sigeberht has a massive reputation, and he intends to grow it. That's why he's joined Edwin and will be the only one of his supposed allies to stand with him when the fight begins.

I don't forget that the others have shown their indifference by not siding with Cadwallon and Penda. I suppose it could be taken as a minor victory of sorts.

King Eadbald isn't here. King Cynegils hasn't journeyed north, and even Bishop Paulinus is hiding away in Kent.

"I've sent one of my warriors home to command my household troops to join us. I'm not sure how long they'll take to get here, but it might be worth delaying until they're here. They'll help even up the numbers."

Edwin raises his eyebrows at me in surprise. I don't think he realised, I'd heard how many men we faced.

"My thanks, My Lord," Edwin says solemnly. He knows when it's important to show genuine respect to another who is, for the time being, his equal.

"It's my pleasure. And my men will welcome the opportunity to fight on your behalf."

For all that it will involve two thousand men, this battle is a deeply personal thing. The feud between Edwin and Cadwallon, his foster brother, has spilt over into this monumental undertaking. It's incredible to consider how something so insignificant can become something so vast.

I appreciate that the king has many enemies and that his actions have converted men and made them almost desperate to join the alliance against him. But still, much of the vitriol stems from a simple disagreement between two men, who were nearly raised as brothers.

I need to learn that lesson. The kingdoms of this island are only held together by the strength of their war leaders and war chiefs.

"Have you seen them yet?" King Sigeberht asks, but Edwin shakes his head.

"No, I'm not looking for them either. I'm intent on choosing the battle site, not letting King Cadwallon gain the upper hand." Edwin growls his response.

"You fancy the river banks?" Sigeberht presses. Edwin shakes his head from side to side.

"I'd been considering it, but I don't want my men to flounder on the marshy ground. I was thinking of making Cadwallon fight there instead."

"But that will mean he's inside your lands," Sigeberht muses.

"He's already within my lands. Elmet is mine now, its royal family dead or in exile. But you're correct in what you say. Should I let him deeper into my lands? Should I tempt him in, or should I act aggressively to drive him backwards?"

"Tell me of the land here," Sigeberht asks, lifting his hand to point at the vista before us. I already know the answer to this, but I listen all the same.

"There are three great rivers that meet near here," Edwin explains. "The River Humber is beside us. The River Trent is further west. The River Don is further south. They all join other rivers. The place can be liable to flood, but it hasn't yet this year. I don't think it will in the short time before we clash. The rivers are all effective boundaries, but which one to choose, if one at all?"

"What would be your first choice if you didn't already know where King Cadwallon was?" Sigeberht asks. His question is intelligent and might help Edwin with his conundrum. He's having a good look around him, eyes narrowing as he tries to interpret the lay of the land so that he can make suggestions as well.

"The Don is close to the River Idle, where I killed King Æthelfrith. I like the symmetry of attacking there. It'll be a reaffirmation of my power and my skill." There's real pride in Edwin's voice as he speaks. It's strange to hear. He doesn't often talk about the victory that gave him Æthelfrith's throne. I thought it was because he wasn't enamoured of his accomplishments there. It appears I'm wrong.

"Then we should take the battle to them, at the River Idle."

Edwin's eyes are distant, perhaps seeing what he did on that long-ago battle.

"It's close to Lindsey as well. It'll be a double victory. I'll reassert my kingship over both kingdoms."

"We'll need to march?" Sigeberht asks.

"Yes, but only half a day, no more. The men won't complain."

"Now or tomorrow?" Sigeberht queries. I wish I could question the king this intently, but even now, after all, cousin Oswald's words, he doesn't treat me as his equal.

Edwin looks to the sky. It's growing dark. It's late in the year. Daylight is to be treasured when it's available.

"Tomorrow. The men need to see where they're going to get there. Come, I'll feast you in my tent. We can talk about battle lines and tactics with the rest of my commanders. Osfrith and Eadfrith, you'll join us and bring Oswald as well. He's been overseeing the provisioning of the men."

Without pausing for confirmation from my brother or me, the king is riding back to our temporary camp, the camp where no doubt, I have no canvas over my head because I was away retrieving Sigeberht.

"Well done, brother," Osfrith calls to me, his gaze focused on the view before him.

"It was no great thing. King Sigeberht was dragging his heels and was barely out of Lindsey when I caught him."

Osfrith barks a laugh at the news.

"He seems keen to do battle."

"More than keen, and he thinks he acts with his God's blessing."

"Bloody hell," Osfrith says, "another man who thinks of what God wants before considering his wants and needs. I almost despair of these gods and kings. They seem inexplicitly linked and for no reason that I can decipher at all."

"They need each other," I say, as though it should be the simplest thing to understand.

"That's obvious, but why?" he presses, his gaze intense as he peers at me. I think he genuinely wants to know.

"Fuck knows," I answer irresponsibly. I don't know, not at all, what happens in the minds of kings. They seem overly concerned with themselves.

Eadfrith laughs at my response.

"I do love you, brother," he shouts to me, turning his horse to follow the line the king just took. "Remember that."

His words fill me with foreboding even though they're lightly offered.

28
AD632 OCTOBER - EOWA OF MERCIA
ELMET / MERCIAN BORDER

King Cadwallon, Penda, Clydog, Clemen, Eiludd, Beli, Domnall and myself sit in the war council. Cadwallon and Penda have been in hiding since the height of summer. How the pair of them have managed to keep nearly five hundred men hidden, I'll never know, but they have. Edwin and his allies had no clue to their whereabouts until two days ago when they purposefully made him aware that they were concealed within the great forests on the Elmet border.

Now we discuss our tactics and wait for the final piece of the alliance to fall into place. I know who's coming because Penda has finally relented and let me completely into his confidence. I'm pleased. I shouldn't have allied with King Edwin in the first place. I'm relieved my brother finally understands my contrition for such actions.

Cloten is not with us, and Cadwallon seems to think he won't come. Not now. Cadwallon has spent much time and effort trying to bring the huge man back into the alliance, but Cloten doesn't share his concern regarding the threat posed by Edwin. Even when Eiludd filled him in with all the gory details of Edwin's attack upon the men of Powys, Cloten closed his ears and refused to listen.

Cloten's not afraid of battle, and his argument is sound. His land lies so far away from Edwin's he simply can't see the danger. For his sake, I hope that Edwin meets his death here and that he never faces the risk of a force of Northumbrian men trying to kill him and his people. I can't see it either, though. I'll be honest. He has more to fear from the men of the divided kingdom of Dal Riata over the sea than he does from Edwin.

The men have been arriving by prearranged intervals for the last two weeks, coming via circuitous routes, some even taking to their ships first and then travelling overland—anything to keep Edwin blind to our actions for as long as possible.

"Edwin will want to keep us from Deira," Cadwallon announces to the assembled men. We sit under the forest's canopy before a vast roaring fire that crackles with the dryness of the wood. I did fear that it would allow the entire forest to catch flame, but Cadwallon's men have built a large stone enclosure for the flames, and they can't connect with the dense leaf matter underfoot or the straggling branches above our heads. Amazingly the space is dryer than under any tent I've slept beneath. Overhead, it could be raining more heavily than at the height of winter, and I'd not know.

Cadwallon wears his war gear, weapons glinting with the light from the fire. He's a war leader come to seek revenge.

"He'll want to dictate where the battle takes place," Penda confirms. He's never met Edwin, but he's managed to decipher the man's nature from everything he's heard about him. I've filled in details where I can.

"He'll want to make it significant," the King of Powys, Eiludd, states, very matter of factly. He, too, has never met Edwin, other than in battle and yet he too understands how he thinks.

"He'll hope to meet you at the River Idle, where he first gained his kingdom," I state. I want to be sure to have my voice heard here.

Penda nods as he considers that.

"Is that near here?" he asks. I know he knows, but for the sake of everyone else, who hasn't spent the last two winters surveying Edwin's land under a deep black cloak and pretending to be nothing more than a wandering mercenary troop, he asks the question.

"Yes, half a day at most, no more."

Beli speaks then. "It would be better to attack him deep within his kingdom." His tone brokers no argument, but he gets one all the same.

"Edwin has been waiting on the Deiran border for almost the entire summer. We can't attempt to sneak past his guard. He'll see us coming and then get to choose the battle site. We need to draw him south."

Cadwallon is just as decisive in his words as Beli was in his. The King of Alt Clut glares at Cadwallon for a long moment but quickly subsides when Eiludd speaks once more.

"Edwin looks for portents and the grace of his new God in every action he takes. He'll see attacking us at the River Idle as some sort of approval from his God. When the battle turns against him, his resolve will quickly crumble. His forces will see him falter, and we'll be able to kill them all."

Eiludd hopes to inflict as much death and destruction against Edwin as possible.

"What about King Sigeberht of the East Angles? He doesn't share the same attachment to the site?" Penda presses. He's enjoying this discussion with men who see him as their equal. He's also curious enough that he wants to draw them into a conversation and listen to their reasoning. His intelligence allows him to realise that his views aren't the only ones or the right ones.

"King Sigeberht is more religious than Edwin. If he survives for long enough for us to cut Edwin down first, he'll be questioning why they've not won as well. It'll make him leave with as many of his men as he can. He'll not want to fight when his God has deserted him."

"So we try and kill Edwin first?" Clemen asks softly, his eyes reflecting the firelight, making them look like black pits. He's an old man, and I wonder why he's come to this battle. He should have stayed at home and died in his bed.

"We try and kill as many of these men as we can. If we can slay all of Edwin's men and Edwin himself, then Northumbria will be neutered for a generation to come. We don't want the kingdom to reform and reassert itself over the rest of the kingdoms."

Eiludd is so fierce when he speaks, I almost think he could kill with the sharpness of his words. He truly does hate Edwin.

Cadwallon talks then, slowly and thoughtfully.

"If we have a river at their backs, they'll have nowhere to retreat to when we gain the advantage. We already know that our combined forces are greater than anything he has. With superior numbers and the deep river behind them, I think the men will become desperate."

"No war leader would choose to have a river at their back?" Clydog counters. He should know. I understand his land is covered with waterways.

"No, they wouldn't, but if we use the River Humber, he'll see it as his land behind him, and he'll want to protect it, come what may."

"I agree," Domnall says into the sudden silence. It's strange to think a thousand men could suddenly fall silent at the same time, but that's what's happened.

"We should ride out from here but split our forces as soon as we're able," Penda announces with decisiveness in his voice. It's really not his place to plan this, but he's not letting that stop him. I'm the king here, not him. Yet he has the respect of every man in the small clearing. I should probably fear that, but there's enough land within this island for both of us to forge a kingdom if we have to do so. There needs to be.

"We'll head for the Humber. If we come across Edwin advancing towards us, we'll bunker down at the closest river crossing to where we are. If not, we'll stake our claim to his kingdom but stop at the most natural boundary. The Humber. Whether it's where he wants to be or not, the threat to him, the realisation that we've pushed so far north without being noticed, will unsettle him enough that he'll panic. Remember, he's been the victor for so long, he's probably forgotten the raw taste of fear in his mouth."

Penda's speech is met with nods and grunts from the rest of the men. I admit that it's an excellent plan. Edwin will be unnerved when he sees a thousand heavily armed men encamped around the base of Deira. For all that he spends his winters in Yeavering and Bamburgh, it's Deira to which he feels the most committed. It is, after all, Deira that King Æthelfrith stole from him, and it's near the Deiran border that he killed Æthelfrith and claimed back that which had been taken from him.

"The land by the River Humber is flat on the southern side and more banked on the northern. It will be a good position."

"However," and now all eyes are on Penda again. "If we've missed Edwin, and he's already in a position more to his liking, I'd suggest we attack on the banks of the River Don. Like the Humber, it's flat to the south and steeped to the north. It's also marshy and boggy, and men might well become trapped in the thick mud. Three rivers meet at one place, which would be the perfect place to fight a battle. Some might drown, and others sink in the mud. I prefer it as the better option but like the idea of making the battle site as significant to Edwin as possible. This attack might well come down to more than just who has the most men and the most skill."

Not one voice is raised against Penda's logic; everyone listens to him as though he's the master here. I sneak a look at Cadwallon, but even he's under Penda's spell.

"Who'll lead the attack?" Eiludd demands. Aggression runs through his voice. He wants to be the man to kill Edwin.

Cadwallon takes over the conversation now.

"Half of us will lead the attack, and the other half will act as reinforcements. I suggest Eowa, Eiludd and myself begin the attack. Clydog, Penda, Clemen, Beli and Domnall Brecc can come from the rear, with Penda and Clydog encircling the front shield wall and extending it outwards. They won't be expecting tactics like that."

A man steps into our circle of light then. Penda smiles with delight. I recognise the man as one of Penda's most loyal followers. I'd been wondering where he was. I'd meant to ask Penda but kept forgetting. If he'd met his death, I'd not wanted to remind my brother of the man he'd lost.

Penda stands then and walks away from the discussion.

Cadwallon watches him go without rancour. This must be something they've decided upon a long time ago.

"Is our discussion not important enough for you to listen to?" Clydog goads, but Cadwallon waves him down.

"Penda and I have one more ally we've kept to ourselves. Not to upset you all," he hastily adds, when the men all as one open their mouths to argue. "But to protect his identity and to ensure he was able to join us. He's just arrived with Herebrod, and Penda has gone to greet him. He'll be here soon."

"Does he bring more men?" Eiludd asks aggressively.

"He does, and more than that, he brings the mental advantage that we also need."

Clydog huffs dramatically.

"How many little tricks are we trying to use to out-think Edwin?"

Cadwallon glares at him.

"As many as it fucking well takes," he growls into the sudden silence.

"Edwin will be trying the same on us," I speak into the quiet, trying to diffuse the tense situation that's brewing between Cadwallon and Clydog. Penda has told me that Clydog is an excellent warrior, and his men, all a hundred of them, will be a lethal force in battle. He doesn't want to lose them. Cadwallon, on the other hand, sees him as a possible enemy because they share a considerable land border. Penda has asked me to do all I can to keep the alliance that he's worked so hard to forge together."

All eyes are suddenly on me. I almost wish I hadn't spoken.

"He'll have his priests speaking to the men, telling them that a blue sky means God's grace is shining on them, assuring them of victory. That a full river is a good thing, flowing with God's love for them. That a rain cloud will be a sign that God will wash away their sins. Never think for a moment that Edwin doesn't know how to use his religion against us."

Cadwallon nods his head to thank me for my intervention. Clydog half shrugs again.

"What is it with your tribes and this new God? There's nothing new about him," Clydog mumbles. He's as unhappy as the rest of the ancient Christians that Edwin has decided to make this a religious war. In all honesty, it's only really me and Penda who are true believers of the old Gods. Even the banished royal families of Elmet, those few who've joined the alliance, are followers of their Christian God.

"No, there isn't, but Edwin sees an advantage in saying there is. As I say. He'll use whatever he can to gain the upper hand. A man's faith is to him and his bloody Bishop Paulinus, a great thing to be celebrated and upon which they can expound. Faith is no longer a man's private concern."

The sound of footsteps and men speaking reaches us through the overhanging branches, and Cadwallon quickly regains the conversation.

"Penda is returning with our ally. I don't think many of you, if any of you, will know him."

At that moment, Penda steps into the clearing, an older man behind him. I stare at him, trying to decide if I know him or not. He has long hair and a full beard, and his brow is furrowed with worry lines, but he wears fine clothes and jewellery flashes on his cloak clasps. Something of value is also threaded through his hair, as though he wears a crown there.

The men all stare at the man, who stands firm under their onslaught. No one seems to know who he is until Domnall stands and reaches out to offer him a handclasp of friendship.

"Eanfrith," he says, his voice holding approval. "I had no idea. If I'd known, I could have travelled south with you."

Eanfrith relaxes at the welcome from Domnall, but I'm still trying to decipher who he is. The clue must be in the knowledge that he comes from the north.

"My thanks, My Lord," he says formally, respect evident in his voice. "My brothers are well?" he thinks to ask, and Domnall falters a little before he replies.

"As well as exiles can be. I'm pleased you're here."

The other men are as unsure as I am about who this is. Penda is enjoying their confusion and doesn't seem too keen to introduce them, not until Cadwallon coughs loudly.

"Apologies, My Lords," Penda finally speaks, his hand resting on the arm of the man protectively. "It's my pleasure to introduce you to Eanfrith, exiled King of Bernicia, son of the man Edwin murdered."

A babble of conversation fills the silence. I find myself watching Penda with utmost surprise. He's even more devious than I've credited him. This will be the mental advantage they need against Edwin. Once Edwin realises his nephew, his sister's son, is fighting against him, even his new God might struggle to offer him his sympathies.

"Well met," I say, standing and reaching out to offer Eanfrith my arm.

"Eowa?" he asks with a question. "You look like your brother?" he says in surprise. I wonder what he's heard about us, but Penda only winks at me and Herebrod, who's standing on the other side of Eanfrith, won't meet my eye. The bastards. I bet they've told him all sorts of lies about me.

"Yes, I'm the pretty one," I say, trying to mask my slight annoyance.

Eanfrith falters and then grins at my attempt to lighten the mood.

"Indeed you are, My Lord," he offers with a wry grin and Penda barks with laughter.

Eiludd watches our new ally with unease.

"Your father was a cock," he growls. Eanfrith tenses at those words. It's not exactly the most politic thing I've ever heard Eiludd say.

"But I respected him a damn sight more than I ever did Edwin. You'll be fighting for your kingdom, I assume?" he continues.

"Yes, My Lord, I will. As to my father. Well, my memories of him are faded. I can't answer for him or excuse him."

"No, you can't, but to win my support, I'll need assurance and a treaty with you that you'll not attack the men of Powys as he did. He killed my predecessor, and whilst I thanked him for that at the time, I'm not about to replace one bloodthirsty bastard with another."

I think Penda might speak for Eanfrith, but he holds his peace.

"I want my land, estates and wealth," Eanfrith answers ominously. "I don't want your land as well. I don't kill people on a whim. Your predecessor should not have earned the enmity of my father, and I suggest you don't do the same."

The words are spoken with a sharpened edge. For a moment, I think he may have angered Eiludd. A deep silence fills the fire lit space, the only noise the crackle of the fire and the far distant sound of the rain falling high above us, audible because of the intense silence.

"Agreed. If we win and you become King of Bernicia, we'll be friends, not enemies," Eiludd says gravely. "Then you can prove to me that you're not a cock like your father."

The men seal the agreement with a handclasp, and the tension in the air dissipates immediately.

Hasty introductions are made to all the other allies, apart from Beli, who already knows Eanfrith, and the conversation returns to tactics.

"Any more secret allies?" Eiludd asks grudgingly. "Any more men who might have killed another's father, brother or son?" His tone is angry, and yet it isn't prohibitive.

Cadwallon considers the question.

"There's the possibility of another, but we can't speak about it, not here and not now. If they truly mean to switch sides during the battle, then you'll all know anyway."

That's a hugely telling admission, and once more, loud conversation develops between the allies. I glare at Penda. What does he know? What by the Old Gods has he done? I thought Eanfrith was a fine addition to the alliance. Who else has he tempted away from Edwin, and by all accounts, right from under his nose?

No wonder Penda doesn't always trust me. He's such a scheming man; he sees conspiracy where none exists.

Or does he? Domnall's following words show how right he is, the king turning to Eanfrith.

"You asked of your brothers?" Eanfrith glances at him in surprise. "I did, My Lord, yes."

"You don't know then?"

"Know what?"

"That Lord Oswald has allied with King Edwin. That he has land within your old kingdom."

Eanfrith looks ill at the news, his face draining of all colour. Penda hisses sharply at the revelation.

"I didn't know, no, but as you know, my brother and I have had little contact since our exile."

Domnall fixes Cadwallon with a hard stare?

"Did you know?" he demands. I wonder why they've not discussed this before today.

Cadwallon turns to Penda, and Penda nods minutely.

"Of course, I knew. I know everything about Edwin's allies."

Eanfrith looks unhappily at Penda, but he only shrugs.

"Would it have changed your mind if you'd known?" he asks, whilst at his side, Herebrod looks as uneasy as Eanfrith.

A stray blast of wind disturbs the fire, sending gusts of super-heated air washing over me. I bat at an errant ember on my sleeve and then look back to Eanfrith.

At that moment, a transformation has taken place.

"It hardens my resolve," he says, his voice like stone. "The kingdom of Bernicia belongs to me, not to that little shit."

The tension scatters again as one man looks to another. Families and brothers, allies and enemies, who can tell who anyone is anymore?

I meet Penda's eyes. I wonder what he thinks behind his hard eyes. Does he know my intentions, or does he only guess?

He'll find out soon enough.

29

AD632 OCTOBER - OSRIC OF DEIRA
THE HUMBER RIVER

King Edwin and Sigeberht have been in close conversation for much of the evening, with Eadfrith, Osfrith and bloody Oswald, almost as though they've forgotten I'm even here. I have just as much right to be consulted on the coming battle. After all, I rule this kingdom in Edwin's name. I know its physical characteristics far better than Edwin does.

I know he'll be regaling them all with tales of when he killed King Æthelfrith at the Battle of the River Idle. He will have to downplay them to avoid upsetting Oswald, his nephew and Æthelfrith's son, but all the same, Edwin was lucky that day. He often forgets just how lucky and my role in stopping the blade that should have killed him.

For once, I feel my anger at the constant side-lining I receive, consume me. I was going to tell Edwin of the rogue troop of men who've been surveying this land every winter for the last two years, but I've decided against that. Not this time. He thinks King Cadwallon will have no clue about the layout of the land. I suspect he's very wrong and that someone, perhaps even Penda himself, has a thorough understanding of the watercourses and hills.

I don't believe I want Edwin to lose this battle, but I do not intend to help him anymore.

At my side, Liefbrun is silent, but his eyes never stray from the tent, from which the sounds of men talking can be heard. We don't stand close enough so that we can hear. I'm not that desperate. Not anymore.

"What will you do?" he asks, his voice half a whisper.

I look at him in surprise.

"What do you mean?"

"You'd get more respect from King Cadwallon than you ever will from Edwin."

I inhale sharply at hearing the words spoken out loud, but he knows me too well. He must know that I've been thinking the same.

"He's my king and my cousin," I say, hoping that my denial sounds half-convincing.

"He's a bastard and an unloyal one at that. You've done everything he's ever asked of you, and what have you received in return?"

I'm still amazed that Liefbrun is speaking to me openly. He is, after all, Edwin's loyal man.

I'd like to ask him if he's testing my loyalty, but I know he's not. Ten years ago, he might well have been, but now he has more sympathy for me than he does for Edwin. Ten years is a bloody long time.

"He's my king," I say again, even more half-heartedly than before.

"He ignores you and treats you as though you're a slave or a horse."

I wince at the image in my head. Liefbrun is being intentionally cruel with his words. I glare at him, and he meets my eyes levelly. He's deadly serious.

"What would you do?" I whisper back. No one is close enough to us to hear, but the wind can do strange things to a man's words when it blows around them, as it does now.

"I'd leave," he says without even pausing for thought. "I'd join King Cadwallon. Tell him all I know and hope to either die in battle or be given some small piece of land to call my own."

It's an intriguing idea.

"My family?" I say, and his eyes are now positively glowering at me.

"Your wife is dead. Your sons have grown to manhood. They can make their own decisions."

He's right. No one needs me at Goodmanham, not anymore. My choice is that stark.

"When would we go?" I query. I know he'll be coming with me. He has even fewer ties to Northumbria than I do. His wife is dead as well, and his sons hate him. He was a hard father. I disapprove of that, but it's not my place to judge him.

"When we march for the place they selected for battle. It'll be easy to slip away in the confusion."

"Let me think on it," I say, and he shrugs at me. "It's your life that you're wasting," he says but stays with me, despite his anger and frustration.

"What do you think of King Sigeberht?" he asks me. We've had this discussion before. There's nothing not to like about Sigeberht. Still, there's something that I don't like, and I've not yet worked out what it is.

"He's a smug Christian git," I say. Liefbrun smirks at me.

"He is, isn't he? Does Edwin have any allies who aren't total wankers?"

We both laugh at that. The tension between us evaporates. In the moment of clarity that follows my laughter, I conclude that Liefbrun is correct. Edwin will never value me. I need to leave.

"Tomorrow then," I say. He understands without me having to elucidate.

"Tomorrow then," he repeats, his eyes showing his relief at my words. "I know the perfect place."

I thought he would. He has an amazing memory. He can remember paths he might have only ever walked once, and he never ever gets lost. I know I'll be in safe hands with him.

A bellow of laughter from inside the tent, Edwin's voice raised high in enjoyment, and I know I've made the correct decision. We might have been childhood friends. He might have been my king, and he might trust me implicitly, but none of those things can come without some reciprocity. He's taken me for granted, and I'm not about to let it continue any longer.

"Tomorrow," I say to myself, mulling the word over and thinking of a life free of King Edwin. It's almost a pleasant idea.

30

AD632 OCTOBER – EANFRITH OF BERNICIA

MERCIAN / ELMET BORDER

The news of my brother's betrayal is unnerving and understandable all at the same time. Oswald, like me, must strive for more in his life than he currently claims. Yet, I wouldn't cast in my lot with the man who murdered our father. Not even if it gained me a kingdom would I be able to speak to the man as though our father's death was of little or no importance.

Yet the greeting from my new allies is unexpectedly warm despite my brother's treachery. Herebrod has led my men and me through the land of my uncle, the land I hope to have returned to me, without anyone spotting us. Herebrod knows secret passageways and hidden caves that have sheltered us each night. I'll be forever in his debt. But coming under the forest canopy to meet with these kings and almost kings have been far more terrifying. I'm glad it's done, and I'm pleased that Penda is the man I thought he'd be and that Domnall is here. Friendly faces are always to be welcomed.

Spread out amongst the forest, it's difficult to know how many men are attached to our endeavour. Herebrod says there'll be at least six hundred men. But he didn't know how many men the other kings would bring; that was just his assessment of Cadwallon, Penda and

Eowa's might. I only have fifty men with me, but they're all fiercely loyal and excellently trained warriors who fight in the ways of the Picts with their square shields and long javelins. King Edwin has some experience against the Picts, with his constant raiding to the north, but I doubt his other allies will look favourably on how my men fight.

Herebrod has been training with my men as well. He knows how to handle a javelin and use a square, as opposed to a round shield, effectively. He's also informed my men about the shield wall. I don't think our square shields will work as well against our enemy, but Herebrod is convinced that we'll have a distinct advantage in close combat. The strength of my men, Herebrod announces, will ensure their javelins are used when Edwin forms his shield wall. We might initially have to fight from the back is his only caution, and my men grumbled at that, but they've had their opinion swayed by his stories of just how we'll help win.

Herebrod speaks well before other men. He convinces them to his will, just as he did me. I know that, and I also can see where he learnt such skills. Penda is an intelligent man who knows how to draw people into a conversation to make them see their worth.

Slowly the meeting between the kings breaks up as they drift away to their individual camps, and Penda sits beside me. His eyes are bright despite the vast quantity of mead I've watched him consume. He seems keen to talk.

"It's good to meet with you at last," he begins. He's grinning at Herebrod as he speaks. I consider what's been said about me in my absence. "I'm also keen to meet the women of the Picts," he adds as an afterthought, and I realise that Herebrod has probably spent much of his time regaling Penda about his exploits with his woman. That makes me grin.

"They can be very beautiful but also quite, quite lethal," I offer and Herebrod nods. I don't want to know what he's been engaged with under my roof, but I can imagine from my own experiences. The women of the Picts are savage beauties and all the more appealing for that. It's a relief to know that whilst my home might have lost the majority of its male warriors, anyone who tries to attack will face the wrath of the women. They'll wish they'd waited until the women were gone to safety and the men left all alone to fight with their skills.

"Your men are prepared for the coming battle?" Penda queries, and I nod.

"They've all pledged an oath to me to support me and stand with me. It's not the usual way of the Picts, but they're coming around to my way of doing things."

"And your wife and son have been left behind?" Penda continues. I wonder what he's trying to imply.

"For safety," I say. "I want to ensure my family line continues."

"You're wise to do so," he confirms. I appreciate he's not forcing a confrontation. "I hope I have many sons to rule should I die in battle. But as of yet, I have only a burgeoning life to rule in my stead, although the child might be born by now. I'm not sure. My brother has two children. I plan to have many, many more than he does."

This amuses me. It appears as though the brothers constantly try to outdo each other, even in the act of procreation.

"I hope my brother has no children," I say then. I'm still upset by the news that he's an ally of my enemy.

"Well, if he does, you can kill them," Penda says so straight-faced that I stare at him in shock. Herebrod cautioned me that he was a pragmatic man and fiercely logical.

"I'd not considered that," I say carefully. I don't want to give him the wrong impression. I'm prepared to do anything to gain my throne, but would I kill children who were my flesh and blood? I hope not. That would make me too much like Edwin.

"It was a joke," Penda clarifies and then grimaces. "A poor one, I accept, my apologies, Lord Eanfrith."

"No apology is needed," I say, but I'm pleased to hear his words even if they're only said to placate me.

"King Cadwallon has asked me to assure you of his support for your kingship."

"His support is welcomed."

"But," Penda says, and I anticipate what he's about to say. "He wants an assurance that you won't ally with King Cynegils of the West Saxons as soon as you become king."

I knew that Herebrod would be forced to tell Penda of our meeting.

"My Lord, I assure you I sent the messenger on his way with words and promises that dissipated in the morning sun."

"Good, I just needed to hear that. But that's not to say you can't forge a friendship with him. We hope for greater peace upon this island once we're rid of King Edwin and everyone holds the kingdoms they should." His words are edged with steel, and I stare at him in shock. He's trying to tell me something, but I'm not sure what it is. I hazard a guess it must be to stay true to him and Cadwallon and especially to him. I hope that's what it is.

"When you're king," Penda continues, his voice suddenly softer. "You can do whatever you deem fit to your brother, but I'd caution you against exacting any revenge on other members of your family. No matter the differences with my brother, I know I can almost always rely on him."

Penda's words are the opposite of what I was expecting. I thought he'd warn me against re-establishing links with my younger brothers. I suppose he has a good point, though. My son will, quite possibly, be the King of the Picts. I don't know if he'll want Northumbria. As my wife is unlikely to give me more sons now, there might be no one to pass on my kingdom. I could marry again, but really, I don't think I want to feel my wife's angry breath down my back. She would, I don't doubt, exact retribution if I left her behind.

"It's always better to be friendly with your enemies," I say, and Penda nods once, decisively. That's all the confirmation I get that I've interpreted his words correctly.

"Now, go with Herebrod, find your men. Make sure everyone is content and ready for when the call comes. It won't be much longer."

His words should be ominous, but they sound like a soft prayer even on his rough lips.

I've dreamed of this all my life. The opportunity no longer terrifies me. I won't die here. Herebrod will ensure it. I just need to ensure that our alliance defeats Edwin. I just need to kill King Edwin.

A small price to pay to assuage my father's memory and ensure my future.

31

AD632 - PENDA OF MERCIA – THE BATTLE OF HÆðFELD

I feel as though this battle has been planned for years. It's the worst kept secret on this island. Everyone has allied with someone. Almost as many have broken alliances or failed to live up to their promises.

Not me, though. Never. I came into this as an underling of Cadwallon's, a much-desired one but one all the same, and I'll emerge as a mighty king. I might have to rule with my brother, but I find that a small compromise to make now. I find I almost like the bastard, and I no longer wish to see his death. It might be good if he were wounded and I rescued him, but really, I want us all to live through this clash.

King Edwin doesn't deserve to cause the deaths of any in my family. He has his Christian God now, but I'm a descendant of one of our Old Gods and Woden will watch me today, keep me safe and ensure my greatest victory yet.

I've offered a sacrifice of blood to my personal God. I've promised him my unending support in return for my victory and that I'll feast with him upon my death. Not for anything will I turn to this new but old God. Never.

My weapons are ready, my shield scoured clean and emblazed

with my emblem picked out on the leather covering, a fire breathing dragon, the enemy of my God, Woden and a symbol of his great power. He killed a great wyrm. I'll use my shield and sword to kill the wyrm that comes against me now in the shape of Edwin and his warriors.

Breaking free from the forest canopy above my head, my men and I are the first to step foot outside the forest that's kept us hidden for the last month. It feels strange to see the glint of early morning sun in the overcast sky, to feel the crunch of frost under our feet, but then, we've hidden our way through the end of the summer. Winter hasn't arrived yet, but it's a close thing. In a few weeks, snow will carpet this land, and I hope Edwin's body will lie half-rotted underneath it, half-gnawed by Woden's ravens. The thought brings a grin to my face.

My horse is as shocked as I am to be free from the restrictive forest. I reach to calm him as he sidesteps all over the place, other horses doing their best to avoid him. He's a black beast and can be vicious when his temper is roused. My father chose him for me when I was too small to appreciate his worth. I've been punished every day since for thinking that my father was giving me a pet pony as a gift.

My father saw my future before me. He must have done. Why else gift a lad of no more than ten a violent, angry animal that can ride faster than any other horse in the entire kingdom? I named him Gunghir as soon as I saw him. My father cackled with delight at such an apt name. He's Woden's spear made flesh. He's nasty enough and sharp enough that he can do significant damage with minimal effort.

He treats me savagely, my beast of a horse. I treat him just as viciously back, but I wouldn't be without him. Never. I've ridden to every battle I've ever fought on him, and he's carried me away as well. He'll let no other groom him, and so I, almost a king, must see to my beast. I don't mind at all. In those quiet moments with him, when he's finally stopped snapping his teeth and stamping his hooves, I find I have my clearest thoughts.

"Come, Gunghir," I caution the beast, and he bites my hand in thanks. I slap his nose in anger and surprise. He breathes into my face, causing me to cough away his stink. It's evident that he's unhappy with his captivity. He'll ride like the wind today. I'll have to fight him every step of the way to ensure I don't leave my warriors behind. It will ensure I'm angry enough to fight the enemy when we encounter them. I often think much of my battle rage comes from my journey-long arguments with the horse. But still, I'll ride no other. Never.

I mount him as he bucks and tries to dismount me. Herebrod looks at me worriedly, but I shoo him away. I'll calm my bloody beast with no help from another.

When Gunghir finally subsides, with a sharp nip to his sides from my leather boots and a sharp yank of his head to remind him who's his master, I gesture Herebrod to come nearer. He sidles closer, giving Gunghir the space he requires and casts me reproachful looks. Herebrod and Gunghir are acknowledged enemies.

"May the Gods ride with you today," I say to my friend, reaching down to clasp his arm with mine. I note the vast number of arm rings that cover his arm. They feel warm under my touch. I remember every occasion he earned one of them from me. He's my friend and my enemy both, just like the bloody horse.

"Keep close to Eanfrith," I caution. "I trust him and you, but make sure none kill him. I want him as the King of Bernicia, no other."

He nods at my words.

"My Lord, you have my oath," he says formally. I knock the side of his head in annoyance.

"I want your word, not your bloody oath," I mutter angrily. Although the force of my blow splits his lip, he grins at me, teeth stained with his blood.

"Fine, you have my fucking word, now go, and don't whatever happens, sodding well die today. I've got a lot invested in you winning this."

He turns and walks away with a jaunty step. I almost call him back and give him the same advice. But he's won our engagement with his words where I failed with force. He always works to ensure I see that there's another way to win every battle I face.

Damn the man.

My two hundred warriors have all managed to tame their equally unhappy mounts, and as one, I give the order to ride out. We're heading to the Humber, and I hope that when King Edwin sees me there, he'll think he faces only me and rush across the flowing river.

My men and I will attack him, raise our shield wall, and then when we're all exhausted, the rest of the force will appear. I doubt Edwin will leave anything in reserve. King Cadwallon and I have decided it's best to leave as much of our force in reserve as possible. This isn't what we initially agreed, but our battle tactics change every time a man speaks with new information or some new insight into the mind of Edwin, and his allies is mouthed.

The day is chill and fresh; the rain from the night before turned to ice and frost in places. It makes the sound of the horses' hooves over the hard surface reverberate loudly in the silent air.

We follow the path of the River Trent as it gushes along at a rapid pace, the threat of ice forming on its top still a far distant possibility despite the deep chill. The horses drink thirstily from the fresh freezing water, too used to stale water within the forest canopy. It's strange the things you miss when you're in hiding.

The morning slowly progresses as I'm on high alert for any sign of an advance force from Edwin. The scouts assure me that there isn't going to be anything of the sort, that Edwin still sits by his Humber river to the north, but I'm not convinced he won't have decided to make his move by now. Edwin must suspect that our numbers are greater than his so late in the year. His allies, with nothing to lose but Edwin's good wishes, will have long since departed to see to their harvests. I would expect him to do all he can to gain an advantage.

It's a dull ride through the landscape as it turns towards the dark time of the year, but finally, as the sun reaches its zenith, one of my scout's returns, two men behind him. One of the men is very well dressed, his mail byrnie sparkling even on such a dull day, and the man beside him is only a little less well dressed.

"Lord Penda," my scout calls.

"Who is it, Egbert?"

I issue a swift prayer to Woden that this isn't one of the king's representatives come to negotiate peace. I don't want any sort of peace that doesn't result in King Edwin's death.

"Osric, My lord, a cousin of King Edwin's."

I reach for my short seax. I'd rather kill this messenger now than hear his words of peaceful intent.

Egbert holds his hand out to stay my hand. He must have expected my response. I'd be disappointed if he didn't know me well by now.

"He seeks an alliance with you?" he manages to interject before I'm leaping from my horse and severing the man's head from his shoulders.

"He what?" I ask, momentarily stunned by the unexpected words, my leg half over my horse as I'm in the process of dismounting. Egbert grimaces at me and repeats himself.

"He wishes to seek an alliance with you."

"What, just him?

"Yes, just him and his companion Liefbrun. They're disgruntled with King Edwin and wish to help you win. They'll tell you all they know."

"Why?" I ask. I'm feeling as though I'm missing something important here.

The man who I assume is Osric speaks then. He's watching me with curious eyes. I wonder if the words used to describe me these days do justice when men meet me. I should ask Eanfrith. He, I like, and he, I think, will give me an honest answer.

"There's no deceit here, My Lord. I've supported my cousin for the entirety of his rule. Yet he excludes me from his war council and includes men he barely knows. I'm no longer prepared to do his bidding."

Osric's formal words intrigue me, although I don't trust him yet.

"To whom does he listen?" I query. Gunghir is restless beneath me, and Egbert nudges his horse away from Gunghir's mean, snapping mouth. I yank his rein once more. Will the damn horse never let me be the master?

"King Sigeberht from the kingdom of the East Angles," Osric

retorts with bitterness. "And Oswald of Bernicia and his eldest sons, of course," his voice dips even lower then. I wonder of whom he thinks the least?

"Then you're welcome to join with my men and me." Two men can cause our vast force no harm.

"How many men does he have?" I ask eagerly, "and where?"

Osric doesn't hesitate with his response.

"Seven hundred and near here, they're heading for the River Idle." I look to Egbert, and he nods to show corroboration with those numbers.

The irony of that statement brings a bitter smirk to my lips. Damn the bastard and his inflated opinion of himself. How much would he like to beat us at the River Idle in stunning symmetry to when he killed King Æthelfrith there? It's a good thing I plan on allowing the irony to have a less pleasant ending for him and that I anticipated this move with every step I took towards the Humber.

I observe the men. If either of them tries to escape now, rush back to tell King Edwin where we are, I'll unleash Gunghir, and together we'll kill them both. It might settle the tempestuous beast if he manages to bite someone other than me today.

"How far away are they?" I ask, and now Osric looks a bit uneasy, his body language giving him away before his words do. Egbert doesn't show any alarm, so I'm unsure what this means.

"They're coming now, but closer to the Idle than here. We veered off and lost them so that we could hunt you out."

Fuck, I don't want to hear that, and I glare at Egbert. He shrugs his vast shoulders at me. He's my scout because nothing riles him, and men could be beating him on the head with their weapons whilst he reports to me, and he'll not raise his voice or show any concern. But I don't want Edwin sliding past us as we head for the Humber, and he heads for the River Idle. If that happens, we'll be fighting to defend the wrong kingdoms.

"My thanks for your information, and please, join with me now, or if you prefer, Egbert will take you back to our supply line."

Osric is unsure what to do, so I decide for him. It's one thing to change sides on the day of a battle, but quite another to fight against a man you once called your king. I understand that.

"Egbert, go back to King Cadwallon. Take Osric and his companion with you. Tell him what we know. He'll want to rearrange the men."

Egbert doesn't question my words and quickly sets off, at last showing a little bit of alarm for the words he's not spoken himself but that he's facilitated all the same. As they ride back the way I've come, I take the time to consider what I know and how this affects my efforts. I need to head west. There's no help for it.

"Frambert," I shout to one of my men. "We're heading the wrong way. Go and retrieve the three scouts. I'm going to head west. Find us there."

He raises his eyebrow in surprise at me. I never make mistakes, and I sure as fuck never admit to them.

"Go," I instruct. "Quickly." Trying not to be impatient but failing.

He kicks his horse, and they're away, skimming along the side of the great river, its roar suddenly loud in my ears.

I just want to find the bastard and kill him. Is that too much for which to ask?

I offer a quick prayer to Woden and turn my raucous beast around. He tries to bite my hand, and in a moment of anger, I bend down and bite his neck. He stiffens at the pinch of the wound, and I spit horsehair from my mouth in disgust.

"Do what you're fucking well told," I shout at him. He jumps to my commands, fleeing across the flat land as though he can outrun the pain from his neck.

That will hopefully put an end to his constant refusal to obey me.

The rest of my men sprint to catch up. I belatedly remember my earlier thought. It will do me no good if I arrive alone to face seven hundred men. I need my warriors with me.

I fight with my horse once more, only this time his resistance is a token of its former self. We slow to allow the others to catch us.

"My Lord? What's happening," Offa cries. I appreciate I've been so angry I've not told my men what's happening. They deserve to know what drives my sudden change of direction

"Osric, Edwin's cousin, has changed his allegiance. He seeks sanctuary with us. He tells me that Edwin is headed for the Idle."

My men have spent as much time as I have to reconnoitre this area. They immediately know that it changes our plans.

"We head west then," Offa calls, and I nod. I know that I'm very close to losing my temper if I try to speak.

"Yes, and quickly. We don't want to be caught behind him or even to the side of him."

As one, we race across the land, the horses all pleased to be doing more than trotting along. They crave speed as much as I do.

All the while, my heart beats erratically in my chest. I pray to Woden that I've not spent nearly three years arranging a battle to have my plan in pieces before it's even begun.

I imagine the confusion amongst the allies with which Cadwallon now has to contend. I wish I were there to rearrange everything. I know this area, not him. I'm hoping that this Osric will help. If he doesn't, I might just kill him when the battle is finished.

The steady sound of two hundred horses flying over the near winter landscape eventually calms me. I take the time to fully consider what's happened. It's not like me to panic or show any weaknesses. I need to remember that, reassert control over a situation that's still of my devising. Whether he's quite where we want him or not, Edwin has walked into our trap. We just need to close it now.

I rein my horse in once more. He's suddenly docile as a baby. I almost bite him again just to feel his pent-up aggression beneath my legs. I sigh deeply and slide from his back, holding his reins tightly.

His huge eyes glare at me. I feel remorse for our earlier argument. It wasn't his fault. It was mine.

I rest my head against him, all the while holding his rein with one hand and stroking his neck with the other. He likes to be caressed like this. I'm hoping he'll realise it's an apology.

The men take the opportunity to eat and drink. I hear their soft voices over my calming heartbeat, and then Gunghir nips my ear, and

I know we're allies again. I glare my outrage at him. He stomps his hoof in response, just narrowly missing my foot.

Bloody horse.

My original scouts finally catch up with me on the open grassland. I listen to their excuses with half an ear. It's not their fault I sent them the wrong way, and they know it, but clearly, my uncharacteristic bad temper has unsettled them.

I repeat the words that Lord Osric gave me, and they're off again, flying over the land, scouting in the correct direction for Edwin.

A swathe of land, boggy and prone to flooding, borders the convergence of not one but three rivers—the mighty Trent, the belligerent Don, and of course Edwin's favourite, the Idle. We need to get there first, make our stand on the southern bank of the river, with nothing but the Don and the marsh at our enemies back. I don't want Edwin to set his defence on the northern side. I don't want a river at my back.

The day quickly passes as we travel forwards, but I think we'll still be able to battle. The night will draw in eventually and far earlier than I want it to, but for now, the sun is high in the sky, the murk of the day has lifted, and there's even the hint of warmth in the wind. Either someone close by is having a massive fire, or a warm blast of air is making its way across the land, undoubtedly from the hills in the far distance.

One of my scouts returns, and he's grinning. He can't have been gone for long.

"My Lord," he calls as soon as he's close enough to make himself heard. "They've been sighted. Still some distance from our new battleground."

My excitement stirs at the news. I offer another brief prayer of thanks to Woden. He labours for my victory. That's good to know.

"We'll get there first?" I demand, just to be sure.

"You'll, My Lord. Yes, see, the ground is already flattening."

He makes a good point. I'd not noticed that we were on the flood plains. Come to a heavy winter storm, and much of this area will lie under water. There are no homes to speak of, not here, although the proliferation of animal dung suggests that the ground is used for grazing cattle nonetheless.

Glancing behind me, I hazard a guess that Cadwallon and Eowa are close. This is it. It's time for me to choose the final place and pitch my men ready for the battle. To jump from our horses and have them removed from the battle site. As much as I know Gunghir would make a fine addition to my force. He's too valuable to lose against Edwin. Just like my brother, my allies, and more importantly, my men.

No one is to die here today. They've all been warned. There's to be no glory in going with Woden today. My men and I have far greater futures in our sights.

I allow Gunghir to take me closer to the confluence of the rivers; the Idle is to my right, the Trent a rushing torrent behind it. I imagine I can hear it, but I can't, not really. It's still too distant, but I can see the Don in the far distance. I've passed the place where Edwin killed his brother by marriage, and that already gives me the mental edge against him.

He won't get to choose where he fights, not now.

The site has its advantages now that I've arrived first. That was always my worry. The Humber is such a great river there were any number of places where we could have forced the battle. Here, upon this vast flood plain, the options are far more limited but still winnable with the Don ahead. I've spent time assessing the possibilities. I have a plan firmly in mind.

Another forward scout rushes towards me, face flushed with the cold, breath pluming before him.

"The enemy are readying themselves to cross the Idle above us."

I don't want Edwin on that side of the Idle. I want him wedged between all the rivers. My good cheer evaporates once more. Edwin is proving to be as contrary as my horse. I'll have to assert my dominance.

I think quickly. There's nothing for it. We'll have to make ourselves more noticeable, make Edwin change his mind.

"Did he see you?"

"No, My Lord," he says without flinching at my sharp tone. I told him to stay hidden. I told them all to remain hidden. I didn't want Edwin to understand our plan before I was ready to enact it.

"Good, but now we're going to need to draw them to this place, not to the River Idle."

"I could lead half the men back the way I came, and then we could race back here."

It's a good idea.

"Yes, but take only twenty. I want the other thirty to split into two forces of fifteen each and escort him this way. I need to send word to King Cadwallon that he needs to send Eowa and his men to support me."

Altagung is sizing up his fellow warriors.

"I need the fastest horses," he says without rancour, and I agree.

"Are there ample places to purposefully show yourself by making it look unintentional?" I check.

"Yes, My Lord. Penda, I know what to do." His voice is warm. He, too, is my friend. All my warriors are my friends. I respect them. I trust them to make the decisions I would.

"Good, choose your men and go," I offer. "We need them here as soon as possible. I don't want to fight under the moonlight."

"My Lord," Altagung simply says in agreement. I dismiss him from my thoughts. He'll do what he said. Now for the other needs.

"Wiglaf," I call, startling the warrior from his battle preparations. He carries an injury that can impact his skill in battle. It's never talked about, but I'll be doing him an unlooked-for kindness by sending him to Cadwallon as my messenger.

I explain to him what I want. His eyes show that he knows why I'm asking him and no one else. Before he rides away, he grabs my arm.

"My Lord Penda," he says formally. I fear I know what's coming.

"It's been my honour to be a member of your war band. I know you'll be the mightiest king the Mercian's have ever seen."

His words are well-intentioned but fill me with a sadness I don't need on this day.

"You're not to fucking well die," I tell him fiercely. He smirks at my annoyance.

"My Lord," he demurs and rides away. Honestly, if he gets himself killed, I'll kill him myself.

Looking behind me, I feel a moment of fear. We're now only fifty men, and a force of seven hundred is riding towards us. Reinforcements are coming, but if the timing of the rest of the afternoon is even a little wrong, I know that I could die here.

Ah fuck it, I think to myself. I sure as shit am not about to let any Northumbrian prick kill me with his ineffectual sword.

I should send the horses' away, form my shield wall, but until Edwin's force is turned to my location, I can't take the risk. I'll just have to wait and then hope that the horses see sense and run back towards the safety of their forest sanctuary without too much fuss. Gunghir will take them. He's a devil of a commander.

My men are used to the long waits before battle. It's a strange thing, really, all that frantic activity to get to the right place, then a long wait whilst you hope your enemy arrives, and then frenetic activity once more.

War is a strange business, complicated by the needs of men to have kingdoms and call themselves kings. I'm guilty of that.

I test the weight of my shield, my sword and my spear. They're all ready for when I need them, my smaller seax is around my weapon's belt, and my war-axe is there as well. I clink when I move. It makes stealth difficult.

My helmet, a darkly polished gift from my father, is resting on the neck of Gunghir, ready for when I'll need it. I'm glad of the chill day now. Within all my war equipment, waiting could be a cold affair, but instead, the clothes and equipment heat me and keep my body loose and ready for the coming battle.

I hope I get to face Edwin myself, but I think Cadwallon and Eanfrith want that honour for themselves. I'm learning from the rift in their family, and that's why I've been so welcoming to Eowa. After all, I don't want an enemy who shares my blood or my family.

Sooner than I'd expected, I hear the sound of an advancing war band coming from behind me. I feel reassured once I see Eowa's face at the front of his men. He commands as large a force as I do. He has two hundred, amongst them my father's oldest ally and friend, Aldfrith. I think he hopes to meet his death in battle here, but I've made sure that he knows I'll not allow his death. I've informed his son of the same, and he, far more scared of me than his belligerent father, intends to do as I've commanded.

Aldfrith cackled at me through his cracked teeth, the holdover from an argument with my father when they were boys when I told him he wasn't to die. He's always worn his teeth as a physical show of his close association with my father. They're his battle scars, and they used to make me reconsider my words when I was a boy. I never wished to excite the wrath of a man who had the jagged teeth of a wyrm.

"King Cadwallon is moving in beside you, as you discussed. The other kings are leading their men in behind him as soon as he's gone. Eiludd is the first to come. They'll wait to attack until they think they're needed," Eowa informs me quickly and before I have to ask.

"Or until they see your skinny arses running home in defeat," Aldfrith cackles. I roll my eyes at him in annoyance. Just once, it would be nice to have his full support without the references to possible defeat.

I seem to be surrounded by men and beasts sent to test my patience today.

"My thanks Eowa," I say, and I mean it. In the pale daylight, I catch his eye, and we both chuckle at Aldfrith's expense. The old man simply beams with delight.

"Good, you're friends and allies as well as brothers. Now, and only now, I hope you understand, I'm released from my oath to your father and can go and damn well die if I please." He turns his horse whilst we watch him in surprise. I never guessed our father had given the stubborn bastard such a heavy task. Poor sod, no wonder he's been so sour-faced for the last ten years. My father gave him a commission that even he couldn't accomplish.

"We fight together, then, brother," I say in response to Aldfrith's words. Eowa reaches over to grab the back of my head, our horses sliding next to each other and, more amazingly, tolerating one another. Gunghir has always been friends with only one horse, and it just so happens to be my brother's.

Like he and I, Gunghir and his brother beast have more often than not worked against each other. He's named Sleipnir, Eowa's attempt to outdo the name for my horse. He's named after Woden's horse. I think the name is better than Gunghir, but then, Gunghir is a sharpened blade; Sleipnir is far more contented. He's a horse built for riding and not for war.

"Yes, we do, and at the end of the day, we'll be named as joint rulers of Mercia."

His easily offered words surprise me.

"No other bugger will be able to stand against us," Eowa hastily assures me as he holds me close to him, almost the embrace of a lover, only this means more. We're brothers, and we're united.

King Edwin can throw anything he damn well chooses at us.

As brothers, we're too strong to be beaten.

This battle is won before it's even begun.

32

AD632 - EDWIN OF NORTHUMBRIA
BATTLE OF HÆÐFELD

I feel the eyes of another warrior on me, even over the seething mass of fighting men. I love battle, but more for the rewards it brings me than for the action itself.

I like to plan and enact my strategy. But this, this is not my scheme. I know I've been fooled into an unwise course of action by Cadwallon and his allies and by Lord Eowa's brother in particular.

I fear it's Cadwallon's eyes that watch me as I try to salvage some order from the chaos before me.

I should have known better than to follow the few stray warriors when I saw my son chasing them. I genuinely thought that my scouts had found the enemy. But the men they found weren't outriders. Instead, they were sent to lead us to this battle site. A place not of my choosing, for who would decide to fight on the wrong side of a river to their kingdom, where the water lies between the safety of retreat? Only a fool, and that's not for what I wish to be remembered.

I blame my son, Osfrith. It was he who raced forward with his men on spying the opportunity. It was he who swayed the rest of my warriors away from their commands. He who caught me with his enthusiasm for what he hoped would be an easy kill.

I could almost think he was working against me if I hadn't been encouraging my men as well.

I'd been fighting with the Northumbrians at the front of the shield wall. But when the first shield wall of my enemy gave way, I knew it was all too easy. I retreated to my horse to see just what damage had been done to my numbers.

The red of bodies swirls around the hooves of my horse. The beast, a stray I found wandering the riverbank, nudging the dead for any sign of life, doesn't belong to me. It's unhappy with my weight upon its back, with the stench of sweat, piss and fear that I bring with me. It's restive, and I think I should let it go, but I need to see what's happening.

As I look outwards, I observe Osfrith fighting to the right-hand side, as though possessed by the devil himself. Eadfrith labours to the left. My warriors take the centre and King Sigeberht of the East Angles, intended as the reserve force, presses his two hundred and fifty men close behind mine. He doesn't see the futility that I do. He thinks to fight for his Christian God. That he'll win with God's help on his side.

I'm beginning to think the Christian God is as much of a fickle bastard as my old Gods because, unless I'm much mistaken, this battle will see my death.

A cry of fury erupts from inside my body. I feel as though the world trembles as my wrath pours from me. A great tidal wave of anger and frustration. Why the fuck did I let myself get drawn into this? Why couldn't I just be happy with what my God had already gifted me? Why couldn't I have practised the conciliation he advocates?

If only I'd made it to the River Idle, the site of my previous victory. I know that I'd not be facing such a complete defeat, then.

My anger drives me to jump from the horse's back, ensuring I land cleanly in the river, with my weapons intact. Then I'm striding forward, my warriors who act as my guard rushing to catch me. They withdrew with me and have been watching me suspiciously ever since, wondering what they should do or whether their lord has once and for all pissed himself with fear and left his men to die.

If today can be saved, I'll have to be the one to save it. On my own. It was my belief in myself that gave me first Deira and then Bernicia to combine as Northumbria. It will be my convictions that holds the kingdom together.

Not my uncharismatic sons with their dark moods and arrogant behaviour.

Certainly not my God.

Still, I say a swift prayer to the Christian God, imploring him to ensure victory, for if I don't win, Northumbria will plunge back into paganism. Without pause for breath, I entreat my old Gods as well. The ones Penda prays to. I can only hope they still hear me. That in their glee at my fate, they see their work at play and the opportunity to meddle with the fate of men. They are the better Gods, the stronger Gods. The warrior Gods. Not this frail God who did little but let his son die on his behalf.

The water is chill around my ankles, streaked with the red of blood and the reek of vomit and piss. The ground on its far side, when I reach it again, is churned with the passage of hundreds of feet. It sucks at my boots, as though the dead men try to drag me to Hell for my failure to protect them all; for putting them in this position in the first place.

They're all good Christian men, but as I've just done, they've probably all said their prayers to the Old Gods as well. Men in battle will do anything to take another breath, live a little longer. There's no glory in death. Not anymore.

My gaze is firmly fixed where I know King Cadwallon was sitting upon his horse. If nothing more, I plan on killing that Christian bastard. He's my foster brother and a man who should have loved me until we both met our deaths, in the arms of pliant women, not here, on a frigid flood plain with winter pressing at my heels and death stalking me.

I heft my war axe into my hand. Feel my shield in my other hand. I've always fought my most dangerous battles with these two weapons and nothing else. A dull helm, a dented thing inherited from one of Cadwallon's father's dead warriors, sits on my head while a byrnie covers my chest, stinking of rust and sweat.

My iron-ringed tunic moves around my body as I walk. I realise that in the past, when I fought for my birthright and when the assassins came to steal my life, I didn't possess this fine piece of equipment. It came when I became a Christian king and not before. Embroidered through the rigid metal rings is a white cross of the new Church. It took half a year to make, but it'll win me no battles now. It's for display, not battle. I hope to be wrapped in it within my grave if I die here, but I have no other use for it.

I shrug it from my body.

I want to fight with the same weapons that have always brought me victory.

The cloak is left behind me, its weight lifting from my shoulders, bringing far more relief than discarding it should have done.

I've been weighed down by my caution and the words of the Christian God who says all men must seek salvation for their sins.

Far better to sin first.

Men move aside as I cleave my way to the front of the second shield wall. Some bob their heads on witnessing their king amongst them, shorn of all his kingly devices. I'm a warrior first and foremost and a king only second. And only because my skills allow me to become a king.

I growl with battle rage. With my shield above me, I stand behind the first rank of the shield wall, just waiting for the opportunity to step into the front line.

It's not long in coming as the man before me falls prey to a slicing action to his lower legs. Forgetting he protects others, he lowers his shield with a scream of pain, allowing one of the enemy to slice at his neck with a massive war axe.

His breath catches in his throat as blood fills his mouth. I yank him backwards, standing on his lifeless limbs and plugging the gap before the enemy can sneak their way through.

I drop my shield to protect my lower legs as best as possible. I don't want the same thing to happen to me.

I brace myself against the attack of the foe-men opposite. I hear his cackle of laughter.

I'm going to kill him, and I'm going to enjoy it, be he Christian or pagan, Mercian, Dal Riatan, Briton or Pict. I'm going to slay everyone here. And then, when I stand victorious on a mountain of dead men, their eyes staring at a Heaven they'll never be admitted to, waiting for a raven from the Old Gods to come and pick their eyes clean, then, and only then, will I chose which God to follow.

But first, first, I must kill this man.

I strain against his weight on my shield, the sudden pressure unnerving me. The man is strong, very strong. Above the roar of battle and screams of terror, I can still hear him, his laughter reverberating around my head as though it were a prayer the monks sing.

I move my shoulder a little to ensure I have my weight as evenly balanced as possible, even though I'm standing slightly off-centre, to the left. Whilst I'd like to kill him with a direct thrust of my axe, I think I need to catch him somewhat off guard and drive my weapon into his exposed body.

Confident I'm as balanced as I can be, I release the pressure from my shoulder, and immediately the shield tries to pivot to the right, the warrior opposite me laughing even louder at this seemingly effortless attack.

He cackles until my axe presses through the cleft made by my rotating shield, impaling his exposed back as he tries to squeeze his weapon through the gap caused by the shield to the right. His screech of rage is almost comical after all of his laughter. As he turns to face me, his eyes wild and bloodshot, blood sheeting his face, I snatch my axe back, maroon dripping through my gloved hand. I slash across his exposed and twisted neck.

He dies with gurgling laughter on his lips. I stamp on his head before retreating behind my shield. I only managed to open a small gap in the shield wall. In order to surge through this second shield wall, I need to open a far larger space. I don't yet know if that would be to my warriors' advantage.

The more men that can be picked off in the shield wall, the better.

Once more, I brace myself for the next foe-man to fill the shield wall opposite me. I'm not left to wait for long. The shield that slams against mine is driven home with such strength, I almost stumble over the body at my feet.

"Move the dead," I shout to the men behind me. They bend to carry out the task.

It's always struck me as ironic how the dead of our side can cause the death of their allies. Bodies fall where they will, with no thought for the next move. And they always, always get in the way.

My weapon is slick in my hand. With my shoulder against the shield, I raise my hand to wipe the weapon on my byrnie. Then, when the grip still isn't tight enough, on my face as well.

My face is slick with sweat from my efforts. The blood that now also covers it will make me look more frightening than the man I just killed. Whether I look like a vengeful angel or Woden made flesh, I little care.

A disturbance behind me. I turn to gaze at my son, Eadfrith. He looks how I imagine I do, his face sheeted in blood, beard dark with the stuff, his helm slightly askew. I ponder what he wants. He speaks to Sigward, raising his voice above the clamour, but still, I can hear nothing. I don't want to be distracted from my role at the shield wall.

A hand on my shoulder and Sigward makes it clear that my son needs to speak with me. Sigward slides into the position that I reluctantly give up. I was getting ready to attack the warrior opposite me.

"What is it?" I demand with annoyance. My son's eyes flash dangerously at me. He's angry with me. We've tried to make amends for my past treatment of him, but even so, I still find it hard to look at him and acknowledge him as a warrior and not just as my son, a boy who can't make the right decisions.

"We're heavily outnumbered. My outriders say they've even more in reserve."

I don't understand why he's brought me from the shield wall to discuss this. I gaze at him without comprehension when he doesn't say anything else.

Around me, the shield wall shifts and buckles, an attack further up the line making the men here groan with the effort of keeping their shields up. I itch to be back amongst them, but my son is patiently waiting for me to say something. His head moves from side to side, his mouth opening and closing, and still, I don't speak.

"What of it?" I finally shout, my anger intensifying with every prolonged moment of his silence.

"Father, we should retreat," he offers softly but loudly enough that others hear his words. I cuff him on the side of the head, not minding that the attack probably injures me as much as him. My shoulder already aches. The new movement makes it throb. I don't even comprehend that he names me his father. I know he never calls me that.

"I'm not fucking retreating before Cadwallon and his allies. Now go and bloody fight," I roar, turning angrily away. But my son has the timidity to call me back.

"But father?" he implores. I look at him with the cold eyes of a man who realises he simply doesn't love his son. No matter what my new God has said, no matter what the old God has said, my son is a disappointment to me. I almost tell him so because my wrath is so great.

"Fight, Eadfrith, get your arse back in the shield wall and don't seek me out again unless it's because you have Cadwallon's head in your hand."

I don't watch him leave. The shield wall is breaking up. I need to fight with my warriors. Dismissing Eadfrith immediately from my thoughts, I rush to reinforce the shield wall.

The shouts of those who are my foe-men reach my ears. Their words are hard for me to understand. It takes me long moments to realise that the men speak a language I've not heard for a long time.

The Picts have come.

I peer into the slowly deepening gloom of the day. I've not forgotten it's nearly winter, and the dark will soon coat the land. My resentment bubbles again as I spy the battle standard I never thought to see again.

That of King Æthelfrith of Northumbria.

My brother by marriage. His son now battles against me beneath that same banner.

The man I personally killed and whose kingdom I inherited on his death.

My ire for Eadfrith and his failed mission to the Picts fuels my fury. I rush against the foe-men, not caring who gets in my way.

The fighting has broken down into stray areas where men fight behind shields and others fight one on one. I want to get to Lord Eanfrith because it won't be anyone else who comes against me. Even his brother, Lord Oswald, has decided his best course is to make a peace with me in order to claim back some small part of his family holdings.

Not Lord Eanfrith, though.

He always was a stubborn young man.

I can't see him amongst the hubbub of men and bodies, but I find a man I know to be a Pict because he attacks with their strange square shield, his face covered by a helm and a nose guard. He's a man with great wealth, perhaps a member of their royal family, but he's not the man I want to kill.

Not that I care.

I raise my axe to step around him, to slice his neck clean open so that I can continue my search for Eanfrith. Only the Pict warrior reads my actions before I can make them. His shield is raised at the crucial moment, knocking my lower arm, sending my axe slipping from my hand.

I lift my shield in a similar movement to his as I frantically try to protect myself from the colossal spear he's pointing menacingly in my direction. The length of the shaft on it is the only thing that currently protects me. He simply doesn't have enough room to aim at me.

"My Lord." A voice from behind me. I feel a long seax being pressed into my hand. I'm grateful for the weapon, but the loss of my axe is a major blow to me. I've bartered with myself that if I only used my axe, I would win this battle with the help of whichever God was the strongest.

It now seems I've made a poor bargain.

The man's eyes are a deep green in the gathering dusk. For a moment, I gaze at him, speculating about who he is and why he would leave his land to fight for a man who's not even his king.

Never taking his eyes from my face, he cautiously moves back two steps, and then three, four and five. I almost don't realise his intent until he raises his spear and aims it. I move my shield before my body and wait for the thunk as the metal hits the leather and wood of my shield.

But the noise never comes. Instead, I hear a voice beckoning me onwards, and when I lower my shield, it's to see the Pictish warrior dead at the feet of Ohtrad.

I lift my eyes to him, and he offers me a slight bow.

I turn once more to look for Eanfrith's standard-bearer, surprised when it's merely a few steps in front of me.

Did I just kill Lord Eanfrith? Why else would the standard-bearer be so close? Only then does the foe-man move aside. I meet the eyes of my predecessor and my sister combined.

The world spins alarmingly for me as he opens his mouth to speak.

"Hello, Uncle Edwin."

33

AD632 - CADWALLON OF GWYNEDD
THE BATTLE OF HÆðFELD

Horses stream past me across the flood plains as though pursued by the coming night as I ride onwards. I've scouted the area during the last month, and I know where I'm going even though the horses temporarily block my path.

The return of the riderless horses can mean only one thing. King Edwin has found Penda or is about to, and battle will soon be joined. Penda and his horses amaze me all over again. I've never heard of horses being able to take themselves back to safety when an enemy threatens them, but that's what Penda's horses do. He doesn't even have a youth who leads them. No, his vicious bastard of a horse does all that by himself.

I half think the animal is possessed by his Old God's spear, as though the name he gave it was simply a realisation of its true spirit. Eowa doesn't have the same way with animals.

As I finally get my first glimpse of the warriors lining up against each other, I see an area that's been put aside within which the animals can shelter. Eowa's men have pulled together a temporary rope structure to keep them safe for when they either have to surge forward and kill the men who are fleeing the battle site or use them themselves to flee the battle.

If we should be defeated.

Penda never takes the same precautions. When he runs after retreating enemies, it's as though he's the horse himself. I've never seen a man quite so fleet-footed.

I've never, ever, seen him retreat either.

Penda's man was curt when he delivered his message, and I asked him if Penda was well. His response was abruptly in the affirmative, but until I cast my eye over Penda, I harboured half a thought that the worry of the battle and these last moment changes might have undone his usual good cheer and unfailing belief in his abilities.

I was wrong.

I'm pleased.

Of all my allies, it's Penda who matters the most. It's he who'll give me the victory I need. A pity I plan on doing more upon the death of Edwin than I've ever told Penda, but by then, I hope Penda will be as keen to engage in my wholehearted acts of revenge as I am.

I don't want Northumbria, but I don't want anyone else to have it either. Not yet.

I want to leave the landscape empty of men and beasts.

When Edwin is dead, I'll have to kill Lord Eanfrith and whoever claims the kingdom of Deira to accomplish my goals.

I've no problem with that, despite the reservations I voiced to Penda about having to choose whether to kill Edwin's nephew or his son. Hopefully, all of his bastard children will die in this battle. It'll make the coming months far easier.

I don't plan on returning to Gwynedd anytime soon. This winter, I'll feast within Yeavering and take my rest at Bamburgh.

Fuck Edwin. I want to live how he did.

Penda and Eowa have arranged their combined strength of men into a long snaking shield wall, far enough away from the banks of the River Don that Edwin will have no choice but to cross it in order to attack them if he decides to do so. And it's either cross the river or defeat. Edwin won't countenance a defeat.

I count about three hundred and fifty men and muse on where the rest are until I see some of them bolting across the far side of the flood plain, splashing their horses through the mild flow of the river. At its deepest, it reaches the front horse's knee height. Ideally, I wanted the river at Edwin's back to be deeper, in fuller flow, but a man can drown in water from his drinking horn. Some foolish men will underestimate the force of the river, and weighted down with their byrnies and swords, they'll sink to the bottom.

It'll be a death like a baptism. I almost wish them peace from it. I've heard drowning is a more pleasant way to die than from a slit throat or gaping belly wound, although I'm not sure who's told me so. After all, the men involved would have been long dead before they could tell me about it in person.

My brother, Cadfan, hurries to war with me, and he has his men close to him. We don't bring a battle standard. There's no need. King Edwin knows who comes to kill him. I wonder if he's always known that it would come to this.

He should have killed me three years ago when he had the chance. I've never understood why he didn't. I would have no such reservations in killing him.

Suddenly, from the far side of the riverbank, the first head of a warrior is seen, and soon many of them face us, still mounted. Two men in shining armour and on fine horses take the time to gaze at us from their very slight elevation. The river is no more than a shallow gash across the landscape. Any riverbank is little more than a build-up of muck and slime that's been dragged from the hills to the point it gets washed up and abandoned on the side of the river, pushed out by its force.

There's no advantage in keeping to that higher ground. It lasts for the length of a horse and then dips down back into the flood plain upon which that I already stand.

It's been an overcast day, and yet, although it should be turning black for the coming night, the clouds suddenly part above us and the day is thrown into the brightness of a summer's evening. I take this as an excellent sign that my Christian God, not Edwin's one, is keen for the battle to take place now.

I'm sure Edwin reads the same portent into it.

I slide from my horse, handing the reins to my servant, who runs with the beast to stable him with the other animals at the rear of the battlefield. If we all lose our lives here, Edwin will ride away with more than enough horses for every nobleman in his kingdom. They'll be set for life.

I'm armed with all the weapons a man can need. I hold my shield loosely in my hand, weighing it in and deciding whether to put it over my back or leave it where it is.

I don't let myself become distracted by what Edwin and his men are doing. Soon enough, they'll advance on us. Or they won't. The choice is Edwin's alone.

A man rushes through the press of bodies and bobs his head quickly to me. He's slight and sprightly. I assume that he's one of the warriors Penda uses for his lightning-fast attacks on the enemy. He's not one of the burly warriors who could kill twenty men without breaking a sweat. No, he can slide between the legs of warriors in the shield wall and slice their calf muscles without them even realising he's there.

Penda loves this man. He thinks of him as a secret weapon as so many mistake him for a boy, nothing more.

"What is it, Willigang?" I ask urgently. Has he come to tell me unlooked-for news?

He bobs again, probably surprised that I know his name, but Penda has spoken of him so often that I can't help but know his name.

"Lord Penda wished to apologise for the abrupt change of tactics, and he wants me to thank you for coming so quickly."

I'm surprised to hear the apology and not at all dumbfounded when he presses something into my hand and then darts back to his place at the front of the shield wall.

I look down to see the sharp object that's been placed there. Slowly I unfold my hand, and then I laugh with delight. Penda, the pagan bastard, has sent me one of his pagan trinkets to ensure I have the support of his Gods as well as mine. Grinning with delight to discover that Penda is as riddled with suspicions and fears about my

God as many men are about theirs, I thread the chain holding the replica of one of Woden's wolves around my neck, being careful to tuck it beneath my byrnie. I wouldn't want a man to strangle me with the weight of the Old Gods.

Eiludd has advanced his hundred men to reinforce the shield wall, and everyone is ready for battle now. All that remains is for Edwin to make his position clear.

Long moments pass, and the men at the front of the shield wall fall silent. The moments before battle are a time for contemplation, but too much silence is bad for a man's soul.

I rearrange my weapons once more, my shield on my back, for now, my seax hanging on my weapons belt with a war axe that another of Penda's warriors gifted to me when I showed a great deal of interest in the weapon. It's a lethal piece of equipment. Held correctly, the axe's head can impact a man on his head or in his stomach, and then with the correct sleight of hand, it can slice open the skin and expose a man's lifeblood to the elements.

Death is normally a welcome relief from an attack with a war axe.

It's a weapon that Edwin uses to great efficiency. That's why I've taken so much time to learn how to use it correctly. If I get the chance to meet Edwin in battle, I'm going to rip his belly open and then his throat. I might even force a hole in his scalp so that I can peel the skin from his head. I've not yet decided on all the injuries I'll inflict on him, but they'll be many and varied.

The men begin to shuffle their feet with impatience. We've waited a very long time for this moment. I'm as keen as they are for the battle to start. For a moment, I worry that in making our intentions so clear, Penda might well have convinced Edwin that he shouldn't attack.

Yet we've ensured that our forces are evenly matched for the time being at least. Whatever Edwin's heard about our numbers, he might well be considering his scouts' poor reckoners and hoping that it means his God is smiling on him, ready to give him the victory.

A roar of wind rushes across the flood plain. As I raise my arm to shield my eyes from the dry dust that blows across the exposed ground, Edwin and his men must decide to move into place because suddenly, as I wipe the dust and tears from my eyes, Penda, Eowa, Eiludd and their men issue a roar of readiness. They'd only do so if they had an enemy preparing to face them.

It's now that we need Eanfrith and his wiry Pictish men to assault the enemy with their extra-long spears and uncanny accuracy. Again, it's as though the wind has conjured them up. They peel away from my men, who escorted them into their current positions and race for the front of the shield wall.

Eanfrith has warned me and Penda that some of his men will wish to rush out into the space between the two forces and will throw their spears from there. He says they know it'll be a greater risk to them, but he also says they prefer to taunt their enemy. Their skills are astounding, and I want to use them for more than a single throw. I hope none of them meets their death before the battle starts.

Penda's men are stamping their feet and striking their shields as they enrage the enemy. I imagine I hear the hiss of the spears being thrown because I certainly heed the cries of outrage. Abruptly, the enemy shield wall is a tightly held physical barrier, as the sounds of swords on wood add their voices to the quiet day.

Battle has begun.

For now, there's little for me to do but await my turn. At the front of the shield wall Penda, or so I hope, will be living up to his legendary status. If he doesn't slay at least fifty of the men, I'll be very much surprised.

A whoosh of air around me and my men and our shields are suddenly above our heads. It appears that Edwin has a few Pictish warriors of his own to use against us. I grin with delight. The odds between our two forces have been evened out. This won't be an easy victory, but nothing I've ever wanted has been comfortable to achieve. Nothing apart from winning the support of Penda.

I can hear the cries of Penda, Eowa, Eiludd and their war chiefs as they encourage their men to hold firm and resist the attack from the Northumbrians. Penda says he doesn't want a single step forward to be taken by the combined force. He wants Edwin to come to him. Then, when he deems the time is right, Penda will shout his orders to move backwards. In so doing, he'll unbalance the first rank of men on our opponent's shield wall, compelling many of them to their knees when the force they were leaning against gives way.

That way, the men in the second rank of Edwin's shield wall will have no choice but to rush forward and take the place of their fallen comrades. And by stepping directly over them, the remainder of the men will follow them, unable to see what's happened. Those brave men from the front will die with their heads pressed down into the marshy ground beneath their comrades' feet.

Even from my place, in the fourth rank of men, I can feel the press of so many bodies, one against the other, and my blood rushes through me, and my heart pumps loudly in my ears.

I'm listening intently, but I almost miss the call for the shield wall to retreat four steps and nearly find myself trampled to death. A hand on my arm steadies me and keeps me on my feet. I meet the grinning face of Lord Eanfrith, would be King of Bernicia.

"Be careful, My Lord," he shouts, but he's running to meet his men, those spear throwers who still live. So he gives me little thought. I don't even have the opportunity to thank him.

A thud on my shield, amazingly still above my head, reminds me of where I am. I tighten my grip on my war axe and brush Eanfrith from my thoughts. He'll be dead by the end of the day, along with his uncle, Edwin. There's no need to muddle my thoughts with that knowledge now.

The shield wall has, as Penda demanded, moved back four steps, making the other men think they might have broken us. But now is the time for our side to start compelling them backwards.

Behind me, I know more than see that the warriors from Powys, Alt Clut and Dal Riata are reinforcing us. I can feel it in the increased pressure along the shield wall. We must now be at least six men deep and a hundred men wide. I can't see how Edwin's side fares, but I imagine it's poorly.

I hope it's poorly.

Soon the fighting will break up into smaller sections, and that's when I'll be able to hunt out all the men I want to kill. Despite any assurances I've given to Penda, I want to kill Edwin myself.

I hope Penda understands that.

A hail of spears flies above my head. I duck once more under my shield to protect my head. I'm becoming more and more impatient. I should have demanded to be in the front rank of the shield wall, not waiting at the back.

The man beside me, my brother Cadfan, cautions me. He knows me too well.

"Easy, Cadwallon, it'll be soon."

I can't see him behind my helm or my shield. His words only anger me further. But that's probably his intention.

Once more, there's a heave of momentum as men rush forward. Then I hear Penda and Eowa's voices again, raised in unison. They're breaking up the shield wall. Edwin's men won't know that a second shield wall has been formed behind us. They'll think that we're weakening.

The roar of an outraged bear rips from my throat. My chance is coming.

The original shield wall divides into four squares of attackers with crystal clear accuracy. I'm to the far left, Penda to the centre with Eowa next to him, and on the edge, Eiludd.

The squares of men will rotate so that the enemy believe they're making progress when all they're doing is being worn out by a steady stream of the enemy who'll never tire of attacking them.

My brother is with me. He echoes my battle roar. I hear my men shout my name in recognition of the sound.

Finally, I get my first glimpse of the enemy as the group of men I'm within rotates slowly. My hand has been so firmly clasping my war axe that I momentarily worry that my fingers might be frozen in place.

I take the time to flex them, and then a weapon is against my chest-level shield. I can hear the man who owns the weapon breathing and feel his weapon beating about my shield. I hope he knows that he's about to die at the hands of Cadwallon of Gwynedd.

I take a deep breath, weave my war axe from side to side. Only then do I seek above my shield and see a mass of dull metal and painted leather on the opposite side. All the men wear helms, but my war axe will see the metal as no deterrent in its desire to spill a man's brains.

My axe hits the helm. I appreciate that the man has faltered, no doubt stunned by the heavy weight of the weapon. It's not light. My brother momentarily drops his shield and uses his sword to impale our enemy. The man would stagger from his head wound if those behind him didn't hold him in place.

My brother is quickly back in place, a faint smile on his lips, which is about all I can see of him beneath his helm. He's had his first blood. Now we employ the same tactic against the man attacking him. As I lower my shield to slash his belly open with my axe blade, I feel the spray of the man's warm blood in my mouth and think of myself in heaven.

Northumbrian blood. I've been waiting to taste it since I became King of Gwynedd.

All around me, the noise of battle is so loud that it's impossible to determine any of the words that men try to shout at me. I simply roar back and hope that's the answer for which they were looking.

The four squares are working well, but I think the fighting will soon become man on man, Northumbrian against one of my allies.

I hunger for that to happen.

Abruptly, I lose my balance on the slippery, marshy land and look down to see the permanently staring eyes of a dead man. I hope he's not one of my men, but it's impossible to tell. His clothing is sheeted in blood, and his face has been stamped on so many times that his nose has cracked open. The sight makes me laugh, a great wave of delight from my belly.

"Cadwallon." A voice finally breaks through my delight. A warrior stands before me. His clothes are bloodied and stained, but he looks to be a great warrior for all that. I muse on who he is as I drop my shield slightly and step into his attack.

He would have done better to assault me. There was no need to notify me of his presence. I've managed to hang my war axe back on my weapon's belt. Now I hold my sword. It's a good weapon for personal combat. I assume that's where the battle is currently heading.

I dance into the warrior, careful to make my body appear as though it's going to the right and not to the left. The warrior stumbles as he watches me. When he decides to defend himself from the expected attack, I follow through with my intention to go to the left, slicing my sword across his byrnie. It has no impact on the outside, but I imagine a deep bruise is already forming on his body. I'm a strong man. I always have been.

My enemy 'woofs' as the air is driven from his body. I step even closer to him. My sword raised to neck height. He tries to bring his shield high to protect himself, but he's too weak without air. The sword isn't the best weapon for slicing throats, but I saw it through, all the same, watching with satisfaction as the man faces his death, almost pitying him for the mess my sword makes of his neck.

He dies in pain. I don't even do him the honour of waiting for him to take the last breath before I move on to the next man before me. I yank the blade from his neck and perhaps hasten his end along the way.

I don't know the man, and I owe him nothing, not even a good Christian death if he happens to be a Christian.

I take the time to look around me to gain some understanding of how the battle is progressing, but I can't see anything. I need to be above the battle to decide who's winning and losing; anyway, the battle is in its infancy. False belief now could be my undoing.

The square of men continues to rotate, and another warrior comes to test his luck against me. He's small and compact and has no idea that he faces a king. I've chosen not to go into battle in my ornate battle gear. It's just as well to kill a man in something that isn't adorned with precious metals. It always takes too long to clean, and anyway, I'm a warrior first and a king second. When I fight, I just want to be a warrior.

Admittedly, when the battle is over, then, well then, I do want to be a king.

My opponent sizes my weapons. I grin at him, probably a harsh face when the blood and grime smeared upon it are considered. Not that he looks much better. He must have killed some of Penda's men, or rather some of Eowa's. Like him, I believe that Penda's men are touched by the Old Gods. No man can kill them. No Old God walks the battle line for Edwin, and so they'll live to fight on and on.

I watch my foe's devious eyes for a time. When he fails even to step forward and attack me, I pool my weight on the balls of my feet and rush into him, my sword sliding across his belly as I do so. He wears a thick padded byrnie, but still, its contents spill open. The trace of blood can be seen pulsing behind the dirty material.

I've not killed him, but I've bloodied him for the first time this battle. The anger on his face makes it clear he wasn't expecting me to act as I did.

I wonder what he was expecting?

He raises his weapon and then stops. What is he looking at?

He hesitates for a moment. I consider if he's realised I'm a king. Only then I hear Penda's battle cry, and I exactly know what's upset him.

No man should ever watch Penda in battle. Certainly not when he's on the opposition.

Penda moves as no man I've ever seen. He's lithe, fast, deadly, and more than anything, his laughter drives even the most Christian men to cross themselves and hope to be anywhere but there.

Really, I'd quite like to let the man watch Penda, but he's an enemy, and he needs to die. I take advantage of his distraction and move into him, using my sword to hack open his neck. Such strength fuses through me that I feel as though one of Penda's Gods does guide my hand. Never before have I managed to remove a man's head with only one blow.

The body falls before me. Confident that my brother watches my back, I follow my dead enemy's example and turn to see what Penda is doing.

He and his men are fighting with the force of giants. They cut and slash with wild abandon, almost too fast for my eyes to witness. Penda's face is wreathed in blood; his eyes black pits as though he comes from my own God's Hell. His armbands are encased in blood that rushes so deeply up his arms every time he moves; a hail of red rain is left to fall over the ground or his enemy.

I pity every man who must face him.

Penda's warriors are just as terrifying. All they lack is his laughter. Their faces are grim and determined. They have only one role today. To kill Northumbrians. To kill Christians.

Stray arrows fly overhead. I duck without thinking as I hear the whistle of one of the weapons. I swing my shield to protect myself and feel the arrow impale itself in the wood of the shield.

As I said, I could almost believe that Penda's Gods are dictating this battle and my actions as well. When we leave here, as victors, I might have to atone for my sins. Or I might just have to hedge my chances and offer a sacrifice to his Gods as well as mine.

Thankfully, my God likes money and treasures, not blood, which is Penda's Gods' currency.

"My Lord." A voice bellows to me. I turn to see the soon-to-be King Eanfrith and his grinning face. He's enjoying this battle as much as I am.

"Edwin is losing huge numbers," he calls and then he's gone, swept away from me by his rotating square of men. This tactic that Penda jokingly described one night is proving to be a great success.

I believe we won't need our reinforcements.

Almost.

Suddenly, a host of new men join the battle for King Edwin. I can see them running along the marshy bank of the river, rushing to reinforce the men who already stand there. This could be it—the time for the ultimate betrayal of the Northumbrians.

I stand battle ready, men glancing blows against my shield and my sword, but for the time being, the killing edge has left us all. We're tired and exhausted after the initial encounter. I think I might welcome what comes next.

I hear a voice, and I imagine it to be Edwin's, forcing his men to greater effort, and now everyone on our side is complicit in letting them think they're winning. Men purposefully stumble and allow the enemy reinforcements to mingle amongst us. That's until Penda, Eowa, Eiludd, and I raise our voices once more and then we're all running, the word 'retreat' on our lips.

I hear the whooping joy of Edwin's Northumbrian warriors and can imagine Edwin's grin of delight.

It won't last long.

As we turn to rush backwards, the new shield wall, commanded by old Clemen and Domnall, opens to allow us to pass through onto ground that's free from blood and the shattered remains of bodies.

As soon as Penda, who of course must be the last warrior to escape through the small gaps, is to the rear of the shield wall, the shields all overlap with a bang that might as well be the crash of the heavens closing against the men of the new God.

They'll gain no admittance here.

Above our heads, the spears of Eanfrith's men fly once more, taking with them a sure death. The wet thuds as the spears find a target makes me wince with sympathy, but I'm too busy regaining my breath and taking stock of my men and the other commanders.

Penda walks behind me and slaps me on the back as I try to recover.

"Fuck, did you see them? Like flies to shit," he bellows, his loud voice permeating over the new roar of battle.

"You fight well," Penda remembers to compliment. I laugh at him, even though my breath is hitching in my throat.

"You fight like a God," I congratulate him, and he just grins again.

"I know," he concurs and struts off to check on his men. The second shield wall is holding firm against Edwin. For some, the battle must begin all over again. This will exhaust even the strongest of Edwin's men.

I continue to walk back towards where the horses have been stationed. I want to mount one, see how the battle progresses and see if I'll be needed again.

I certainly hope I am. But with so many allies, it's imperative that they all be given the glory of the victory. I don't like to share, but I will on this occasion. I don't want bad blood to flow through my allies as it does through Edwin's.

Near the back of the line, I come across the well-dressed man Penda allowed into our fold. He's watching the battle with hardened eyes. He might have wanted Edwin dead, but to see so many other men die for a lost cause is hard to do. I know. I've seen it myself.

"Might I?" I ask, gesturing towards the horse, and he dismounts quickly and without speaking, probably pleased to be given the opportunity to tear his tortured eyes away from the view before him.

I heave myself into the saddle, careful to heft my shield over my shoulder and replace my sword in its scabbard. I don't want to injure the man's horse inadvertently.

In the dimming light of the day, it takes me a long time to decipher what I'm seeing. It's just a heaving mass of moving men. A few steps forward and then a few steps back. Some fall as flying arrows or spears hit them. Others stand even though they have arrows or spears embedded in their bodies, their bodies allowing them to fight on provided they don't move from their position. Their death will come only when they dislodge the weapon that'll kill them but hasn't just yet.

I admire the resolve of all the men. This isn't a pleasant battle.

And then, above all the flying weapons and cries of battle glory, I see a man mounted on a white horse doing the same as I am. I meet the eyes of my foster brother, King Edwin. Even at such a great distance, his eyes are defiant, but they show me all I need to know. He's losing, and he knows it.

34

AD632 - EANFRITH OF BERNICIA
BATTLE OF HÆðFELD

I watch the fighting play out before me from behind the second shield wall. I can't see everything because the land is too flat, but I know one certain fact.

Cadwallon and the rest of my allies are winning the battle. King Edwin will surely need a miracle from his new God to ensure he doesn't die here.

I can taste his death on my tongue.

My warriors and I have made an enormous impression on the men we fight with side by side. All of the war leaders, every single one of them, have made use of my spearmen. I didn't think we'd need the thousand spears we carried from the kingdom of the Picts, but I know that the men will soon run out of spears to throw. They'll have to resort to more traditional weapons unless they take the time to retrieve the spears from the silent bodies of the dead.

Soon it'll come down to single combat, and I have my uncle firmly in my sights. I plan on killing him. I don't much care that King Cadwallon wants that honour. It should fall to me as the most aggrieved family member to kill my traitorous uncle.

Beside me, Herebrod shouts in my ear to let me know he can see

Edwin. My eyes follow where he points, alighting on the figure of my uncle. I can see his standard-bearer just behind him.

I don't understand why he's advertising his position to me, but I'm relieved all the same. The worst part of this battle is that it's impossible to see who everyone is. The land is too flat to differentiate between the men of Northumbria and those of Cadwallon and Penda's alliance.

I keep my eyes firmly on Edwin's position in the shield wall, trying to fight my way directly to Edwin, warriors at my back. But the press of bodies is too great. I can't find my uncle and keep all my men together.

I slash at foe-men who try to stand in my way, knocking them to their knees and stealing their lives with my short sword. But still, more and more come, as though they wish to die on the weapons my men and I carry. As though Herebrod and I are lovers, they can't stay away from even though it will mean their death.

I kill one man, two and then suddenly I know ten men are dead on my blade, and I'm still no closer to Edwin. Panic begins to grow within me.

I can't miss this opportunity to kill my father's killer.

It would be dishonourable.

Abruptly a clear path opens up before my men and me. I rush toward Edwin's standard. They all know the real task for today is to allow me to slay my uncle.

Slowly I walk forward; my eyes fixed only on Edwin. He stands within a cohort of men who are trying to kill the warriors of Eiludd. They're not making any headway. My men flood into Eiludd's defensive position, strengthening it while allowing me to make my way to the front of the fighting.

I position myself in front of Edwin in his shield wall, just waiting.

And I'm rewarded with a vision of him standing in front of me. I get to meet his eyes for the first time in nearly twenty years.

This man killed my father, and I will take his life in revenge.

But first, I introduce myself.

35

AD632 - OSFRITH OF NORTHUMBRIA
BATTLE OF HÆÐFELD

I don't know who's winning this battle. I don't much care. If my father is winning, he won't be for long—the smug bastard.

I wish I'd managed to stand closer to him. It would have made it easier to attack him, to literally and figuratively stab him in the back. But he's placed Eadfrith and me away from him. I don't know if it's because he trusts us more than his other allies or less.

It's not always that easy to tell.

The battle has been raging since late afternoon. Thank goodness it was cold last night and the ground crisp beneath our feet. The location is not ideal, as close as it is to the river that flows at our backs. If we're forced to retreat, or rather when the few survivors are forced to flee, I imagine many will fall foul of the shallow water and marshy terrain. It will suck them down. Then one of the enemies will make a killing stroke and take the life from them with minimal effort.

I should be upset, but I'm not. The fewer of my father's faithful adherents there are upon his death, the better for me. He made no secret of his growing unhappiness with me. I intend to be proclaimed king in his place once I've killed him. Then it'll be advantageous that Northumbria has lost some of its best warriors. It would have been those men who would have wanted to defend the honour of their dead king, but I won't have time for that. Not when I'm the king.

I've pledged my allegiance to King Cadwallon, and he's given many assurances that I'll be king once my father meets his death. That's good enough for me. I'll be a better king than my father. I have more skill with my weapons. I'm about to prove that by becoming the reason for his death.

As my father once owed his position to the great king Rædwald of East Angles, I'll owe mine to Cadwallon of Gwynedd, my father's foster brother and his greatest enemy. I doubt we'll remain allies for long. Eventually, I'll have to turn on him and punish him for slaying my father, as I can hardly take the credit for that act.

I wonder what will happen between my brother and me? I'm sure he'll be shocked when I walk away from this battle with Cadwallon and Penda's support. Or maybe not. He's not the easiest man to decipher. He might already know what I've done and have just decided to keep it a secret from our father. Only time will tell. Either way, I'll be the king, and he won't be.

My father certainly erred when he failed to secure the allegiance of my brother and me. A fatal error for my father, the king, and a man that other men admire. A man that my brother and I do not.

I'm exhausted but nearing my goal. I've fought my way through wave after wave of the men from Gwynedd and Powys, overcoming my amazement that they've united together. I thought they hated one another.

My father's power to unite his enemies never fails to astound me.

I've slain at least ten men so far. They all died with anger and rage in their eyes. They hated the Northumbrians, my father most of all. Their fury made them easy to kill. I hope my wrath makes it easy for me to slay my father.

I signal to Actulf to follow me as I try and make the necessary move to get closer to my father. The battle is almost lost. I need to make the killing stroke to seal my bargain with Penda and Cadwallon.

Actulf has shared in my conspiracy with the alleged enemy. He's keen to help me now.

A foe-man steps into my path as I skirt my way along the second battle line. Cadwallon's changing tactics must have stranded the man. The first shield wall of Cadwallon's held for some time. Then he tricked everyone by making them think he was retreating before forming a second shield wall. I know my father labours to break through the second wall. I can see his standard-bearer near the point where the two opposing sides meet.

I'm holding my war axe in my left hand. My shield is draped over my back. The warrior is menacing with his iron helm and his well-worn leather byrnie. He's a man who fights for his living. I pull my sword loose and return my axe to my weapons belt. This won't be an easy fight.

He grins at me. I don't know if he recognises me or not. Maybe, he just thinks I'm a worthy kill.

At my back, Actulf beckons to say that he'll dispatch the enemy, but I have a mind to do it myself. I'm a deadly killer. I've had plenty of opportunities to hone my skills in the yearly raiding parties that attack the people to the north of Northumbria.

Actulf shakes his head at my decision and steps back regretfully. He respects me enough to know that I can beat anyone. He stands a watch against the coming attack.

I square off in front of the foeman. He's holding a sword and a shield, just as I do. He's bloody from the confrontations he's already won. His gloves flash with fluid that must be blood, and his arms, beneath his byrnie, bulge menacingly, the linen threatening to rip.

As I said, he's a man who's trained for this skirmish. But I don't recognise him as Cadwallon's warrior, so I can't talk my way out of this by saying that I fight for his lord's side.

I step forward, keen to get this over and done. My sword raised his sword clashes against mine. I place all my power behind that stroke, pressing my body weight onto the weapon. I'm tall and bulky, a great weight to press onto my enemy as he tries to fight. He'll have to work hard to get me off him.

The clang of battle surrounds me. But I'm smirking at the man, and he at me. I'm not sure which of us is in denial about our skills. I hope it's him. Obviously.

He surprises me by meeting my weight with his own. I feel stupid now. Effectively we're just both leaning against one another and doing little else. He's stalemated me when I thought I'd beaten him. If I step back, he might overbalance, or he might simply lower his sword and sweep it around so that it impales my body. Alternatively, he could do the same to me, and I might over balance.

I only have a moment to think about it before losing the advantage.

Decisively, I press forward again, doubling my body weight so that he'll think I'm trying to push him backwards. When I feel his stance shift, I drop my sword immediately and step back from him. Predictably he staggers forward, as I hoped he would. I slash my blade across his exposed back as he tumbles past me.

The byrnie he wears deadens the full impact of my manoeuvre, but it sends him to his knees behind me. Before he can recover, I pivot and grab his head, thrusting his neck upwards. As I still hold my sword, although I've dropped my shield, I reach for Actulf's seax. I exchange my sword for his weapon as mine is wedged behind the enemy's neck.

With a tug across the wounded man's neck, I hack him open, from side to side, his hand flailing uselessly at his side until it stills.

"Another kill, My Lord," Actulf offers appreciatively, making no mention of the savagery of the attack.

"Just not the one I want," I respond quickly, my eyes already scanning where I hope my father is fighting.

Actulf looks around me, ensuring no one takes advantage of my distraction. Really, we should have been the brothers, not me and Eadfrith.

The fighting is deadly. I can't deny that. Pockets of fierce attacks dot the landscape. I dispassionately watch as men I might know are hacked down in their prime. Many will not leave this place with their lives intact, my father being one of them. But I will, and I will be a king.

I grin as I roll that idea around my head. I'll be a king, King Osfrith of Northumbria; I like the sound of that.

"There," Actulf says. I look where he's pointing. I squint against the late winter sun shading the fighting with yellow hues and see what he's trying to tell me. Only two hundred feet from where I stand, my father's men face a concerted attack from some of Lord Eanfrith's men.

That mars my good mood. I've still not managed to rationalise why Cadwallon and Penda felt it necessary to include him in the war, my father's predecessor's son. He has no right to be here. He sure as fuck isn't about to fulfil my end of the bargain by killing my father. Eanfrith's standard-bearer upset me when I first saw it on the battlefield. Cadwallon could at least have warned me of his ally.

I wonder if that's the prize. If Cadwallon and Penda have both sold our involvement on whoever kills Edwin first becoming the king of Northumbria. I hope not.

His determined attack allows me the opening for which I'm looking. I face Actulf and nod. He calls five of our fiercest men to his side, shouting his concern for the safety of my father. With their rage stoked, they follow me into the band of warriors my father commands.

Actulf has not spoken to my men of what we hope to do once we're amongst my father's warriors. It's a secret I've only shared with him.

I rush over fallen bodies, discarded weapons, the ground turning to its more usual marshy texture as the press of men warms it. I'll have to watch that. It would be terrible if I suddenly fell to my knees before my father.

Actulf runs with me, and his voice is raised in a roar of outrage at the onslaught my father's enduring. I could almost grin with delight at his fraud, but I'm exhausted. The fighting has been fierce and has lasted a long time. I'd hoped to kill my father at the beginning of the battle when I was fresh and full of vigour. Now I know that it'll be a brutal altercation, and I'm not even close to him yet.

My father's warriors are ready for an attack against Lord Eanfrith, reinforcements coming in the shape of some of the men who fight under King Sigeberht's banner. They're trying to force a wedge through the second shield wall.

Coming as we do from behind, no one thinks us anything other than more reinforcements. No one even looks at my men as I slide into the rear of the shield wall.

I can hear my father issuing instructions to his men at the front of the shield wall. I consider what he felt on discovering Lord Eanfrith was amongst his enemy. I know my rage was vast, but then, Eanfrith and I both want the same thing, and only one of us can have it. For my father, it would have been a meeting with his fate, with his past, with something that he says he's made his peace with, although I have my doubts.

It can't have been as easy as he says it was to kill the man who fathered his nephews and bedded his sister.

But Edwin has an interesting way of remembering the past. He's forgotten that I'm more a part of the southern lands than him, that my mother was a daughter of a Mercian king. In light of that, it seems only fitting that I ally with Penda. Somehow, we're relatives, although it would take a man more skilled in genealogy than either he or I to work out how. For King Cearl, the previous king of Mercia was my grandfather, but he's not Penda's father, and neither is he his grandfather, uncle or cousin.

I could ask one of the priests, but I don't trust any of the fucking bastards to tell me the truth.

My father has a way with words that can turn almost anyone to do his bidding. He's employing his skills to reinvigorate the men. I can hear his voice clearly even over the din of the battle.

I hold my shield firmly in my hand, but instead of reaching for my war axe, I feel around my belt to ensure that I know where my seax is placed. This is the weapon I plan on using to slay my father. In secret, I've had it blessed by a priest of the Old Gods. I hear the Gods calling to me as I shove and push my way closer and closer to my father's back.

Edwin fights in the front line against his enemy, or rather, one of his enemies and the one he most fears will take Northumbria from him.

"Eanfrith has some fierce warriors," Actulf cautions at my side. I understand what he's not saying. He wants me to let my father and his men kill as many as possible before attacking Edwin. He has a good point. There's no point in killing Edwin only to fall prey to Lord Eanfrith's attack.

"Keep fighting for now," I huff.

I handle my war-axe. It's the best weapon for close fighting. Any moment now, I'll be beside my father. His most skilled warriors support him, but Eoif is older than my father. He looks unsteady on his feet. I imagine another few clashes with our foe-men, and one of them will sneak in an attack that finishes him. I position myself behind Eoif, much to the disgust of his son, whom I offer a smile of apology. He doesn't recognise me. I'm pleased about that.

Battle is the great leveller. Anyone can die, and anyone can survive. Many men have already pissed themselves with fear and run back to the supply lines. They'll be the ones that either escape or who'll offer apologies. Or become reinforcements if they run from the battlefield and then regret their choice. They might be forced to use the weapons they carry at some point. Men might be scared or terrified, but when someone tries to kill them, and they have no one at their back, they'll fight as though possessed by Woden himself.

My father fights well in front of me, his actions intentional and never hurried or forced by his opponents. This is how he won his throne. In battle, against King Æthelfrith, the father of the man he now faces.

I've never said my father isn't an excellent warrior, for I know him to be one. He taught me much when I was a young child. A pity really that he was so keen to keep many of his special moves to himself. A shame for him that I've since learnt many for myself.

The heave and heat of battle are overpowering. I've had nothing to drink since the late winter dawn. My tongue is dry. My throat is a little painful. I don't count the occasional mouthful of another man's blood as a drink. Not that it doesn't sate a little, take the dryness from my mouth and leave me keen to destroy the next man.

Eoif is close to the end of his endurance. I can see him trying to meet his son's eye and have him take his place. He would fight to his death. I know he would. But my father has so much vigour left in him that Eoif appreciates he needs to have himself replaced. If he should fall now, my father would take precious few moments to mark his passing, and that would distract him from the ongoing battle.

Eoif's son attempts to shove his way past me, get to his father, but Actulf bars his way. I want my father to be distracted.

A vast thunder of noise from our enemy and Eoif is looking about frantically for a moment before turning back to the man trying to kill him. Whatever he thinks of his son's failure to take his place, it won't be a problem for long. The enemy has been reinforced. They're about to renew the attack.

I feel it as a rumble through the ground. So many feet turning towards my father. So many men crying for his death. The reverberation worries me. I want to fight and die as a warrior, not crushed to death by the weight of a herd of Cadwallon and Penda's warriors.

My shield above Eoif's head, I steady myself for the coming onslaught. I deliberate if my father has other men who'll reinforce the line. I can't remember who yet lives and who's perished. I know I live and that my father lives, but other than that, I've not taken the time to calculate how many others still survive.

I think it's a fairly evenly balanced battle. Or at least it was. Until now.

Braced for the ambush, I feel a monumental thud on my shield, either made by a giant or by a man jumping over his allies to get to me. I've seen this tactic before.

My arm throbs painfully with the power of the attack, but my shield holds. It's a solid thing and has saved my life many times before.

Eoif shudders with the blow. I imagine another foeman is attacking his outward-facing shield whilst the giant attacks mine. It's a double attack.

My father stands firm against the assault, the shield above his head, held by Actulf at my side. I wonder how Actulf managed to arrange that. If the worst should happen, we can allow the enemy to kill my father and take all the credit. All we need is his severed head. That will be the proof that Cadwallon and Penda use to proclaim me as the King of Northumbria.

Eoif stumbles backwards, his feet connecting with mine. I know this is it. He can't fight any longer.

I reach out with my weapon hand and place it on his shoulder. This is the signal for him to step backwards and let his son take his place.

As he steps back, his eyes alight on my face with surprise. I appreciate that he recognises me. That's not good. I step quickly into the gulf left by his retirement from the battle line, my hand clasping his shield so that the enemy can't take advantage of any physical gap.

I hand Eoif my shield as we rotate places. With my suddenly free hand, I clasp my sharpened seax and slice it cleanly around the man's belly where it extends over his weapons belt. His eyes bulge open in shock, but I've turned my back on him. I hope the old bastard dies quickly. I liked and respected him far more than I ever did my father.

My father grunts when I slide into the shield wall beside him, but he doesn't know it's me. He thinks I'm Eoif's son, Eomar. They've fought together far more times than my father, and I ever have.

See how easy it is to win the unquestioned support of a king. Simply don't be his son.

Lord Eanfrith's force continues to battle energetically. I find myself distracted by the task because I want to kill as many of these men as possible.

Using my shield and my seax, bloody once more, I stand firm against the assault. I maintain a wide stance, balance even, and shoulder behind the shield, but stationary. Somehow, I manage to work my seax between the gaps of the overlapping swords, stabbing at men opposite me, worming my weapon between their shield and their body, spearing any part with which I come into contact. Time and time again, my blade returns to me, bloodied and slick.

I grin with delight.

Kill all the fucking Pictish bastards. This isn't their fight and never should have been.

Actulf continues to cover my father's head. From behind, I can feel the harsh breathing of one of my men, Hahmund. He's a great bear of a man, ridiculously strong and able to pull trees from the ground without the need for an axe. He'll keep me protected whilst I battle.

A war axe snakes its way beneath my borrowed shield. I look at it in surprise. I'm not going to let them pull my shield away from me. I'd rather hack the edge off my shield than have someone try such a sneaky move.

I reach for my weapons belt, replacing my bloody seax for something with a better reach. The war-axe should do it. Casually, I reach as far down as I can and then I make a short stabbing motion with the axe, smashing the fingers against my side of the shield. The fingers smear bloodily all over the shield. I hook one and pull it towards me.

A screech of pain from the warrior on the other side of the shield wall. I know I've injured him, hopefully in such a way that he'll be no more of a threat to me. The warrior tries to snatch the wounded hand away, but I raise my foot and stamp it to the ground. Just for good measure.

Distracted, I feel my shield give slightly. I pivot quickly to see what I've missed.

My shield is being forced down by a foe man's war axe, slowly but surely. It's all I can do to keep it upright. I scream to Hahmund behind me, and he seems aware of my peril.

"I'll deal with it," he rages, his voice so loud in my ear that I temporarily lose the ability to hear anything. I keep my focus exclusively on the warrior in front, surprised when I'm blinded by sunlight a moment later. I look behind in confusion, and then I understand.

Hahmund leans over me with his free hand whilst his other maintains its holds on his shield. He plucks the foeman from the other side of the shield wall and lifts him high above my head. The man kicks and screams, blood dripping from a wound onto my helm and down my nose guard as I feel the gap in their shield wall being replaced by another.

Godfrid quickly takes Hahmund's place as Hahmund removes the screaming enemy deeper into our shield wall so that he can kill him or keep him captive. It'll depend on his identity.

As I say, Hahmund is a giant and his great height and reach are very useful in a shield wall. I hope he doesn't take too long to decide what to do with his captive. I could do with him at my back.

Suddenly, our side of the shield wall surges forward. I rush the few gained steps with the rest of the men, our shields remaining tightly overlapped. It's just possible that we might be winning this battle.

That's good and also bad.

I need to kill my father, and soon.

Then I almost howl with rage as the battle line opens up before me. I see Lord Eanfrith and hear him speak to my father before a surge along the shield wall moves my father away from him once more.

I know my father saw him. I understand he still stands and stares at the place where Eanfrith stood only moments ago.

I sigh with relief.

Actulf leans towards me, his shield over my father but a strange look in his eyes that are half-hidden by shadow and his helm. He's plotting something.

"What are you doing here?" my father asks Actulf, finally deigning to notice who surrounds him. In a strange slow motion, he turns to look at me, his eyes narrowing.

"And what the fuck are you doing here? I told you to fight the men from Gwynedd."

"I did, father," I respond, my voice dripping with condescension. "And we beat them and came to help you because you weren't winning against Lord Eanfrith, and I didn't want to be a victor without you."

My tone is singsong and belittling. He bites back his incensed retort. At that moment, I notice how old he is now. Well into his fifth decade, his hair is wispy and greying, the stubble on his chin looks like ashes from a fire, and his eyes are flat and black.

Whilst we converse, we retain our vigilance and strategy against the enemy, almost as though we're not fighting for our lives.

"The rumours are true then?" he says, his shoulders sagging as he looks behind him but sees only the eyes of my men. Eoif has gone. Eomar seems to have disappeared as well. I wonder if Hahmund has him. He never liked him.

"What rumours, father?" I ask, disappointed to think that he might have been expecting my betrayal after all.

"That you're now a mightier warrior than me?"

I wasn't expecting that response. His sudden compliment knocks my resolve. My father hasn't offered any words of encouragement since he turned his back on our old Gods and embraced his new one. Even with the intervention of Lord Oswald, he's never thought to praise my warrior skills.

"Yes, father, that's it. A mightier warrior. Far more able to command men and attain my goals than you ever were."

Another surge from the shield wall. We advance another four paces. At this rate, we'll be well on the way to crushing Penda and Cadwallon. I can't allow that to happen. I only become king if my father loses the battle and his life.

Edwin laughs at me then. His derision reignites my anger, where his commendation had me reconsidering what I'm about to do. Not anymore, though.

"You only have even the remotest chance of being a king because I'm your father. You're no Penda, no Cadwallon. Your men don't follow you through love and devotion and because they believe in you but because you bloody well scare them."

Actulf moves a step closer to my father, fury evident in his body language.

"And you only became king because you became Rædwald's man and were lucky enough not to be killed by the first assassin. What were you doing again when he came to kill you? I think you mentioned you were drinking with your men and with Rædwald and his wife, or something like that. Mind, I hear you were in bed with the old man and a few other women as well. That they all died in your stead whilst you scrambled from the bed, piss running down your legs even though your cock was still half up."

My father glares at my outrageous accusation, for it is disgraceful and very untrue, but I want to upset the equilibrium of his thoughts as much as he's upset mine.

The bastard.

Abruptly, the shield wall collapses in on itself, and because I wasn't paying any attention or even listening to the sounds of battle, I stagger forward and land on one knee. More alert than I, my father is on me immediately, a seax at my throat that I know isn't his. Now it's my time to laugh at him.

How ironic that the situation has completely reversed itself.

My laughter takes him by surprise, and that's all I need. As the rest of Edwin's force cries with delight and chases after the backs of the retreating men, I stand, my free hand clutched around my razor-sharp blade.

It's said that the young have far better reactions than the old, and that's why with barely a blink, I'm behind my father, his scrawny neck pulled back in my shield hand that's discarded its weapon, my blade pressed close to his gulping throat.

I hate my father, and his death will be too quick for him, but it must be fast, or his men will realise what's happening.

"Osfrith, no," I hear him gurgle, but it's too late. My blade slices across his throat, hot blood spewing to the floor.

"Goodbye, father," I whisper harshly into his ear. Actulf and Godfrid surround me, hiding what I've done from the men rushing past, chasing the enemy back to their land.

I lay my father's body on the floor and reach for Actulf's war axe. Only Hahmund is back. He takes one disgusted look at the dead king and swings his mighty axe, the noise of the head completely leaving the body, turning my stomach with its wet, sucking noise.

"My Lord King," he offers with a grin. I eye him grimly. I didn't know he knew about my plan.

"Hahmund?"

"I believe you might need this." He leans down and plucks the head from the still body, unheeding of the blood pulsing from it. I reach out and take it, breathing heavily but exulted all the same.

Damn, the old bugger's head is heavy.

I turn to the battlefield, the head in my hand, and slowly word leaks of my father's death. Hahmund triumphantly holds the severed head of the man he pulled over the shield wall earlier in his hand, tears of grief streaking his filthy face. His intent is clear. That man killed our king.

Screams of anger erupt from the Northumbrian warriors who are streaming past us. Abruptly, the battle has turned again. Eanfrith's men have played the Northumbrians for fools, pretending to retreat and then counter-attacking.

Quickly men stream past me in the opposite direction, their faces confused and fuming in equal measure. They thought they were about to win and now find that they have a dead king and an army howling for their blood at their backs. In order to retreat, they must crest the river first, and it's no longer a sullen, meandering little brook, but a river in full flow, as though it works for the enemy. It's not been raining, and I don't know where the extra water has come from, but it will kill these men as surely as a sword, spear, or seax will.

The pebbles will be slippery, the men will be panicking, and none will care what happens to others, provided they live to go home to their family.

The enemy, now my allies, rushes to chase them.

My five men close around me, protecting me from Lord Eanfrith and his men. I gaze into my father's dead eyes as I hold his head level with mine.

A king no more.

I hope he goes to his idea of Heaven. They'll be no room for him where I'm going after my death. I expect never to see the cocky bastard again.

36

AD632 - EADFRITH OF NORTHUMBRIA
THE BATTLE OF HÆðFELD

The king's anger and dismissal of my fears stalk my path back to where my men fight.
This battle is a bloody mess.
We shouldn't even be fighting here, not now. If I can see that, why can't the king?

I can't deny that I saw the outriders earlier and thought that King Cadwallon and Penda had made a strategic mistake. But as soon as the king realised that this was all a trap, he should have had the courage to turn the men around.

He's going to die here. I know he is, but he's too delusional to realise.

The battle has broken up into four distinct areas. My brother fights. King Sigeberht leads another force. The king another. And I direct the last one. I've not seen my cousin Oswald anywhere, although he said he would fight. My uncle, Osric, hasn't been seen since this morning either. I muse on where they both are, but only briefly.

I think enemies dressed up as allies surround the king.

I've not yet decided what I am.

My body groans as I stride back to my force. Battle is for young men, but even then, it takes a strong man to weather the painful blows of the enemy. I've seen a lot of our foe-men. I've killed men from Powys, men from the land of the Picts and other men, perhaps those from the kingdom of Dumnonia and even Dal Riata. I didn't recognise them, and they didn't recognise me. I know some of them didn't use my language.

Cadwallon and Penda were thorough when they made their alliances.

If by some slight chance the king should win here today, he'll know that every other kingdom that surrounds him wishes him dead.

I think it might be better if he died here rather than live with that knowledge.

It would undoubtedly be better for me. My brother and I could then split the kingdom between us. Or I could just kill my brother and command myself.

As though I've conjured my brother with my thoughts, I look to see him entering the rear of the latest reformed shield wall that stands for the king against the Picts and Lord Eanfrith, the man I met and who refused to allow the king to communicate with his king of the Picts.

He's turning out to be an enemy worthy of watching, but it's Penda I wish to see. Rumour has it he fights as though he's the wind himself, driving through men without pause or thought for them, tumbling them to the ground and leaving them there, uprooted, to die.

But it's my brother I watch with interest at the moment. Perhaps too much interest, recalled only by my warriors when their outrage reaches my ears. I gaze back to the front of the small shield wall with some confusion. I see I might just get my wish after all, for before us can be none other than Lord Penda, come to kill us all.

He is, as my brother told me, a hugely tall man. I could almost think of him as a giant. He wears his hair long under his helm, and it's dyed with the blood of so many men it glints red even in the dull glow from the waning sun. Penda crashes against the shield wall. I watch with horror as it staggers under the weight of just him.

Suddenly it's falling apart, men tumbling to the ground or jumping out of the way to avoid their falling comrades. I feel the weight of my sword in my hand. I'm minded to go and face Penda, but then, maybe I'm not.

Edwin has made it clear that he thinks little enough of my skills and little enough of me in general that I'm not sure I wish to die at the hands of this massive man. I hesitate as I flick my eyes back towards where I know my brother and the king fight and then towards where Penda and his cohort of warriors are cleaving their way through my remaining force of a hundred men.

A cry from where the king fights distracts me. I see that their shield wall has been overwhelmed as well. My eyes turn back to Penda.

He's slugged his way inside the group of men who protect me, who've vowed to fight until my death, or their own, whichever comes soonest.

Even now, Penda squares up to attack Frambert, the tallest man amongst my warriors and yet still dwarfed by the size of his foeman. I watch Penda raise his war axe in slow motion as Frambert reaches for his shield. I imagine it fracturing before my eyes, the wood and leather of the shield serving no purpose whatsoever against Penda's blow. Abruptly, I can't do this anymore.

I know the king is losing. I know he's going to die here. But I'm not, and neither is Frambert.

I raise my voice, bellow to the God of a man before me, but he doesn't seem to hear me, too focused on his impending fight. Frambert ensures his feet are well balanced, and a small enclave has opened up around him. No one else wants to face Penda.

The poor sod.

I sprint forward, grabbing my war standard from the man who's watching the coming fight with morbid interest. Then I'm before Penda, my breath heaving in my lungs and my knees shaking.

Shit, he's a scary-looking man.

I'm so winded from my brief run across the flood plain, from avoiding the bodies of my comrades; from trying not to look into the forever staring eyes of men I used to drink with, share tales of women we'd bedded, and stories of how we'd be mightier warriors than Woden and Thor put together, that I can't speak.

Penda eyes with me with disdain. So I reach up and pull my helm free from my head. I hope he'll recognise my eyes, see that I am related to Edwin. He's met Osfrith; he knows what the men look like in my family.

Recognition slowly gathers in his eyes. He notices my war standard.

"Are you surrendering?" Penda asks, his voice even and steady. This battle has had no physical impact on him other than to turn his clothes to the red of death.

"I am," I announce loudly and clearly and above the howled denial of my warriors. I'll not have them die here, not for the king. Not for a man who doesn't believe in me.

Penda nods once and then lowers his weapon. He reaches out to grab my hair roughly and bring me level to him.

"Tell your men your wishes again."

Some of them still hold their weapons. They look as though they would kill rather than surrender.

I open my mouth to say the words, but a huge snarl comes from further down the battlefield, and Penda is distracted. He releases me to determine the source of the noise. But I already know.

He thrusts me towards one of his warriors.

"Detain him and his men," he instructs and then he's gone. Off to see what's happened on the battlefield. I sink to the floor, my arse resting on the feet of the man Penda's ordered to guard me.

Grief consumes me.

The king, my father, is dead.

I know he is.

37

AD632 - EOWA OF MERCIA
THE BATTLE OF HÆðFELD

The battlefield is a sea of bodies. I could never have imagined that just under two thousand men would make so much noise and cause so much death and destruction.

I know one thing for a certainty. I made the correct decision when I turned away from King Edwin. He doesn't have anywhere near the sway of power, he thought. If he did, I'd be doing more than fighting King Sigeberht's men. I'd be facing men from Wessex and Kent, maybe even the men from across the sea who share a heritage with the people of Dal Riata but who hate them more than any other.

I've not seen my brother during the battle, but I know he'll battle with his usual prowess. I can be proud and jealous of him in equal measure. I'll never have his reputation, but I can at least bask in the glow of his reflected greatness. My name will go down in history as 'the other brother', the one who couldn't kill a man with a stare.

My men and I form a shield wall to deflect the attack from King Sigeberht. Penda warned me of the man. He said his techniques might well be different to ours and that I might need to think on my feet. I think he meant it respectfully. He gifted me the opportunity to defend against the man and his strange ways. I only wish it had proved to be the case, but Sigeberht fights much the same as any other man. In fact, of everyone on this battlefield, it's the Picts and the men of Dal Riata who employ techniques so different to the rest of the warriors.

They fight with strange square shields, and the accuracy with their throwing spears could put any of my warriors to shame. We like our spears, but we use them sparingly, preferring to fight with seax or swords and war axes. I have a whole new appreciation for the work of the humble spear now.

King Sigeberht calls to his men on the other side of the shield wall, his words carrying over the noise of battle and stupidly for him, broadcasting his plans. In response, I send whispers up and down the line, letting my men know how we'll counter the attack without telling Sigeberht as well.

His constant commands come with appeals to his God. I swear he has a priest standing amongst his men because I hear the muttered 'Amen' of a prayer every so often. I doubt it's coming from the warring warriors.

We're all too hard-pressed against each other.

Sigeberht commands a force that's fairly evenly matched to mine. His men are strong and well trained, but so are mine. The outcome of this attack may very well depend on what happens on the rest of the battlefield.

Ideally, I want to line myself up so that I'm attacking Sigeberht, but it's difficult to move in the press of so many bodies. I don't want to undermine my solid shield wall because of vanity.

As I said, I'm not my brother. I have the skills needed to be a king, to command my shield wall, to earn the respect of my men, but I'm not half God and half man. I'm just me, and my strength is all mine. My skills have been gained through hard practice and my bouts with Penda.

He's taught me much, but he doesn't know that. It would simply make him even more insufferable.

A thud on my shield from the opposition has me turning my thoughts to the battle. That my mind has wondered so far is simply a reflection of how long the standoff between Sigeberht and my forces has been ongoing. I've sent a man to try and tempt Lord Eanfrith's men to rain their hail of deadly spears amongst the East Anglian warriors, but so far, they've not come.

I assume they will when they've stopped helping my brother or Cadwallon.

I force my body weight against my shield. My war axe is slippery in my hand. I've been holding it for a long time without any action. A few unfortunate men have died when they stumbled or were pulled under their shields, but really all the men have done so far is to shout insults, retreat and then reform a second shield wall.

The welcome sounds of spears flying overhead has me spreading the whispered words to the men on either side of me so that our attack can finally begin. I'll welcome the opportunity to move.

This second shield wall we've formed is more chaotic than the first and threaded with men from Powys and Mercia. I hope that they can all work together.

Cries of anger fill the air. I know the time is right. As one, my men and I apply more and more pressure to the shield wall, forcing the men opposite to groan with effort as they try to combat the spears above their head and our movement against them. I can hear Sigeberht bellowing commands, urging them to hold firm, to protect their heads, to make themselves ready. He knows that something is coming. But he thinks it's coming from in front of them, not from above.

As one the men in the third rank of my shield wall lift their legs and fairly fly over the first and second ranks of the shield wall, skipping their way over the same formation of our enemy before jumping onto their exposed backs.

It's a movement I feel and hear but don't see because I have to hold my shield firmly before me and brace myself for the weight of the man as he passes overhead.

I feel its consequences quickly, though, as the shield wall suddenly gives way. Men can't protect their backs as well as their fronts.

My warriors are braced for the disintegration of the shield wall.

Abruptly, I finally face an enemy I can see and size up. The shields are up, but they no longer overlap and warriors are fighting for their life, exposed in places they never thought they would be.

I can hear Sigeberht's bellows of shock, but I can't see him. Instead, with a war cry that forms deep in my belly before exiting my mouth as a hoarse scream of rage, I'm walking towards a man who holds his shield tightly but seems to have forgotten he might need another weapon as well.

I step into his shield, my war axe ready. With dazed eyes, he watches my movements but appears unable to move. I slash my axe across his exposed upper body, pounding on his byrnie before hooking the head of the axe under his neck on its return. Its passage opens his delicate skin there, unleashing a torrent of burgundy against his dull clothes and the grey day.

He dies without so much as a sword in his hand.

I hope he's a Christian and that his new God doesn't worry about things like that.

I look for my next victim.

My men who risked their lives to jump over the shield wall are making an easy job of killing the men at the back. I grin with delight. I've often wanted to try this trick, but Penda, brave and valiant Penda, was always so convinced it wouldn't work that I've shied away from trying it. Not that my men and I haven't practised it. We have, and now I know that it works. Possibly too well.

Penda will be pissed off about that.

Good.

The flash of a sword catches my attention. A young man stands before me with no protection but his obvious rage. I wonder how he's managed to make his way through the shield wall. Surely, he's only one of the squires? But his determination is clear to see. I almost envy him the fiery blaze of outrage that burns from grey eyes.

The battle rage is upon him. He probably won't even feel the death blow.

It'll be a pity to kill him, but I must.

With my shield in front of me to ward off any attack from his blade, the weapon too long for his short arms, I skip towards him, the power of Woden infecting my movements.

He opens his mouth to scream his rage at me. Once more, I admire him, but his shriek never issues from his mouth because I rush past him, my war axe ripping open his exposed back. He sinks to the ground, turning soggy with the blood and piss of dying men, and tumbles face-first into the muck.

What a waste. If only men could control battle rage, I think battles would be far shorter and result in far fewer fruitless deaths.

Men mill around the dismantled shield wall. I move through them, offering a slash of my axe as I go, wounding men where I can and slicing through their necks when it's necessary.

I do enjoy a good slaughter, despite my brother's assertion that I don't. I hope that today I get to slay more men than he does.

Shit, I could earn a name for myself today that's as powerful as Penda's.

The thought makes me smile.

Eowa and Penda has a better sound to it than Penda and his brother, Eowa, the one who's not as good with a sword.

38

AD632 - PENDA OF MERCIA
THE BATTLE OF HÆðFELD

I'm streaked with blood from head to toe. Not mine, and that's all that matters. Around me, bodies lie still or twitch in the throes of death on the blood-soaked ground. I laugh, a long joyous noise that reaches from my belly to my head and my toes.

It might be battle joy, the berserker in me, but I don't give a shit what it is.

The day had been grey and cold, a terrible day really for such slaughter and annihilation. The Northumbrian force is in tatters, and I have a prisoner of real value. The Northumbrian king's son. I think his name is something 'frith', but I can't remember the name of all the men on this battlefield. There are too many fathers, brothers, cousins and uncles.

King Edwin. Fuck the man. He had his head turned by this new but old God, the one towards which Cadwallon also directs his prayers. He saw portents everywhere, and they meant nothing. Edwin's battle against Cadwallon and me was not preordained to any sort of victory.

I wipe my bloody hand across my bloody face as I take the time to catch my breath and stride to see what the recent shout means for the future of the battle.

One overwhelming victory, that's all I need, and that's what I'm going to get. I'll be a king now, almost as powerful as Edwin, even if I share my victory with Cadwallon.

There are just one or two more events that need to happen, and the victory Cadwallon and I claim together will be complete.

I'm hoping that the cry from where the Northumbrian king was fighting is one of those things.

I'm striding towards the broken shield wall, my men running to catch up with me and form a protective shield, only I'm focusing on someone in front of me as a slow smile spreads across my face.

Fuck it if he hasn't come through on his promises.

He bows his head at me a little as he catches my eye. One of my warriors has already run off to deliver the news to Cadwallon.

This will truly make our victory complete.

"My Lord Penda," he says, and for the first and only time in his life, I smile at him and bow my head. A rarity, I never acknowledge the superior claims of others, but he's earned my respect for now.

"King Osfrith," I respond. His joy splits his face showing delight at hearing himself so-called.

My warriors have closed around him, cutting off any men who might have accompanied him across the muddy, bloody battlefield.

He holds out his trophy still, his mouth open and blood staining his teeth. He looks frightful and victorious, his helm firmly on, while his clothes are ripped and torn. He has several nasty looking wounds that pulse with fresh blood. He's fought hard for the honour of killing his father, for that's whose head he holds in his hand.

"Ugly bastard," I offer, bending down to look at the forever-staring eyes of Edwin, the most Christian king of Northumbria. His helm has come loose with his death, and his son, his bloody son, holds his head upright by a few pieces of straggling, grey hair.

I reach out instinctively to take hold of the head, but Osfrith tightens his grip and swings it from my reach.

I see how this is going to be played now.

"It was a long and bloody battle. He was a fierce and arrogant warrior who only pissed himself with fear when he realised he was being attacked by me, his son."

Osfrith laughs with delight as he replays the battle in his mind. I gulp over my uneasiness. Even I'm surprised by the anger in the voice of Osfrith, but then I reconsider; there had to be a reason why Osfrith had been swayed to our side.

"I'm ecstatic that you had the victory," I offer, and I mean it, for Osfrith has just solved a massive problem for me. I almost regret what has to be done now, but only almost. I have no choice. I don't want Osfrith as my ally. Not now he's done what was asked of him. It makes him difficult to manage if he'll do absolutely anything demanded of him.

I step forward, offering my arm to clasp Osfrith's free hand tightly in mine. Osfrith still holds the head of his father, blood dripping onto the battlefield.

Osfrith is caught in my firm embrace. Unable to do anything, and utterly incapable of defending himself when I slide my seax into his stomach, through a handy hole in his byrnie that some other warrior has made in a previous engagement.

Osfrith's eyes open in shock and horror. His mouth works as he tries to speak. I hear the thud of his father's head hitting the floor. I hold him upright for long moments yet, waiting for his breathing to stop.

It was always this part of the plan that would prove to be the trickiest. The father is dead, the son as well, and the other has just surrendered to me. There's only one other enemy out there. I don't believe we'll sway him to our side, not yet.

Before my eyes, I see the press of my warriors being forced to take a step back. I know that Osfrith's warriors want to see their new king. Pity they'll all have to die as well.

Finally, I feel Osfrith slump against me. I let him slide down my front, his mouth catching on the metal at my shoulder and forcing me to raise him a bit higher and then lower him down. It would be a gruesome task for many, but it's just an annoyance with which I must contend.

Death is one of those things. Provided it's not your own, you just need to get on with it and not overthink it.

I lie the dead prince down next to his father's staring eyes. I eye them both speculatively.

What great king is this to fall in battle, and not at the hands of his enemy but rather at the hands of his son? I believe Edwin must have been a poor king, all good luck and the divine intervention of a useless God who's deserted him now. I hope he finds his dull Heaven to be to his liking. I know what I intend to do in my afterlife.

None of Osfrith's men has survived their assault on my men, just more of the enemy to rot in this field.

I don't fancy forcing my men to bury them. They can pillage and take what they want. I'm a happy man already.

My warrior, who sought out King Cadwallon, is back, breathing heavily. He bends double at the waist to catch his breath and, as he does, catches his first view of the body lying beside the severed head of Edwin.

He stands and begins to laugh, a dull sound that starts deep in his belly and reaches to the top of his head. He points at the body and then at the head and then looks at me. He's still trying to catch his breath from running and overcome; he slides to his knees. His breath rasping.

"I only bloody ran because King Cadwallon wanted to make sure you remembered about Osfrith."

I grin then because I finally understand what's made him laugh so much.

"You can bloody run back and tell Cadwallon that it's done."

The man continues to laugh, and I glare at him. He's shaking his head.

"No, he's coming. He's right behind me. Only he's walking, not running."

Once more, my warriors move aside to let someone through. Cadwallon runs his greedy eyes over the scene before him. I've not seen him since this morning when he looked resplendent in his armour and his helm, his sword gleaming and his shield brightly painted.

He looks faded now, his armour streaked with rusty stains and his face covered in dirty sweat and with spots of blood.

He grins and stops beside the body and the head. Just as I did, he bends down and stares Edwin in the eyes.

"How do you like that, brother?" he spits before standing and kicking the head. He's rewarded with a dull smacking noise as the back of the head concaves at the force he uses.

The head impacts that of his son beside him. I feel my stomach roll a little. As I say, death is to be born, not tormented.

Cadwallon walks towards me, his hand outstretched. I reach mine out to join his. No matter how I've just betrayed Osfrith, I know that Cadwallon is my ally and my friend. He doesn't want the same things that I do. Yes, we both wanted Edwin dead, but he doesn't want my land, and I don't want his.

Not yet.

We hand clasp firmly, our arm rings marking the occasion with their dull thuds against each other.

"We've won," Cadwallon says, his voice smug and self-satisfied. "Everyone's fucking dead," he hollers, his words high and delighted.

"Everyone?" I enquire. I know that Osfrith and Edwin are dead. I wonder who else he knows has fallen.

"Everyone who's bloody important," he corrects. We stand together, looking out over the total destruction before us and the retreating backs of King Sigeberht and his remaining warriors.

Our argument isn't with him. We let him go without ordering the men to follow him and cut down any who still stands.

This was a great battle.

There is death and destruction all around us, the groans of men who yet live drift in the still air as night finally closes around us, the blackness masking the mess of men who lost their lives here.

This was our great victory.

In the morning, we'll be faced with the prospect of burying our comrades, of deciding whether to bury the enemy in a mass grave or whether we should leave them where they are, to feed the animals of winter, the wolves that stalk the land with their coats turned all to white.

Haeðfeld.

We are the victors, and the kingdoms of this island will once more undergo tremendous upheavals.

I will be a king.

And so will Cadwallon.

And so too, Eanfrith.

I might share my kingship with my brother, Eowa, but that no longer concerns me. If we rule together, we'll be the brother kings and mightier because we both have strengths the other lacks.

I might share my kingship with my brother, Eowa, but that no longer bedevils me. Not now. I see his face across the battlefield. He raises his bloodied arms in victory, and I mirror the celebration.

We are the brother kings of Mercia.

EPILOGUE
AD632 WINTER - CADWALLON OF GWYNEDD - AD GEFRIN

Northumbria is the land I always imagined it to be. I can see why Edwin was so keen to return to it and claim it all himself. All of it.

It's a place of extremes; wide-open rivers, shallow trickling streams, vast open spaces and tiny haunting caves. It stretches wide in places and shallow in others. The wind can be fierce and the sun gentle, but not often at this time of the year. I've seen the rain sheet in over vast hills, hailstones as large as an arrowhead have fallen in one place and only ten horse lengths away, have fallen only as small drizzle, almost a caress. I've seen storm-tossed seas, the crests of the waves towering high, their tops white with foam, and I've seen its deep blue depths, its moody grey as well.

It reminds me of my homeland only on a far grander scale. Gwynedd is a place of contrasts. The lush green grasses of the summer when sheep graze the fields and the wind-blown winters when no one can walk upright because the wind is too strong.

I think I prefer my homeland, but I can still see the appeal.

I've ridden far and wide since the death of King Edwin and his son, Lord Osfrith. Sometimes in the company of Eanfrith and sometimes not. I wish he'd met his end at Hæðfeld, but he didn't, and now

I find I almost like him. He might just hold onto the Bernician kingdom after all. He certainly likes it when I call him King Eanfrith, a smirk of joy spreading over his face.

I have to grudgingly admit that the majority of the men and women he meets are pleased to see the return of his dynasty. They didn't like Edwin as their king. He should have been King in Deira, never in Bernicia and never in a united Northumbria. Eanfrith need only make a few changes to his personality, make some promises that'll be easy to keep, and the people will love him. I know they will.

For now, I'm wintering in Yeavering. It's a grand hall, and I could almost love it if it weren't for the howling wind, the falling snow and the bitter chill. I don't much like winter in Northumbria, although Eanfrith tells me that this is nothing compared to winter in the lands of the Picts. Herebrod agrees with him, and with both of them so compelling, I've assured everyone that I'm never going to the land of the Picts. Never. They laughed with good cheer to hear my words. Everyone smiles all the time. There's a wave of happiness spreading throughout the kingdom.

The battle might have been catastrophic for King Edwin and Lord Osfrith, but, as is the way with women, beasts, and even men, that battle is now a thing of the past. All that matters is the future. Never the past, not when lives are lived from harvest to harvest, year-to-year.

The aftermath of the battle has been surprisingly muted. The changes in kingship have been accepted without any complaint.

Only King Sigeberht has even raised his voice in outrage. I believe he does it because he was humiliated at the battle, not because of any great respect for Edwin. Not even his brother-in-law, King Eadbald of Kent, has so much as mouthed an angry comment. Edwin's children and his second wife are gone into exile, and when this winter is done, and I've considered all my options, I know that I'll pursue them. Even Edwin's young grandson. Not one of his spawn will live a full life, not one of them, and it's all his fault.

As to my allies, they all left the battle site with their lives intact, every single one of them. Domnall, Eiludd, Clydog, Clemen. They lived through this great victory and returned home with plunder and victory on their minds. It was truly a dazzling spectacle of how one man can rouse all others against an enemy.

As to the bodies of the dead king and his son? Well, they've been returned to their kingdom. Lord Osfrith was accorded far more respect than King Edwin, but Osfrith was less of a plague on this island than Edwin. He was also, and this is important to remember, a martyr to our cause. He turned his allegiance to myself and Penda. He killed his father, and few knew it. His death will be recorded with that of his father's. None shall ever know of his traitorous actions.

I think that's enough of a slur on his character as it is. We shouldn't say that he died fighting for his father, but it's almost the truth.

As to the other son, Eadfrith, Penda holds him prisoner. He treats him well enough, but I don't know whether that will continue or not.

I don't much care either way. Eadfrith surrendered and put up no more resistance once his father and brother were dead. He either knew his family's reign had come to an end, or he was pragmatic enough to want to ensure his survival.

I doubt he's managed to do that, but time will tell.

So King Eanfrith rules in Bernicia. For now and he has forsaken the new God and returned to the Old. He thinks our victory at Hæðfeld was the work of Penda and Eowa's Gods, and I'm happy for him to believe that. This war wasn't about religion. It was about the bonds of family a man makes and how he should never, ever forget that family. This battle pitted family against family and made me more than aware that men should look closer to home for their allies than Edwin ever did.

He was a fool, and he died because of that. I hope I'm never betrayed by my sons or by my brother.

And in Deira. Well, Lord Osric attempts to rule there. Another man who turned his back on his family in the heat of battle. I don't think he's to be trusted, not at all. I know Penda allowed him to desert Edwin and seek sanctuary at the back of our attack, but really, he did nothing but give us a small amount of warning that Edwin was coming to the River Idle. We'd have won the battle without that knowledge and forewarning.

I'll watch him carefully. I have half a mind to kill him.

And Osric? Well, he, too, has forsaken the Christian God and returned to the ways of Woden and his ilk.

Kings and Gods should never mix. Never.

A man's faith should be his concern, not that of his king or his neighbour.

If the war leaders of the petty kingdoms of this island allow religion to influence them, then it will be plunged into centuries of war.

The Old Gods do not give up their hold on the minds of men easily.

No.

Not that I much care. I believe in my God. He wears the same clothes as Edwin's new god, but he's older and wiser. My kingdom has saints enough to tend to his needs and his wishes. He leaves me well enough alone.

Not like this new incarnation of him that King Edwin and King Sigeberht insist on worshipping.

And not like the Old Gods.

As I say, they don't give up their hold on the minds of men easily.

AUTHOR NOTES

I've studied this time period before but I'd never, ever, considered writing a book set in it. I was very surprised (all over again) by both the wealth and dearth of available information.

The wonderful and most Venerable Bede is the 'go to man' for the time period, but to choose a Northern phrase as is only apt for a book about Northumbrian aggression and his desire to legitimize it, he was a 'canny' man and sometimes Bede wrote events that seem to be the truth but where it's all in the phrasing and as much about the information that he misses out as those pieces he includes.

He tells us that Edwin and his son Osfrith die at Hæðfeld. He certainly doesn't say that they die fighting on the same side. This is inferred because of the way he writes it. It would have gone much against Bede's narrative regarding 'The Ecclesiastical History of the English People' if Edwin's son had turned against him. Edwin was one of Bede's anti-heroes, the first man to accept Romanised Christianity in Northumbria, his own homeland, and it's fair to say he might have been circumspect with the truth. He probably didn't approve of Edwin's pagan roots, but as a converted Christian, Edwin had to be given a 'role' in the Ecclesiastical History of the English People. His death at the hands of a pagan Penda and a Christian

Cadwallon would have been a blow to Bede who liked things to be more clear-cut. Christianity trumps Paganism every time for Bede.

Much of the basis for this story comes from an assertion by the wonderful historian, D.P. Kirby about a possible alliance that may have been mounted against Edwin. "The Earliest English Kingdoms" is one of a handful of books I've held onto for over twenty years and is a constant 'go to' book for mining information about the Early English Kingdoms. I've taken a number of monumental leaps with the ideas he postulates and made them even more extreme, but hopefully, just as believable.

I've used place names to explain where people come from not because they were used at the time (I assume they weren't) but because the names need to 'hang on' something, and it will also work as a clue as to which side of the alliance the people ultimately end up on.

Pagan Warrior is the first in a series of books that will tell the tale of seventh century Britain and have Penda as their unlikely hero. There are other great kings who came before Penda, and many battles that are obscured in the mists of the past, but I planned on starting with Maserfelth before I realised that all good stories need to start at the beginning. Once more I find myself with such a wealth of possible stories to tell that I have to work hard to concentrate on only one story thread.

All mistakes are my own. Remember, this is my idea of Early England, and I'm a passionate proponent of the idea that the men and women who ruled and held sway within the United Kingdom can't all have been blood thirsty bastards who wanted to do nothing but kill people all day long. They must have had endearing qualities, and they thought before they acted and more importantly, were just as manipulative as politicians in modern times.

As to the Gods. Well, they were a matter for a person's conscious but religion was just as much a political weapon as it still is. However, the history of Early England has passed to modern times through the medium of men of Christianity – they wrote our history and they imbibed it with their prejudices. Whether or not religion was quite so important to the minds of men remains to be seen.

The Words of Bede from "The Ecclesiastical History of the English People

"EDWIN reigned most gloriously seventeen years over the nations of the English and the Britons, six whereof, as has been said, he also was a servant in the kingdom of Christ. Cadwalla; king of the Britons, rebelled against him, being supported by Penda, a most warlike man of the royal race of the Mercians, and who from that time governed that nation twenty-two years with various success. A great battle being fought in the plain that is called Heathfield, Edwin was killed on the 12th of October, in the year of our Lord 633, being then forty-seven years of age, and all his army was either slain or dispersed. In the same war also, before him, fell Osfrid, one of his sons, a warlike youth; Eanfrid, another of them, compelled by necessity, went over to King Penda, and was by him afterwards, in the reign of Oswald, slain, contrary to his oath."

http://legacy.fordham.edu/halsall/basis/bede-book2.asp

The quote from The Anglo-Saxon Chronicle at the beginning of this story comes from Michael Swanton's *The Anglo-Saxon Chronicles*. I have discussed the Anglo-Saxon Chronicles at length elsewhere. These are a series of chronicles, with regional difference, but which weren't even begun until the late ninth-century, at King Alfred of Wessex's instigation. It can be supposed that they rely heavily, for this earlier period, on the words of Bede.

MEET THE AUTHOR

I'm an author of historical fiction (Early England, Vikings and the British Isles as a whole before the Norman Conquest), as well as three 20th-century mysteries, and fantasy (viking age/dragon themed), born in the old Mercian kingdom at some point since 1066. I write A LOT. You've been warned! Find me at https://mjporterauthor.com, mjporterauthor.blog and @coloursofunison on twitter. Sign up for my newsletter via my website and blog to receive a free short story set after the Gods and Kings trilogy.

facebook.com/mjporterauthor
twitter.com/coloursofunison

BOOKS BY M J PORTER (IN SERIES READING ORDER)

Gods and Kings Series (seventh century Britain)

Pagan Warrior

Pagan King

Warrior King

The Eagle of Mercia Chronicles

Son of Mercia

Wolf of Mercia

Warrior of Mercia

Eagle of Mercia

The Ninth Century Series

Coelwulf's Company – Tales from before The Last King

The Last King

The Last Warrior

The Last Horse

The Last Enemy

The Last Sword

The Last Shield

The Last Seven

The Tenth Century Series

The Lady of Mercia's Daughter

A Conspiracy of Kings

Kingmaker

The King's Daughters

<u>The Brunanburh Series</u>
King of Kings
Kings of War

<u>The Mercian Brexit (can be read as a prequel to The First Queen of England)</u>

<u>The First Queen of England (can be read as a prequel to The Earls of Mercia)</u>
The First Queen of England Part 2
The First Queen of England Part 3

The King's Mother (can be read as a sequel to The First Queen, or a prequel to The Earls of Mercia)
The Queen Dowager
Once A Queen

<u>The Earls of Mercia</u>
The Earl of Mercia's Father
The Danish King's Enemy
Swein: The Danish King (side story)
Northman Part 1
Northman Part 2
Cnut: The Conqueror (full-length side story)
Wulfstan: An Anglo-Saxon Thegn (side story)
The King's Earl
The Earl of Mercia
The English Earl
The Earl's King

Viking King

The English King

The King's Brother

Fantasy

The Dragon of Unison (fantasy based on Viking Age Iceland)

Hidden Dragon

Dragon Gone

Dragon Alone

Dragon Ally

Dragon Lost

Dragon Bond

As JE Porter

The Innkeeper

20th Century Mysteries

The Erdington Mysteries

The Custard Corpses

The Automobile Assassination

Cragside – a 1930s house party mystery

Printed in Great Britain
by Amazon